A REAL GOOD WAR

A REAL GOOD WAR

SAM HALPERT

CASSELL

Cassell Military Paperbacks

Cassell
Wellington House, 125 Strand,
London WC2R 0BB

First published in the USA by Southern Heritage Press 1997
This Cassell Military Paperbacks edition 2001
Reprinted 2001, 2002 (twice)

British Library Cataloguing-in-Publication Data
A catalogue record for this book is available from the
British Library

ISBN 0-304-35855-X

Printed and bound in Great Britain by
Cox & Wyman Ltd., Reading, Berks.

For Susan and Suza

A REAL
GOOD WAR

ONE

I want to keep track of all this. We're a new B-17 crew just in from the States, temporarily stationed at this Army Air Force Replacement Depot. What they call a repple depple — fifty or so Nissen huts about twenty yards long, shaped like long barrels sliced in half lengthwise and plopped down in the countryside here in Bovingdon, fifteen miles west of London. Lots of hurried comings and goings with no one paying any too much attention to us. Just another dumbass crew. Ten guys, raw as stumps and not half as smart, waiting to be assigned any day now to operations at an 8th Air Force Bomb Group somewhere in England. Two months since D-day, but those damn Germans show no signs of giving up.

We goof off as best we can from all the hurry up and wait calls, the gas mask and air raid drills, and the medics insisting we take every one of our shots all over again. Most of the time we hang around with the other new crews spreading shit just about as far as it will go, mostly about girls and sex, though I'd bet that the guys talking the most haven't had any much more than me, and I've had zip.

With not too much else to do, this becomes a great place for swapping rumors back and forth. You dream one up and before the day is out some character looks you straight in the eye while he tells the same damn story back to you and swears it's the straight goods he heard from a couple of guys in Intelligence, which could be the truth for all you know. The one about Hitler being dead and how they've put in an actor to impersonate him flies non-stop around here, and while I thought it was a joke when I first heard it, I'm not so sure now. Yesterday's blue plate special had the Nazis ready to launch a guided missile against London, and the day before we heard that the Luftwaffe has developed a fighter plane powered by a jet engine; and Fearless, one of our gunners, fed us a good one he got in a letter from a cousin in Tennessee about how we're building some kind of secret super bomb back there in the hills around Oak Ridge. Believe it or not.

The one that keeps coming up about how they're going to increase the tour from thirty-five to fifty missions passed through us this morning like a dose of salts. Then we got into figuring out the group that has lost the most crews. Nobody had the answer to that one, but we knew for sure that had to be the group we were headed for. Then that turned into a rhubarb over what we're fighting for, almost like the one that broke out the other night over the chances of us ever having world peace.

I don't know how many times I've been told that General Motors is sitting on an engine that can run all day on a secret powder you mix in a quart of water, or that Gillette is holding back on a blade that never loses its edge, and the government is going to make them both release the patents soon as the war is over.

The Mouse, our co-pilot, came up with a real wild one. He swears he read that with so many ballplayers in the military, they're thinking of signing up colored guys to fill in. Nothing flies in this depot but rumors, and we switch from believing all of them one minute to none the next.

You hear so many that some are bound to have a touch of truth in them. I heard a real beaut today from our bombardier. Six two and about two fifteen, all chest and arms, we call him Caves or Caveman after his full name Aubrey Benford Cavey. He takes a lot of razzing about where he comes from, out west in Wyoming somewhere. Like we'll say you know damn well there's no such place. It's about as real as Oz. They could just as well have made it The Wizard of Wyoming.

"Hell, that's what you hear when you get a pack of hungry coyotes wyoming into the night," says Earl, our pilot.

"Yeah, and how about license plates?" says The Mouse. "Every state has them. Who's ever seen tags from Wyoming? Nah, it just doesn't check out, and how come you're the only creature from there any of us has ever laid eyes on?" You'd think Cavey would be fed up with that crap by now, but he shrugs it off and takes the needling in stride.

We were loading up at the PX this afternoon. The Butterfingers hadn't come in, so I had to settle for Mounds, but Cavey made out as usual. That cowboy sure loves his Milky Ways. He buys four, the PX limit, then gets me to buy four more for him.

We chomp away on our candy bars. Cavey slowly unwraps his second Milky Way as if he was handling the crown jewels. He gazes at it with adoration and says, "Nothing's too good for our boys in service."

We mooch around the magazine rack, and he shows me a picture in Modern Screen of Ida Lupino in a sexy, low cut, tight nurse's uniform with her knockers about falling out as she bends toward us waving a banner reading For Our Brave Lads Overseas. Cavey puts his finger in my chest and says, "Just in case you forget what we're fighting for."

"Thanks for reminding me," I say. "When do you figure

they'll move us out? We won't be worth shit if they keep us hanging around here much longer."

Cavey thumbs his way through a few more of the girlie books and picks All American Sweater Girls. "Easy there, partner," he says, "we haven't been here but a week. Hang loose. They know we're here. Don't get your bowels in an uproar. It's bad for the digestion."

Both Time and Look are featuring articles about how the war will be over by Christmas. I pick Life which has Rita Hayworth on its cover flexing in a negligee damn near showing it all. I flash it at Cavey. "Eat your heart out," I say.

He takes a deep breath and says "Now that's what I call qualified quail, but way too rich for your blood, bad for your pimples." He riffles through the pages of *Sensational Hollywood Starlets of 1944* and shows me a two page picture of the healthiest sweater girl I've ever seen. "Oh man," he says "those mallomars sure make a guy proud to be American, they belong carved up there on Mount Rushmore."

When I reach out for a closer look, my arm still throbs from this morning's tetanus booster. I tell Cavey there was a real good rumor flying around the infirmary from one of the medics who claimed they'd received a ton of malaria vaccine this week, and that could mean they're planning to ship our ass out to the Pacific somewhere. How about that?

"Sure," Cavey says "and Schlitz is running out of beer." He flips the pages to Marie (The Body) McDonald smiling at us in short red tights and a white angora sweater with a blue ribbon marked Miss Victory '44. He moans as he turns the picture around bit by bit, squinting his eyes, checking every curve and angle. "How can we lose?" he asks.

He buys four girly books and a Zippo lighter that blazes like an oil well fire at night. "You want a rumor," he says, "try this for size. This one came straight from a returnee."

Returnees are the guys here, not too many, waiting to

ship home after finishing their tour of missions. They generally keep to themselves and don't have too much to say, but sometimes if they're in the right mood and not just staring off into the blue, you can pick up a thing or two.

Cavey checks to see if I'm listening. I'm listening all right. "I won't go into all the details," he says "but the way the returnee told it was that one day the 100th was catching hell on their way into Dusseldorf. Three crews down before they even crossed Belgium and three more shot up so bad they couldn't keep up with the formation. A shithousefull of German fighters looking for an easy kill jumped the three stragglers. So to keep from becoming a statistic, one of the pilots wig-wagged his wings and lowered his landing gear, you know like hands-up surrender. The Germans knocked off the other two stragglers, then signalled him to follow them back down to their base. Then just as they were all about to land, our great big fuckin' hero orders his gunners to shoot down the German fighters. They catch the Krauts with their pants down, knocking off all six of them, and then scoot like hell low level back home to the 100th."

I put Rita slowly back in the rack. "Holy shit," I say.

"Yeah, wait till you hear the rest," Cavey says. "The next day just about the whole goddam Luftwaffe was out to get the 100th. They ignored all the other groups in the bomber stream. Just tooling around up there, out of range, looking for the 100th's big square D on the rudder. When the Germans spotted those markings, they pounced on them with every fighter they had. A fuckin' massacre. In a few minutes they shot down the entire Group. Blitzed, wipeout, no survivors, no 100th. It was all kept hush-hush while they shipped in new planes and rounded up replacement crews to get them going again, but they still are the Group the Luftwaffe seeks out, and they're still called the Bloody 100th."

I hear myself whistle. No tune, just whistling. Cavey takes

long chews on his Milky Way. "Now don't get all worked up over this," he says, "for all we know, it's probably just another one of them shithouse rumors."

That was one rumor that really grabbed me. I figure that Don, a returnee I met in the chow line day before yesterday, should be able to tell me if there's anything to it. We had both taken our navigation training in Monroe, Louisiana where he had gone through five months before me, and we got along fine swapping stories about some of the wild instructors we had shared. I told him how we got even with one of them. a real meatball, by dripping a few drops out of an oil can around the fly of his pants while he nodded off on one of our training missions. When he woke up, he saw the stains and was convinced that they were pecker tracks from a wet dream. The stupid bastard even made one up and ran off all the gory details for us.

"Was the guys name Beemish?" Don asked.

"Yeah, right, how'd you know? We used to call him Squeamish Beemish."

It turned out that a friend of Don's back at Selman had included that story in a letter telling him how Beemish, six cadets, and a pilot had all gone down when they tangled with some power lines during a thunderstorm outside Shreveport last month. Don shook his head and said "Damn, doesn't that beat all. Poor ol' Beemish had pulled every string in the book to stay out of combat."

After that we talked mostly about movies and baseball where it looks like it's going to be an all St. Louis World Series this year with the Browns having a shot at their first pennant. Don's from near Des Moines, but he's a dyed in the wool Cards fan, and hoped he'd make it home for the Series. We got into who's better — Musial, DiMag, or Ted Williams, and though after that I had all kinds of questions I wanted to ask about combat, I didn't think it right to push him on it right then. I figured he'd get around to it when he was good and ready. Later, he did drop a few tips about how to stay healthy, and a little about how things work at the groups. Nothing heavy, mostly procedure stuff. Any questions, he said before he left. Hell, I had a thousand, but couldn't come up with one.

I catch up with Don again today outside the mess hall after lunch. I want to check out the stuff Cavey fed me about the 100th, but I don't know where to begin. So I go like a complete moron, "Hey, do you have any more hot tips for me?"

Don wipes his sunglasses slowly. "Hot tips?" The sunglasses are back on. "About the best I can tell you is that when you're up there, remember to keep a tight asshole even though lots of times that won't be any too easy." Don sees I'm not smiling and says, "Don't worry, you'll be O.K. It's still plenty rough, but getting better all the time. Hell, I made it."

That doesn't do a thing for me. I ask "What about the groups? Which are the good ones?"

He lights up a Chesterfield and inhales about a quarter of it on the first drag. He speaks without ever taking it from his lips. "Good ones? Look, as far as that goes, none of them are a picnic. You go where they send you, hope for the best, and say your prayers that it's not one of the real rough ones like the bloody 100th. You've heard about them, right?"

"The 100th? Oh sure, who hasn't?" I feel like such a jerk, so I try to cover up with "Hell, there's tons of wild stories around here, but how do you seperate the shit from Shinola?"

Don swivels his head every now and then as though checking for enemy fighters. It's a habit, almost a twitch. He says "I don't know if this is going to do you much good, but if it's the same story I heard when I came through here six months ago, the most I can tell you is that all the shit you hear about them dropping their wheels and then shooting up the German fighters, maybe that's exactly how it happened, maybe not.

That really doesn't matter. The part about the 100th being wiped out, now that's all too goddam true."

I'm no longer so sure I want to hear this. Don's cigarette butt is down to a centimeter and he pinches it off his lower lip with yellow brown stained fingers. He squints his eyes at me and lights another cigarette. "Yep," he says "they're called the jinx group, the bloody 100th." This is definitely not what I want to hear. Don grins, slaps my shoulder and says, "Gotta go now. Piss call. Just remember what I told you about keeping a tight fisteris."

It's about three in the afternoon and I'm horizontal, logging more sack time in our hut. I tell Cavey in the next bunk all about what I heard from Don about the Bloody 100th.

"You know," he says "I figured there had to be something to that one." He's quiet for a while, then we talk about this morning's escape lecture that dealt with tips on survival after bailing out over enemy territory. If escape was impossible, we were told to surrender to the nearest German military unit. Too many of our boys have been beaten to death or hanged from lamp posts when they fell into the hands of an angry civilian mob.

That's another subject I'd just as soon not think about. I ask Cavey to toss me one of his girly books. I flip through the pages but it's no use. "Caveman," I say "between the Bloody 100th and the stuff we heard about lynchings this morning, a little bit of good news wouldn't be too hard to take around here."

"Hell," Cavey says, "that is the good news. They're not about to dish out real bad news. That could damage our morale."

We're quiet again then Cavey says, "hey partner, are you asleep?"

"Yep."

"Good, what's the toughest job in the world?"

"I give up."

"Japanese skywriting."

I guess I dropped off along about then, because next thing I know, Earl, our pilot, is shaking me awake and saying, "Come on you guys, lift your ass. Help me round up the crew. I was over to the orderly room trying to get us a pass, but forget it. They just cut our orders."

Cavey lying flat on his back with his hands clasped under his head says, "My poor aching, breaking, shaking young ass. Oh boy, Earl, that last dream was one of my all-time greats. I was this close to coming. Give me a break. Just two more minutes. Let me work down easy. I'm still in heaven."

Earl yanks the blanket off him, then spins his cap over Cavey's boner. "You better come down from that damn quick," he says, "we're assigned to the 91st and the orders are for immediately if not sooner."

Cavey sits up. "The 91st?" he says. "Isn't that where they sent ol' Clark Gable?" He squints his eyes, puckers his mouth, and in a real bad imitation of Gable says, "Frankly my dear, I don't give a damn. Anyway, it's about time we were moving on out."

Earl is impatient to get going. He helps us stuff our bags. "Maybe it's just another rumor," I say, "but I hear the 91st has been hit real bad lately."

"Reckon that's where we come in," says Cavey.

Earl grunts and says, "Shit, these things all average out."

We gather the crew together, shake hands all around, wish each other luck, and inside an hour we're all piled every which way jammed in a compartment on one of those little toy English trains on our way to Bassingbourn, home of the 91st Bomb Group.

"Not any too comfortable in here," I say to Cavey folded over in a corner with no room for his arms or legs.

"You're not just whistling Dixie there," he says. "this here's worse than a sardine can, and I don't know where the hell we're going."

"Bassingbourn, the 91st." I remind him.

"Well, at least it ain't the Bloody 100th."

TWO

The train chugs its way through the English countryside, stopping every ten minutes at, and often between, each little station along the way. Cavey snores away, his body slumped against mine. Earl sits opposite, turned sideways trying to look out the window. The rest of us lean against each other more or less asleep, stacked in a heap like cars in a junkyard. The Mouse crosses his legs and we all adjust in turn down the line like falling dominoes.

I look around the compartment and wonder again how in the world they go about forming up a crew. Probably like everything else in the service, by guess, by God, and by the numbers. They throw you in with a bunch of strangers from all over, and you're told from now on you're a crew, an inseparable team, all for one, one for all, and stuff like that, but you soon discover that while you get along O.K. with most of the boys, and may even hit it off with one or two of them swell enough to become good buddies, you also find that they've managed to come up with a few real bad apples. Guys who turn out to be just plain jerks you want no part of, but it's best to keep in mind that, jerk or buddy, any one of them is in a position to save or kill us all in a split second when we're in the air, though no regulation requires you to have anything to do with him when we come down.

Earl turns away from the train window, catches my eye and says, "You know any time our compass goes out on us, we can still count on the old Caveman here. I swear that big dick of his was pointing only a degree off true north when I woke you boys."

I laugh with him though it's nowhere near as funny as he thinks it is. Every now and then Earl gets the notion that it's part of his job to keep our spirits up, but that doesn't necessarily give him a sense of humor. He's a stocky little guy out of Milwaukee, about five eight or nine and a hundred sixty, with shoulders hunched up into his neck in a constant shrug. Twenty-one with a crinkly worried frown that makes him look nearer to forty-one. He and I are not ever goimg to be what you'd call real buddy-buddy, but he seems to know how to pilot a B-17, and I figure that's what really counts.

We first met up when I joined the crew three months ago in Alexandria, Louisiana, where I'd been sent fresh out of navigation school at Selman Field. My total flight time then consisted of ninety-nine navigation hours in a small twin engine Beechcraft bobbing around somewhere between Texas and Georgia, usually with six other equally bewildered aviation cadets, trying to conceal our anxiety and airsickness, and doing our damndest not to become irretrievably lost or commit some stupid error that would slam that Beechcraft into a fogbound hillside deep in the heart of Dixie.

At Selman, Beemish, the instructor who later on ended up tangled in that power line outside Shreveport, loved to trot out his statistics proving we had a lower rate of survival than those in combat. He'd laugh his damfool head off telling us we were taking a crash course. Our tactical officer, drunk, disorderly, and out of his mind, would often lunge howling into our barracks at 2 A.M., carom off a few posts and walls, and line us up at attention while he tore the place apart searching for whiskey. He'd confiscate any bottles he'd find, then march us out to the parade ground for close order drill and calisthenics in the darkness. This would go on until that chicken shit passed out with a bottle still in his hand.

I went through the training baffled and befuddled, squeaking through somehow, and after ten weeks graduated with my class as a navigator and 2nd Lieutenant in the U.S. Army Air Force. A few of the boys were asked to remain as instructors, others were able to pull strings for good deals with Pan Am in Boca Raton or with the Air Transport Command, but most of us were assigned to join crews for combat training on either the B-17 Flying Fortress or B-24 Liberator.

Grassy green, and not at all sure I was cut out for this line of work, I reported as ordered to the air base a hundred miles down river at Alexandria to join a B-17 crew that had formed up two weeks earlier. When I met Earl, Cavey, Fearless, The Mouse and the rest of the crew that first morning on the flight line, I had never seen a B-17 before except in the movies and magazines. I had not imagined it would be so big. I knew the navigator belonged somewhere up front, but I hadn't a clue as to how, or even where to get into the thing, and I wasn't about to betray my ignorance by asking, not on my first day.

Everyone was on board in position ready to go when Earl, puzzled as to what in the world this weird new guy pacing up and down outside the aircraft was up to, suggested if it was not too much trouble, perhaps I would care to join the rest of the crew. He then ushered me to the forward hatch door six feet off the ground, where he showed me how to chin myself up and swing into the ship by kicking my legs in. He still razzes me about that, but not often when anyone is around. I'll say that for him.

The first few weeks training was spent mostly flying out over the Gulf of Mexico where our gunners would shoot at a sleeve towed by the most frightened pilots in the service. Those tow plane pilots, terrified as they watched tracer bullets zipping by closer to their cockpits than to the sleeve, were climbing all over each other trying to sign up for combat duty, where they hoped to have a better chance of coming out alive.

You get a pretty good line on the boys in the crew when you're up there in the blue training with them every day. We all have our faults, and any crew can have a screw-up on board who couldn't hit water if he fell out of a boat, but we had one loony who was truly out of his skull. He hardly ever spoke to any of us, but he spent a lot of his time muttering to himself as he polished up his set of hunting knives that he kept hidden in his foot locker. He finally popped out of his cage on one of our gunnery training flights where we had spent a leisurely, sunny afternoon cruising around the Gulf shooting at sleeves and endangering all other aircraft and shipping in the area. We were all relaxed, enjoying our smokes as we headed back to base. Then on final approach one of our guns starts blasting away. I shout at Cavey, "Now what the hell was that?"

Cavey is as baffled as I am. "Beats the shit out of me," he says. We look out the plexiglass nose and see a herd of cattle in a pasture below. Cavey grabs my arm and yells, "Sonvabitch, look out there, one of our asshole gunners is shooting at those critters."

I see the beasts lifted off the ground by those big Browning .50 slugs slamming into their sides. We land a few minutes later. Cavey is about to blow his top. He stomps off saying, "I'm going to get that misfit bastard and string him up by his balls."

I snag Earl and say, "That dumbass gunner's a menace to us all. Get him the hell off the crew quick. There's no telling what he'll pull next. He's certifiable."

Earl, looking more worried than ever, stares down at his shoes. He didn't join up for shit like this. All he can say is "My aching back, let's not make a big deal over a few lousy cows, no sense making waves, I'll think it over."

I grab Earl's arm. "Goddam it, this geek is out of his fuckin' mind, he's shooting cows, and all you can say is you'll think it over?"

"Yep, that's what I said, I'll think it over." Earl pulls his arm free, hunches his shoulders up further into his neck, and walks off in his short, quick Jimmy Cagney steps. He's showing me he won't be pushed around, and we have to put up with that moron of a gunner for another week before he's gone, shipped off to cooks' and bakers' school.

For the next few weeks the training is stepped up and devoted mainly to tighter formation flying. "Think of an accordion," an instructor says, "now think of a goddam closed accordion. That's what we're after. Overlapping wings." He's a tough old timer, and I remember him lecturing us on the second day of training. "Flying B-17's in tight formation" he said, "is a lot like driving one of those jumbo Fruehauf trailers at top speed in heavy traffic while keeping close to the vehicles front, behind, and to each side, plus those above and below." Then he said, "No, strike that, there's just no comparison. On an airborne 17 you have no brakes, and must rely on hand controlled throttles for each one of four engines to control the velocity to keep with the formation, while holding the plane level and true no matter the wind, air pockets, or the constant atmospheric changes. You must maintain your assigned spot at all times, still keeping in mind that what would be a mere fender bender on the road means mid-air explosion and pieces of bodies falling to earth. Do all this for seven to ten hours and you've had yourself one hell of a day. For combat situations add a sky polluted with flak bursts, and a hundred Messerschmitts and Focke-Wulfs with machine guns

and cannon zipping through and tearing holes in the formation, shake well and try to keep from staining your shorts."
That lecture had us squirming for a while.

A couple of days later on another training flight, Cavey
and I are stripped down to our underwear waiting for takeoff. When we climbed into our positions in the plexiglass nose
a half hour ago, the B-17 had been standing all day in the
Louisiana summer sun. It is hot in here, sweltering, and no
windows that we can crank open. The sweat drips off me, wet-
ting my maps and charts. Behind and above us, Earl and The
Mouse are grappling with their endless checklist, reading their
manuals, examining their instruments and radio, and whatever the hell else they do up there. My temperature gauge
reads outside temperature 96 degrees. Here inside the
plexiglass nose it is close to 125, with humidity somewhere up
around a thousand. They finally get squared away and we taxi
to the runway, only to be held up another ten minutes while
Earl fidgets over a light that won't go off and one that won't
go on. Cavey shouts over the roar of the engines, "Come on
Earl, cut this horseshit! Let's get this bucket of bolts up into
the fuckin' blue."

A half hour later we shiver in sweaters under our sheepskin jackets. We're at 21000 feet, outside temperature is 11
degrees, inside maybe 20. We cruise down to the range where
we repeat bombing runs for two hours, while Cavey and the
bombardiers in the other ships drop practice bombs, hope-
fully somewhere in the vicinity of a white circled target lo-
cated six miles out from the little, and previously sleepy, town
of Jasper, Texas.

We have a 24 hour pass. Earl asks me and Cavey if we'd
like to drive over to Jasper with him. "What the hell," he says
"check out the place, nothing happening here, and it's a
chance to see what this little baby can do on the open road."

Earl has bought a dinky beat up '33 Ford roadster from one of the mechanics who told him it needed a little work. I'm not too eager to spend my pass on a long drive to Jasper with Earl in his jaloppy, but Cavey convinces me that it has to be better than hanging out here in Alexandria. When all the troops come in on pass from Camp Polk and Claiborne, Alex becomes a real madhouse. Nothing to do but roam around drunk and disorderly, fighting over the few girls in town or just for the hell of it, and waking next morning in the stockade with a bandage around your head.

Earl has spent every free minute working on that flivver until he now believes it's ready to go if he could get his hands on enough ration stamps for the gas. That's taken care of when Cavey cons the crew chief out of a tankfull of aviation gas. Earl worries that the high octane will carbon up his valves, but he gets over that when the speedometer needle on that old V-8 hits and sticks at a hundred more than once on our way to Jasper. We pass around a bottle of Swiss Colony brandy, which is all that's available since the shelves have been bare of anything resembling whisky for months.

We're driving due west on the black flat asphalt road. Earl's eyes are scrunched almost closed against the sun setting crimson and low on the horizon, while Cavey and I howl out She Has Freckles On Her But She Is Nice. Cavey breaks off and says "Let's stop this ol' heap at the next filling station, I'm going to show you greenhorns how to drink Wyoming style."

We wait at a Sinclair station until Caves comes out carrying three bottles of Seven-Up in each of his big mitts. "You boys are in for a real treat," he says, pouring about half of each bottle out on to the road. He holds the green bottles up to the light, twirling and examining them like a chemist, and lets a few more drops trickle out. When he has it just right, he refills each bottle to the top with the brandy, as careful as

Louis Pasteur. He presses his thumb on the open end of the bottle and shakes it vigorously.

"Yeee-haw!" he yells, and raises the bottle an inch from his lips, tilts his head back and lets the mixture shoot into his mouth.

"That's downright disgusting," says Earl. He takes one of the Seven-Ups, shakes it up, holds it up near his mouth and lets it fly. Then I do too, and next thing you know, we're whooping it up, shooting the drink into our mouths and at each other.

"Great balls of fire!" Earl sputters between swigs.

"Truly refreshing," I say between coughs.

We pile back into the jaloppy, drive down the road with that damn cowboy singing Brandy 'n Se'm-Up, and Earl and I trying to drown him out with Flat Foot Floogie while we fizz up Cavey specials until we run out of brandy.

"Pilot to navigator," Earl says, "what's our estimated time of arrival for Jasper?"

My eyes are fixed on the dark crimson clouds on the horizon. "Jasper?" I say "fuck Jasper, I'm hungry. Let's find us something to eat."

"Yeah, doublefuck Jasper," says Cavey. "Let's find us something to drink."

We stop at the next honky-tonk down the road. It's pretty dark inside Tiny's Blue Magnolia. Other than a woman with a boy of about eight sitting at the bar, and three old fogeys playing dominoes, the place is empty. The woman calls out a name that sounds like Tolliver. Nothing happens. She slaps her palm hard on the bar, and in a Cajun accented deep voice calls out again. "Tolliver! Godammit, man, come on out, you got some people here."

She looks kind of old, maybe thirty-five, on the plump side with tight beady eyes under pencilled eyebrows, dark lipsticked mouth with bad teeth, and it looks like she has given up trying to be blonde for a while. She puts her arm around the kid who pulls away from her. The kid's long black hair slanks over one eye, and he looks as skinny and sloppy as any other eight year old you might find in a bar slurping his lips around a bottle of Falstaff. The woman catches me looking at the kid's beer and says "What you staring at, boy? It's good for him, Doc says it contains nutrients."

She reaches into her purse, and Earl slides his cigarettes down the bar to her. When she pulls one from the pack, he goes over to her and lights it. He winks at us as he introduces himself to her as Tom Swift. She squints through the smoke, looking him up and down slowly, measuring him.

"Lou Annette," she says, "Lou Annette Bisonette, and this is my boy Lamar, he's real sharp for his age."

Lamar squirms out of her grasp again and takes a seat at the end of the bar. "Tom Swift," she says to Earl, "now where'd you pick up that name."

She's wearing a yellow halter top dress that keeps sliding off one shoulder showing a soiled bra strap. When she crosses her legs, I see her stockings rolled down to her ankles over scuffed, worn down high heeled red shoes, but there's nothing wrong with those legs. She reaches for her beer, and knocks the ash tray over on her dress. Earl is quick to help, but takes his time brushing her down.

Tolliver, a squat, dirty looking runt of a guy, comes out from wherever he was. He twitches like a horse shaking off flies, and looks like he hasn't seen a razor for a while and isn't planning to. I don't know if it's good or bad when he wipes his hands on the bar rag.

Cavey leans over toward him and asks, "What do you have to eat here today?"

Tolliver takes his own sweet time before answering, "Baloney and cheese, or I could fry you up some burgers, that's about it, not much else I'm afraid."

"You got any booze stashed away here mister?" asks Cavey.

Tolliver leans on the bar with one hand and scratches himself with the other, trying unsuccessfully to avoid the scabby spots. He points to a few bottles of Thunderbird and Ripple and some cheap rum on the shelf and says, "What you see is what I got. There's a war on I'm told. No shortage on Falstaff and we just put in some cases of Lone Star."

We order a couple burgers each, and tell Tolliver to keep the beer coming. Earl asks Lou Annette if she'd like something to eat. "Like what do you have in mind?" she asks, nudging him.

Cavey and I snicker, and Earl pulls his bar stool up close to her. "Hey, sweetheart," he says "how much further to Jasper?"

She rolls the beer bottle around her lips making sucking sounds. "Right here," she says "we're forty minutes to Beaumont, but why the hell would anyone in their right mind want to go to Jasper. It's a real shithole."

I tear a half dozen bags of chips and pork rinds off a black wire stand, pass them around and toss one down to Lamar. He makes a good catch of it, pushes the hair away from his eye, and jams a handfull of rinds down his mouth. The kid hasn't said a word yet. Earl's arm is around Lou Annette's bare shoulder as he talks quietly to her, giving her the business. She's running her hand up and down inside his shirt. Tolliver serves up our greaseburgers and keeps the beer coming. We're having ourselves a little party.

Lou Annette asks us for nickels to feed the juke box. She loads it up, kicks off her shoes, pushes her hair up, then clasps her hands behind her head and grinds away slowly to That Old Black Magic, throwing in a few bumps at the end. Earl stands up to dance with her, but he is not too steady on his feet. The brandy and the beer is getting to us. I feel warm and take off my cap and place it on the bar. Lamar picks it up and plays with it, then puts it on his head. It's way too big on him. I smile and ask him if he could go for another beer. He nods, but he doesn't smile back. I order another Falstaff and slide it down to him. Lamar is not too happy when I take my cap back. He slurps his lips around the bottle, but his eyes are on the wings pinned on my shirt. Cavey and I knock down a couple of more beers, while he tries to teach Lamar the words to Pistol Packin' Mamma. The kid ignores him. After a while I notice that Earl and Lou Annette have gone off somewhere.

"Might as well get comfortable, Caveman," I say, "looks like our good buddy Earl has taken on a project."

"Shouldn't be too long," says Cavey "ram, bam, thank you ma'am."

Lamar pulls his lips away from the beer bottle. He plays around with the wings pinned to my shirt. I pull his fingers away. I find a few coins in my pocket and put them on the bar in front of him. He grabs them up in his little fist, then looks at me sideways as if he's trying to make up his mind to break silence. After a while he says, "She seek."

I swing around on my stool to face him. "Seek? What the hell do you mean seek?"

"Seek," the kid says again, "you know, seek." He points to his crotch.

I grab and shake him. "Where the hell did she take him?" The kid points to the parking lot. Caves and I scoot out to Earl's Ford, but it's empty. I make out one other car in the lot partly hidden behind a tree. I get there a step before Cavey. Earl is on top of Lou Annette in the back seat. I don't know how far he's gone.

I pull at his arm and shoulder and say "O.K. Earl, come on, the party's over."

I hear him grunt "Have you gone crazy? Get the fuck out of here. Both of you."

Cavey reaches in and helps me tug at him. Earl stumbles

from the car, rears back and throws a wild punch at me. He misses, loses his balance and falls face first down on the gravel.

Lou Annette screams from the car. "You bastards! You dirty fag bastards! Who the hell do you think you are?"

We pull Earl up on his feet. He staggers away from us. His face is a bloody mess from the little sharp stones, and there's no fight left in him. We loop his arms over our shoulders and carry him over to the Ford, where we dump him like a barracks bag into the rumble seat.

"How much dough do you have left?" asks Cavey. I pull a few crumpled bucks out of my pocket. He folds them neatly inside a ten dollar bill and gives it to Lou Annette who hasn't stopped swearing at us.

"Here, get something for the boy," Cavey says, holding the money out to her.

She draws his hand over her body. Cavey yanks his hand back. She snatches the money and clenches it in her palm, glaring at him. "Fuck you, lieutenant," she says.

Lamar picks my cap off the ground. He asks if I want to buy it back. I'm broke. Cavey empties his pockets of change and hands it over to him. Lamar grabs the coins, then the little bastard runs off toward the bayou with my cap before I can stop him.

We speed back to Alex under a three-quarter moon bright enough to cast shadows. After a while we hear moaning and groaning from back in the rumble seat. Cavey says "It looks like we might have some activity in the bullpen."

I stop the car, and Caves spits into his bandanna and wipes as much of the blood off Earl's face as he can. "I hope some relative comes to claim this body," he says "he sure looks like shit and a half."

We lift him from the rumble and cram him in front between us. Earl coming out of it, waves his arm over us like the Pope greeting the crowd from his balcony. I pull him down as he tries to stand up to bestow the blessing. "We better get that dick of yours to a pro station, your holiness. No telling what that old bag has crawling around inside."

"It's O.K. good buddy," Earl says, "no need, I didn't even get close. I was so shnockered, I was still working to open the goddam buttons in my fly when you dickheads jumped me. My good old dependable buddies."

We're just a few miles out of Alex when the radiator boils over. Not a gas station or any water in sight. Cavey says "Well I guess it's about time to unload some of this used beer." I stop the car and he climbs on the bumper and pisses about half a gallon into the radiator. I add my share, and most of Earl's contribution lands fairly close to the aiming point.

We drive on. Cavey says, "This old heap is beginning to smell like a Trailways men's room on Sunday morning." He tilts his head back and howls "Lou Annette yahoo!", and I yell out Lou Annette Bissonette a few times like a football cheer until Earl and Cavey join in. Cavey mimics the way she said fuck you, lieutenant and we're soon shouting that out loud. Earl stinks and his shirt is torn, Cavey looks like he's been in a losing drunken brawl, but we try to quiet down and act semi-respectable when we arrive back at the base. A disgusted MP waves us through as the radiator overheats again spawning a steamy cloud of boiling piss that rises softly into the muggy blue Louisiana night.

THREE

The Kearney Army Air Force Base is small, neat, and quiet. Every structure on the base white and freshly painted. The pretty rose gardens around headquarters, the mess hall, and even the barracks are tended by a sullen squad of German P.W.'s, who avert their eyes and bow their heads when we pass.

We're out here in the heartland of the U.S. of A., smack dab in the center of Nebraska and it's nothing at all like the large active bases down south where we've taken our training. No training here. Training is over. Next stop is combat, and every dumbass cook, medic, and supply clerk on this base considers it his patriotic duty to inform us that it's combat where they separate the men from the boys. "If that's the case, hell, they can separate me right now," says Mighty Mouse. "I'm no man. I'm just a great big overgrown kid, and I'd like to stay that way for a while, if you don't mind."

Crews arrive here from all over the country and process through in five days. No more, no less. Just long enough to pick up a brand new B-17, take a check flight, then fly it west to the Pacific, or east to the European Theater of Operations.

Most of our time is spent in medical checkups and getting more shots.

Earlier today they issued us the new type oxygen masks, and the sergeant who adjusts them to fit, a real wiseass pops up with "Keep it under your hats, boys, but for sure you're headed for the Pacific."

Zibby rattles the jerk's cage by making up some shit that actually we've received our shipping orders for weather patrol out of Miami. When the guy starts swearing because he's having a devil of a time working the mask to fit snug around The Mouse's scrawny pimpled face, Zibby acts shocked. He whispers to the guy that the Mouse is a divinity student and is about to be transferred to the chaplain's office here on the base.

Zibby is last in line for his mask. It doesn't matter whether it's the sick list or the mail line, everything is alphabetical in the service, and with a name like Zybisko he's always last. "The only time I ever had a break," he says "was once at the end of a pay line of about a thousand guys at gunnery school at Tyndall Field. Some iron ass major didn't like the way we were slouching around. He stood us at attention, marched us up and down in close order drill for a half hour and got it all screwed up with the formation turned completely around with me at the head of the line. A day I won't forget soon. You know, if they lined up everyone in the whole goddam Army, Navy, and Marines for a parade, it wouldn't be over until you saw my ass fading down the road."

The Mouse says "I knew a guy back home named Arthur Zyzyvic, but he had a 4F deferment for being some kind of retard."

"Maybe he wasn't so dumb after all," says Zibby.

The Mouse has no confidence in his ability as a co-pilot to ever handle a B-17, and he's given up on the transfer he requested for fighter plane training ever coming through. He's six one and doesn't weigh an ounce over one thirty. His elongated legs, beak-like schnozz, and pinched narrow face still covered with teen age acne gives him the look of a pimply, undernourished stork. He enlisted two weeks after he graduated from Skokie High and still carries the school yearbook in his footlocker. The quotation under his senior photo is "Here I Come to Save the Day", the theme song of Mighty Mouse.

"I'm way too skinny," he says, "to push around a big old truck like the 17. I hate the fuckin' thing."

Earl gets flustered and acts as if the Mouse is just kidding when he pops off like that. Cavey and I get on Earl to ask for a replacement for the Mouse before it's too late. "Take it easy," Earl says, "you'll see, the ol' Mouse will be O.K. when the chips are down."

We have an entirely different can of worms when it comes to dealing with Skiles, our flight engineer and top turret gunner, a real loudmouth who has managed at one time or another to piss off everyone on the crew. Last night Earl dropped by and says "You won't believe this, but our pal Skiles has come up with a royal dose of the clap. How about that?"

"That sad sack," I say, "he's unfuckenbelievable. Are you sure? He could be making it up. I wouldn't put it past him. That guy has more shit than a racetrack."

"Oh, he has it all right, the genuine article," Earl says, "They've slammed him into the stockade. Sixty days, salvarsan up his dick, the whole enchilada. What really pisses me off is that jerk is almost proud of it. It doesn't bother him a bit. He told me he'd a lot rather have salvarsan shot up his gazoo than a load of flak, and if we wanted to be a bunch of dead heroes, it was O.K. with him."

Earl cusses Skiles out a dozen different ways. We have to get a new guy and Earl doesn't like changes. Then I see his face take on a peculiar expression, and he almost chokes as he tries to hold back a laugh. "Hey, take it easy there, Earl," I say, "what's going on?"

He calms down after a while and says "I just have to tell this to somebody or I'll go nuts, but you have to promise that this is strictly between us. It goes no further."

I promise. He goes on, "This is so wild I don't know how to tell it, but on our leave just before shipping up here, I didn't let my folks know I was coming. It was supposed to be a big surprise. When I get home, Mom sees me at the door, screams and throws her arms around me. She kisses me and I kiss her back, but the crazy part is that before I know it, through force of habit I slide in the old tongue. I can't believe I did it. She can't believe I did it. I can't believe she did it. Yeah, the thing that happened was before she knew what she was doing, she reacted by slipping her tongue in on me. We stare at each other paralyzed, and all the time dear old dad is standing there smiling at us without a clue to what the hell's going on, as usual."

"O, you dirty old pervert," I say. "I bet there's a medical term for that kind of shit."

Earl looks worried again. He scrunches his neck down into his shoulders and says "Remember this is strictly between us, don't be passing it around."

"Mum's the word," I say. I cup my hand to my mouth and whisper "How was it?".

The troop train coming here to Nebraska crawled up from Louisiana through Arkansas and Missouri for two and a half days, but it wasn't as bad as I had expected. Not too crowded either, as many of the boys chose to climb up on the luggage racks where they stretched out and squeezed in, arms folded across their chests like mummies.

The food situation was really screwed up. We could take all we can eat, but all that was on board besides plenty of coffee was K rations, apples and baloney sandwiches. A food fight started at the other end of the car, and apples were flying around like baseballs. I joined in, more for the hell of it than in any kind of protest about the food. Hell, baloney and K rations are a banquet compared to a lot of the slop I ate before I signed up.

I don't have much luck, and even less sense when it comes to cards, but I know enough to steer clear of the cut-throat poker in the next car that started up ten minutes after we left Alex. Those boys would clean me out in no time flat. Not much to do but look out at the empty Missouri corn fields. Nothing to read but girly magazines or comic books, and I'd had about all I could take of them for a while. Nobody I feel like writing to, so it's just old Cavey and I in facing seats, chewing the fat for hours on end.

Early on he tells me that it's about time he owned up to not being a cowboy. His dad's a pharmacist in Casper, and Cavey grew up in town with two older sisters and a younger brother. He says, "I was almost through my freshman year at Wyoming, when my high school sweetheart sent me a Dear John with the news she intended to marry her minister. That letter about drove me nuts. I went home to plead with her, but she wouldn't even let me in. I beat on her door every day for a week until my dad told me to stop making such a witless fool of myself, I was the talk of the town. I finally packed it all in and grabbed the bus back to Laramie where I wandered around deadass drunk for a few days. I don't recall much from that time except a poster in the window of the recruiting office showing airplanes and Uncle Sam pointing straight at me. I lurched in and signed up right then and there. Uncle Sam needed me and that girl would be sorry for the way she treated me once I won my silver wings as a pilot. Now here we are a year later, and I'm a dumbass bombardier on a troop train to Kearney fuckin Nebraska yak yak yakking away while she's married to this Holy Joe old enough to be her father." Cavey bangs his fist down hard on the train seat raising a ton of dust and says "Sonvabitch probably putting the blocks to her right now while I sit here blowing my top."

I hate to see the guy like that, and me without a clue how to handle it. All I can come up with is "Who knows, maybe it's all for the best. Anyway you're one up on me. I've never even come close to having a girl." That's not much help. I try again. "It's not that far from Kearney to Casper. You could try for a day off before we fly out."

Caves presses his lips together and shakes his head. "No," he says "I don't think that would be too great an idea. Not now. Maybe not ever." He digs into his B4 bag and comes up with a bottle of Bayou Queen rum. "This ain't too bad once you get used to it," he says "Got it in a barber shop in Alex."

After a couple of swigs I quit trying to identify its odd smell and aftertaste - maybe dry cleaning fluid. Cavey thinks it's more like a touch of Vitalis. We slouch down in our seats passing the bottle between us. It's eleven twenty when the train stops to take on water outside Joplin. I pull up a balky train window and breathe in the warm, humid July night and look out through the darkness at the few lights still left on in town. The train starts up again, and the yellow lights fade off until it's dark out there again.

I lean back and dream up a beautiful girl, something like Daisy May in Li'l Abner, looking out the window from one of those few lighted houses out there. She waves when she catches sight of me going by on the train and then we're in the back seat of a car kissing, and she helps me slip the clothes off her gorgeous body. I hold her close, fondle her bare firm tits, and she rolls around on me pressing against my dick. I'm getting hard.

I hear Cavey say, "Better close that window. The cinders are all flying in here." He helps me tug the window down, then passes me one of his Milky Ways he has stashed away. I unwrap it slowly and with care, still hanging on to some vague image of a nude Daisy May. Cavey takes a long pull of Bayou Queen then rotates the mouth of the bottle inside his broad palm wiping it clear of all possible killer bacteria before passing it on to me.

"Caveman," I say with the Milky Way in one hand and the bottle in the other, "this is really living. You sure know how to put on the ritz." He takes another swipe at the bottle and says "Hell, if you must travel, always go first class."

We swap stories about the other boys on the crew, and after a while we come to realize that, all things considered, basically they're a great bunch of guys, every mother's son of them, even Skiles. Then for no good reason that I know, I start telling Caves stuff that I'd never told anyone, mostly because it was about my father.

I tell Cavey "When I was a kid he'd make me hot cocoa on winter nights and tell me stories in the cold kitchen of our fourth floor Brooklyn tenement. I must have been around nine when he first told me about being out west and driving a motorcycle in the army when he was young. I'd hang on to every word about that motorcycle. He pronounced it like popsicle, and told me what it felt like to be zipping through forests of tall green pine and wide open spaces, then pulling into the clean, small towns out there with quiet streets of neat wooden houses with trimmed hedges and shrubbery out front.

He was a tall good looking guy, wavy brown hair and trim Errol Flynn mustache, a bricklayer when he could get work, but they weren't laying too many bricks in those days. He tried selling brushes door to door for a while but that didn't pan out too well, so when he wasn't looking for work he'd hang out at a motorcycle shop run by an old army buddy who'd manage to scrounge up a couple of bucks for my dad fixing up a bike every now and then.

One hot summer Sunday he took me on the Fulton Street trolley over to the bike shop for the first time. When we got there, he lit up his Sunday Stogie and told me to wait a minute. He went inside and next thing I knew, I heard a blasting roar and there he was right beside me gunning the throttle on this huge monster motorcycle. It was red, dark red, with gold trim and the word Indian painted on it in CocaCola script next to a profiled Indian head. I'd heard his stories, but had never seen him on a bike before.

He told me to hop on, showed me how to hold the grip, and zowie away we went. If I live to be an old man, I'll never forget that ride. It was my first look at the New York skyline, and there it was spread out for me from high up on the Brooklyn Bridge. He drove up Broadway slowly weaving through the traffic before turning on to Fifth Avenue, following the double decker busses to the horse and buggies outside Central Park where we stopped to feed peanuts to sheep in the meadow as he waved a leather gloved salute to the women who smiled at him, and then up through Harlem and zipping across the shiny, brand new George Washington bridge to New Jersey. Oh man, was I one happy kid.

Over in Jersey, he sped along the highway and I had the sense, which I've never had again except in dreams, of truly flying, different than what I feel in planes now. We loaded up at a roadside stand on hot dogs, sauerkraut, and root beer, before turning off the highway and coasting slowly through the silent Sunday streets of Hackensack.

He parked the bike, took my hand and walked me down the middle of those shady streets under arches of huge old elms. I peeked between the leaves and saw the neat small wooden houses just like the ones he'd told me he had seen out west with shrubbery and hedges in front. A Good Humor wagon rolled by jingling its bell, and he bought me a tooty-fruity on a stick. We came across a small park with an empty playground where he pushed my swing for a while to get me started, and then holy mackerel suddenly there he was beside me standing straight up on the next swing singing Clementine and soon flying way up there, much higher than I could, no matter how hard I pumped. At the top of his swing he waved at me the way he'd saluted the women in Central Park.

We walked again under the elms, past more of those neat houses and he mussed my hair from time to time smiling at me in a way I never saw him do at home. He held my hand and asked if I was having a good time. I couldn't begin to answer. All I could do was nod.

When he dropped the bike off, he took me inside the shop where he let me help him wipe the grease and road tar off that bike until it sparkled in the yellow light of the bare electric bulb hanging from the ceiling. I can still remember the smell of the gasoline soaked splintered wood floor inside that musty shop.

The evening had turned kind of chilly by the time we left the shop, and I drowsed off feeling his arm around me keeping me warm on the trolley all the way back home. I asked him when we might do it again. He patted my head, tucked in my shirt, and said sure kid O.K., maybe some day real soon.

About a week and a half after that ride, I pretended to be asleep when I felt his mustache pressed against my forehead one morning early about five o'clock. I didn't move when he ran his fingers through my hair, but our eyes locked when he turned at the door for a last look before he kept on going. All he had with him was stuffed in a knotted pillow case. I haven't seen him since, not that I give a damn."

Cavey rubs off the mouth of the bottle again, passes it over to me and says, "You just never know, maybe you'll catch up with him some day. It's possible."

I lift the bottle and say "Not where we're heading, it ain't. Ah, what's the use talking about it, fuck him."

I take a pack of Lucky Strikes out of one of the cartons I'd loaded up on at the Alex P.X. before we left. It's one of the new white packs which don't seem like real Luckies. I call out, "Lucky Strike Green Has Gone To War!" I try to sound like the deep voiced announcer on the radio.

Cavey pops two cigarettes in his mouth, puts the torch to both of them at the same time with his Zippo he's so proud of and passes me one of the cigarettes. He got that out of a Bette Davis movie. Then he stands up on the seat and bellows out "Aubrey Bentham Cavey, Red, White and Blue Has Gone To War!" He shouts that out a few times before tumbling down into the aisle when the train bounces through a crossing. I haul him up and prop him back in the seat, then I look out the window at the dark fields and fall into that mood again. Daisy May is wearing Rita Hayworth's negligee and is begging me for it.

I'm awake enough to know that I'm dreaming, but I go along with it until Cavey about dislocates his jaw with a monster yawn. We slow down as we pass through a town with a few dim street lights and I'm back with Daisy May.

Cavey says "You know, partner, this is turning out to be one long fuckin' train ride."

I close my eyes and give him, "You can say that again, Cowboy."

He starts in again "This is turning out to be one ..."

I shove a cigarette in his mouth. He leaves it there unlit, then falls down into his seat bent like a question mark and closes his eyes. I throw his jacket over him, then unscrew the light bulbs overhead until it's dim around us. The train whistle wails out at a crossing. I knock off the last of the Bayou Queen, fold up my jacket for a pillow, look out the window into the darkness and drift back to where Daisy May always waits for me.

FOUR

There she is waiting for us on the flight line, brand new and brightly gleaming in the clear Nebraska sunlight. The latest model B-17G, a four engined silver beauty, completely equipped straight from the factory in Seattle, and she's all ours. Not much chatter as we walk slowly around her in groups of twos and threes like kids in on a field trip to the museum, until The Mouse breaks the spell. He kicks the tires and we all join in. Soon we're climbing on, around, and all over that aircraft as if it were a jungle gym. A lieutenant drives up in a jeep, asks for the pilot and hands Earl a clipboard full of papers. Earl skims through them then signs the bottom sheet. He strokes the propeller on #1 engine and says "Well, I've signed the receipt for this vehicle and now before our friendly Boeing dealer can pick up his check, we have to take her around the block a few times to check her out. Any of you tramps want to hop in?"

It does have that great new car smell inside. Nothing at all like the stink in those old beat up ships of our training days with their stench of gasoline, rubber, and exhaust fumes blended with stale cigar and cigarette butts, sweat, and vomit. I snoop around in my little area. It's all so neat and clean, but just as cramped as ever. No seat and the little map table jammed with gauges and instruments is only fifteen inches above the floor. A navigator spends a lot of time on his knees in a B-17. The table is made of one of these new plastic materials, but I knock wood on it for luck anyway.

I see a small envelope tucked under the drift-meter gyro. Inside is a perfumed note with two lipsticked mouth prints and a message, Our Hearts Are With You Always- Drop One For Us - Mildred & Mary T. - Hydraulic Inspection. I make the first call on our intercom to tell Earl about the note. The Mouse breaks in and says, "Hey we got one of those up here too. It's from an Alma Somebody, I can't make out the name, but it has her phone number and she says to look her up if we ever get to Tacoma."

Eriksen calls in his excited schoolboy voice, "Radio to crew, radio to crew. Guess what? I got one taped on the command set from a guy who says he prays for us daily." That would have drawn a horse laugh if it came from anyone else on the crew, but nobody wants to squelch the kid. Our voices crack, and are often raspy and garbled over the intercom, but his always comes through loud and clear. Lopez says it sounds like Judy Garland's happy voice. These love notes pop up all over the ship. Zibby calls in with "Top this one. Mine is covered with lipstick and says Our Hearts Go With You To Victory with seven signatures and four phone numbers."

This is a great check flight. No tension, an easy happy ride. I reach out to give Cavey a pat on his back. He turns around, gives me the O.K. sign circling his thumb and index finger. I call JoJo who has moved up from the waist to fill in for the missing Skiles in the top turret. "Hey, JoJo, how's it going?" He swivels the turret around rapidly back and forth. "Oh, this is like a regular merry-go-round," he says.

I call each position, and everything is fine or can be easily fixed. The only glitch I can find requires only a minor adjustment in the new type flux gate compass. Earl puts the ship through her paces in a series of sharp turns, dives, and climbs. Smiles and back pounding all around when we land after two hours cavorting up there in the blue.

Flying is still some kind of miracle to me. Only a year ago, neither I nor anyone else on our crew had even come close to being inside a plane. Earl was then a part time grease monkey in a Milwaukee gas station, Cavey was pining away his freshman year at Wyoming having all that trouble with his girl, the Mouse was just goofing off after graduating from Skokie High, and I was an apprentice typesetter in a grimy Buffalo print shop making the forty cents an hour minimum wage and forget overtime no matter how many hours I put in.

The other guys didn't have it too much better. Eriksen was a stock-room boy in a pump factory in Wichita, and Skiles busted his balls on the loading dock in an Akron tire plant. Conrad Lopez was a picker for whatever was in season in the Imperial Valley and had been beaten up and kicked off of every job he ever had for trying to organize. Comrade Conrad. Zibby had just started on his first job in a Denver lumber yard, and our waist gunners, Jojo Cooper and Fearless Fosdick were farm boys. Jojo on a small dairy farm outside Rhinebeck, New York, and Fearless on 384 prime acres in soy beans and corn near Huron, South Dakota.

Well, baby look at us now. Lieutenants and sergeants in the U.S. Army Air Force can you believe it. Aren't we the cat's meow and each one of us making a lot more money than our dads. Ten plain Joes out here in Kearney, Nebraska with this brand new four engine B-17 airplane they've given us, and sometime tomorrow we'll be taking this great big silver bird up into the wild blue yonder and fly it across the Atlantic fuckin' Ocean. Hot diggety dog, how about that!

After dinner, we go into town for our last night in Kearney. The only halfway decent bar in town is the Cornhusker Cafe in the only hotel in town. We tell the owner to keep the Stroh's flowing. Most of our talk is about Skiles and his dose of clap, and how we're lucky to be well rid of him, and whoever we get for a replacement tomorrow is bound to be an improvement.

When we take that as far as it can go, we move on to the possibility of an all St. Louis World Series and what a great year Stan Musial is having, and how about the brother battery of Mort and Walker Cooper. We kick that around, then somebody mentions F.D.R.'s bid for a fourth term, and even though only Earl and Skiles are old enough to vote, that doesn't stop us from flinging it around thick and fast.

Zibby pops up with "If I could vote I'd go for Roosevelt. He got us out of the depression, and now we have minimum wages, Social Security, and all that. Besides we're in a war, and in a war you stand by your leader."

"Right, he'd get my vote too. My dad says we shouldn't change horses in midstream," says Eriksen.

JoJo says "We haven't had anybody else in the White House since I was in first grade. It's about time we gave someone else a chance. I'd vote for Tom Dewey. I heard part of a speech he gave once on the radio, and I know he stands four square behind the Constitution."

Lopez raises his hands and says "You guys are just repeating the lies of the vicious capitalist press. Time, Reader's Digest and Chicago Tribune propaganda. Believe me friends, the only candidate with any kind of program to help the masses is Earl Browder." I like Lopez and he's really a good kid at heart, but I've told him over and over that if he keeps talking like that, he's going to find himself in trouble.

JoJo is for F.D.R. because he ended Prohibition and he's a friend to the farmer. Fearless says, "He kept the country from going under when all the banks were either closing or kicking farmers off their land."

"I don't know where we'll be on Election Day," says Earl, who turned twenty-one last month, "but if it's anywhere I can vote, I'm taking Tom Dewey. No way in the world for Roosevelt to be re-elected. The public will never stand for it. A fourth term! Hell, that would make him a goddam dictator."

Cavey has been putting the Strohs away without word one to anybody all night. Now he explodes. "What the hell's the matter with you guys? Do you have rocks in your head? Don't you know it makes no nevermind which one of those blowhards gets in. They're both nothing but a pair of lying politicians freeloading on us, and neither of them have even the least clue as to how to end this war. You jerks talk like you've got paper assholes."

That almost breaks up our little party. It goes quiet for a while, as if he broke the rules of a game we were playing. Then Zibby and Fearless argue over who's more valuable to his team, Bob Feller or Di Maggio, everyone joins in and it's as if Cavey hadn't said a word. I put my hand on his shoulder and say "Take it easy, Caves, we're all pals here."

He shakes me off with "Ah, this goddam buddy buddy, all for one and one for all horseshit can make a guy puke. And let me tell you, partner, I'm mucho disappointed in you going for it too. I gave you credit for more sense." He jabs his cigarette toward me almost putting it in my eye.

I get him to sit down and we have a couple of beers, but he's still in a foul mood. I ask "What the hell's biting you? You worked up about us shipping out tomorrow? Nothing you can do about that now, so you may as well relax and join the party. Come on, Caves."

Earl comes over and I'm afraid he's only going to make things worse, but he says "Hey, I need a volunteer. See those two gals —." He tilts his head toward a booth where two girls turn away when they catch us looking. "I'm in like Flynn with the tall one, but they come as a matched pair and I can't break them up, so who's going to be a good buddy?

Caves says "Count me out. I'm nobody's buddy. Take him." He points to me. "He likes being a buddy. He just eats it up."

"Ah, fuck you, Caveman," I say. I go with Earl over to the booth. The girls are Vinnie and Minnie, short for Elvina and Minerva. They're cousins from Peru. Peru, Nebraska, that is, where they teach third and fourth grade in the consolidated school and are now here taking summer classes at Kearney State Teachers College. They're older gals, around twenty-five, and I feel kind of nervous being out with teachers, but Earl is doing fine. He and Vinnie get up to dance when Artie Shaw starts in on *Begin The Beguine* on the jukebox.

I apologize to Minnie. "I don't know how to dance."

"Don't worry," she says, "it's O.K.", and we sit there with her making conversation about the weather and shortages until she runs out of anything more to say than it's so close in here and would I care to go out for a bit of fresh air. We walk slowly around the empty Kearney streets, looking in on store windows, where I sneak looks at her figure reflected in the plate glass, and while she isn't built as good all over as some of Cavey's sweater girls, she sure looks good to me. She tells me how much she enjoys teaching, and all about younger brother Merlin, who just sits around the house now in silence, chain smoking cigarettes and drinking booze after losing a foot on Guadalcanal. She asks me about what I did back home, and she hopes I don't have the wrong idea about her. She never goes to cafes, but she's gone this once only because Vinnie had told her that's where she had met some very nice boys from the air base before. Tonight was her first beer.

She talks and talks, but she catches me more than a couple of times staring at her reflection in the windows, and

she knows what I'm looking at, and probably what I'm thinking. She takes my hand, and I feel the beginning of a boner as
my arm keeps brushing up against her side. She says, "There's
absolutely no boys at all left up at school, and they're having a
dance Friday night, would you like to come?"

I tell her that though I very much want to see her again,
there's not much likelihood that I'll still be around, not that
I'm much use at a dance anyway. I can tell right off she thinks
I'm dusting her off, and the way she stiffens up and purses
her lips together doesn't make me feel too much like spelling
it out any clearer for her. She pulls back her hand and says
"It's time we were going back, Vinnie must be wondering whatever happened to us." I've struck out again, and she's cold
silent as we walk back to the cafe.

Vinnie and Earl hadn't even noticed we were gone. Earl
is one hell of a good dancer and is leading Vinnie through
some real fancy steps in Tuxedo Junction. After a while, they
come over to our table. Minnie stands up to excuse herself to
the little girls' room. She nudges Vinnie until she remembers
she has to go too. They walk off hand in hand.

Earl is all smiles when he says "Boy oh boy, that Minnie
really has a pair."

"Oh yeah, I really hadn't noticed."

"You must be going blind. How're you making out with
her?"

"Like a bandit, can't you tell."

Vinnie looks like she's upset with Minnie when they come
back to the booth. She says, "I really hate to leave when we're
all having such a perfectly wonderful evening, but poor Minnie
isn't feeling well."

Earl gets her to stay for one last dance and one more
beer, and it's plain to see the way she's dancing with him that
the last thing in the world she wants to do is leave, but all Earl
gets is it's getting late and we truly have to be running.

After they skip, Earl gives me a dirty look and says "What the hell did you do to screw up this deal."

"Oh," I say, "probably what I always do, whatever that is."

Now I've got Earl sore at me too. It's just not my night. I go back to Cavey who's half plastered by now. I put my arm over his shoulder. "Come on, Cowboy, time to take you home. We have a big day tomorrow. Say good night to everybody."

Cavey sizes me up through narrowed eyes and says, "You sure didn't have to dump that gal on my account. Just looking at that sweet pair of corn fed beauties of hers makes a guy proud of his country." He grins and takes a poke at me. I duck under his arm and help him out of the place.

He says "I know I can always count on you, partner."

"Sure," I say, "remember I'm your good buddy."

It's nearly four when we wake to the sound of a guy running around in the company street in his pajamas shouting I won't go, you can't make me. He yells variations on this for ten minutes until the M.P.'s drive up. I feel sorry for the poor bastard, as they work him over pretty hard before hauling him away. The street is silent again. I go back to sleep.

I'm up at six for the briefing on the Atlantic crossing. The briefing navigator has an R.A.F. mustache, and calls England the United Kingdom or U.K. in a weird British accent that has more than a hint of pure New Jersey. We are to make three overnight stops after we leave Kearney. First stop is Bangor, Maine, then up to Goose Bay, Labrador, then across to Keflavik, Iceland. He tweaks the ends of his mustache before giving us our destination after Keflavik. Near as I can make out, it's Utterly Unpronounceable, Wales, in the U.K., part of the British Empah, chaps.

Most of the crew are on board busy with pre-flight chores when I get out to the ship. I'm puzzled to see Skiles loading his gear on the aircraft. I wave and say Hi, which he acknowledges with a not too friendly grunt. Earl is talking to a couple of guys on the ground crew. "Hey," I say, "am I seeing things? What's the story on Skiles? I thought they'd slammed that jerk deep in back of the stockade and we were getting a replacement."

Earl hunches his neck deeper into his shoulders. He says "Well, shit, so did I, but I'm afraid we still have him on our hands. They have a new miracle drug now. Peninsula, it's called, something like that. The Army just started it last week. It works pretty good from what I hear. Anyway it's made a new man out of Ol' Skiles." Earl laughs. "You should have seen him when he reported for duty, talk about being pissed off— You get the clap and it's no worse than catching a cold now. One jab in the ass and he's now clean and kissing sweet."

"I'll bet he just loved that," I say. "I know where I would have stuck that needle."

One of the ground crew guys hands us a beer, and we click bottles against the side of the plane. "Take care of this baby," he says. Earl promises we'll do our best. I wince when I hear him trying to sing *Off We Go Into The Wild Blue Yonder* as I throw my gear up into the plane. It's time to go.

I call out our position to the crew every half hour or so. It's a bright July day with clear visibility all around, only about 3/10ths low cumulus. We fly at our briefed altitude of 8500 feet, though two or three times Earl takes us up to eleven or twelve thousand where we get a slight buzz from the thin air. He takes us down to 3000 for a good look when we're over big cities like Omaha, Chicago, Cleveland, and we even go down to 1100 when we circle empty Yankee Stadium twice. Too bad the Yanks are playing in Washington today. The sun is dropping toward the tall pine forests as we land in Bangor, nine and a half hours out of Kearney.

We take off for Goose Bay, Labrador right after breakfast the next morning. When we cross into Canada, I call over the intercom, "Navigator to crew, navigator to crew. If you look out to the rear, it's your last look at the good old U.S. of A. for a while. Hats off boys." I get no replies. We cross the Gulf of St. Lawrence heading northeast. Nothing below us but forest after forest, and ten thousand lakes scattered below us like shattered glass from a broken window. No houses, no towns, not even a road. Cavey makes himself comfortable, curled up on the floor with his parachute for a pillow. I point outside and say, "We go down here and they'll never get us out, Caveman. This makes Wyoming look like the big city."

"Getting closer," he says.

He stretches out on the floor and offers me a couple of Oreos from a box. I keep busy. This is no place to screw up. We make Goose Bay six hours out of Bangor. The operations officer at Goose says, "I expect you guys are ready to make the big trip to Iceland in the morning. I have four crews holed up here checking all kinds of shit on their plane. Each day a different malfunction. Two of them have been here a week now. Their main malfunction, if you ask me, is a bad case of the heebie-jeebies, gangplank fever. I hope you guys don't give me any grief."

I know I should turn in and get some sleep, but I'm too charged up. Besides at ten o'clock, the July sun up here is as high in the sky as back home at four in the afternoon. Earl asks if I want to join him, Cavey, and Mighty Mouse for a walk around the base. They can't sleep either.

We're four guys hanging out in Labrador, moseying around in the outlandish eleven o'clock night-time daylight. The Mouse turns to me and says "Fuck 'em all. It would serve them damn right if you gave us the heading for Bolivia tomorrow. What do you say, guys?" We walk toward our plane on the hard stand. It glistens pink as it reflects the red shafts from the sun emerging behind the clouds.

Earl says, "You're way too weird, Mouse. We try a stunt

like that, and we'd all end up chopping rock in Leavenworth the rest of our natural lives plus six months."

Cavey slides his big mitts slowly across the skin of the plane. "Yeah, that'd be tough duty," he says, "but it sure as hell beats bleeding to death with your balls shot off in a burning ship twenty-five thousand feet somewhere over Germany. How many infantry guys do you think would be heading for the front lines if you gave them a plane with full gas tanks?"

I climb up on the plane's wing, suck in my gut and the crystal clear air of Labrador. A yellow-red three quarter moon shaped like a Shell gasoline sign covers one fourth of the horizon as it rises in the rosy eastern sky. I look down on Earl, Caveman, and the Mouse. My boys. I pound my chest, and give out my Tarzan yell. They look at me up on the wing as if I'd gone completely whacko.

I shout out, "Hey you goofballs, how about Zanzibar?"

FIVE

Well, this is it. On our way across the Atlantic to Iceland. CAVU, clear and visibility unlimited, two tenths high cirrus, wind from 195 at 16 knots. Ten minutes after we reach our assigned altitude of 8,000 feet, Earl goes on autopilot. It's a smooth ride, and I call in corrections of a few degrees only about once every hour. He doesn't tell me until we land that he had picked up the powerful Iceland beam when we were halfway across, and had used it as a cross-check on my navigation in case I screwed up.

An old timer at Goose Bay had warned me not to rely on radio up near the magnetic pole. I listened to him and stuck to good old dependable dead reckoning textbook navigation, reading drift off the whitecaps for my wind velocity and direction, shooting sunlines by sextant for ground speed and longitude, picking up latitude off my astro-compass, and verifying position as we crossed the coast off the tip of Greenland. I could hardly believe that all those navigational aids pounded into my skull by those goofy instructors at Selman Field could actually work up here, one thousand miles from land and eight thousand feet over the North Atlantic Ocean. Cavey asked

"Why the smile partner?" I said "Oh, nothing special. Just thinking about some guys I used to know."

That old timer at Goose Bay knew his business all right. He was Major Omar Stang, grizzled and heavy set, about forty-five. He looked as if he slept in his uniform and smelled like a bar rag. One of those genuine boozers who somehow manage to function between their morning hangover and the start of another day's bender without ever appearing totally loaded. He belched his way through the same briefing he'd given every crew that had come through Goose Bay since he was a scout for the Byrd expedition ten years ago. Omar had always been on the booze, the operations officer told us, but he hadn't made a career of it until he heard he'd lost his son with Patton in Sicily.

He seemed sober enough, decked out in a clean uniform and freshly shaved with only a few nicks here and there, when he came out to see us off. He spoke to each of us separately, asking if there was anything he could do for us. "Like what for instance?" I asked when it came my turn. He seemed almost as puzzled by my question as I was with his. He shrugged and said, "Why like anything, anything at all. Name it."

I tried as we all did, but none of us could come up with anything except Eriksen who asked him if he would take our crew picture. Later, Lopez asked him to pose with us as an honorary member of the crew. We put Omar in the middle, and we all gathered around that old walrus. Some of us asked him to pose with us individually. That made his day.

Before we took off, Omar pulled me aside, put his arm around my shoulder and said "Look son, you're going to do fine, but this is serious stuff. Accept your responsibility. And number one, stick with what you know. Don't deviate from the instructions in your briefing kit. There's a lot of water out there, so don't do anything stupid like trying for short cuts. Number two: the only land you'll see after you take off will be the tip of the Greenland ice cap when you're around three hours out. Be sure to spot your position over it as a check on your D.R., but don't stare at the snow without your protective goggles. And number three, I'm sure you've found out by now that at these latitudes magnetic forces and sunspots can play hell on radio bearings up here. So if you're counting on picking up the beam and homing into Iceland, well I just wouldn't if I were you. Sure it works fine most of the time, and it's easy to sit back, fat dumb and sloppy, keeping that needle on zero all the way, but where the hell are you if that crutch is pulled out from under you by interference, or a storm that will swing that needle crazily all over the lot, or if you get a short or some other malfunction and you have no radio at all. You're in real deep shit, that's where you are, up the well known creek without a paddle. And also, don't forget there's a flock of German subs sitting out there with heavy transmitters working day and night at bending that beam. I'd hate to add you to the list of all too many poor dumb kids who followed it smack into a fjord in Norway."

I kept my head turned away to keep from being knocked over by his breath all the time the old geezer was briefing me, but you can bet I listened. "Drop me a note when you think of it," he said. "Let old Omar know how you're doing when you get there. Damn, I wish I were going with you." Then I didn't know what to say or do when he grabbed and hugged me. The last thing he said as I climbed on board was "And don't forget to send me the pictures we took."

We were about four hours out over the ocean when Lopez and JoJo came visiting down to my area. They said they'd had a couple of drinks with Omar the night before and Omar had confided that he felt a special kinship toward me because I reminded him so much of the son he had lost. Lopez remembered that Omar said it wasn't only that we looked alike and had the same peculiar way of walking, but we both even had pretty much the same attitudes. They waited for my reaction, but I was so flustered by their news that all I could say was I hope I have a little better luck on my side.

One half of our bomb bay was loaded with a couple of extra fuel tanks, and the other with well over a hundred sacks of mail for the boys overseas. Once we were airborne, Earl and the Mouse scanned the dials and took turns at the wheel, but there wasn't much for them to do after we went on auto-pilot. Eriksen radioed out position reports I gave him every half hour, but the rest of the crew just hung around or slept their way across. Not much for them to look at but hour after hour of empty dark green ocean and whitecaps.

They're all awake when we run into a bit of sudden tur-bulence in heavy weather about a half hour before my E.T.A. for Iceland. Cavey presses his face to the plexiglass as we de-scend, but he can't see through the soup and rain out there. We break through the undercast at three thousand, and he's the first to see Keflavik ahead and four miles to the left. He spins around, waves a circled thumb and index finger at me, and heaves a sigh of relief. He's nowhere half as relieved as I am. Earl calls on the intercom, "Nice going, navigator". I think of Omar Stang back at Goose. "Piece of cake," I say. Caves tosses me a Milky Way. "Getting closer," he says.

We've been socked in here in Keflavik for three days. Other than all around goofing off and dedicated sack time, there's not much to do. Yesterday, we all gave the Mouse a going over after he dragged into our hut what looked like a ragged, dark gray sheet of plywood that smelled like mothballed fish. "No kidding," he said "it's a genuine seal-skin pelt. I got it for a song from a guy in the instrument shop. It's going to be fine after a little thawing out."

He spread it out carefully over the coal stove when we went to lunch. We would have needed gas masks to get back into the hut when we returned. The stink hit us from fifty yards out, and the Mouse ran like hell to save his valuable pelt. We held our noses, and gawked at the smoking, vile mess spread out on the ground. It stank like a combination of burnt feathers and tires, and most of the hairs had fallen out. We got buckets, poured water over it, and the rest of the hairs washed away leaving a shrivelled, reeking heap in a puddle of mud. The Mouse took such an awful razzing from the guys that I almost felt sorry for him, but it was all I could do to keep a straight face when Earl told him, "Tough shit, ol' buddy, that was one beautiful skin." We all felt better when even The Mouse joined in as we hooted at that one. "That's Earl for you," Cavey says to me later "what he really wants to be is chaplain."

I've gone to the base movie with the guys yesterday and today, seeing For Whom The Bell Tolls both times. It's a real good movie with Gary Cooper and a beautiful new actress named Ingrid Bergman in it, but I hope they show a different one tomorrow. Coming out of the movie this afternoon, we had a little situation going, and naturally it had to do with Skiles again. I still wish we could get rid of that creep.

The way it started was we noticed a small detail of German prisoners, about twenty of them, seated in back of the movie, guarded by M.P.'s. They sat stiff and straight up in their seats, some with shaved heads, three or four with monocles, and all with thick necks and pressed uniforms. They looked nothing like the P.W.'s we saw back in Kearney. These guys, an M.P. told me, were all Wehrmacht officers captured in North Africa and Sicily. They're still in command of their men who work for us building barracks and extending the runways here at the base. Anyway, sometime during the movie, Skiles sneaks off and works a deal with one of the prisoners, swapping a carton of Pall Malls for the prisoner's medal. Of course, we don't know about it until we leave the movie, and there's ol' Skiles strutting around with the medal on his chest hung from a black ribbon.

We stare at him, puzzled. Zibby says "Hey, other than your ugly head, what the hell is that you have hanging from your neck?" Skiles goes into his version of a goose step. He marches right up to Zibby and says "It's nothing but a fuckin' Iron Cross, that's what."

Zibby takes a closer look at it and says "If that's an Iron Cross, I'm Eleanor Roosevelt. Looks more like what you find in a box of Cracker Jacks. You've been screwed, Skiles."

"What the hell do you know? You think you're so fuckin' wiseass, all of you guys. I'll get hold of the guy and prove it to you."

Skiles starts goose stepping again.

"Cut that shit. Take the goddam thing off," says Lopez.

Skiles stops, glares at Lopez and says "What do you know? Another county heard from. Who yanked your chain you little pisspot?"

Lopez has his fists clenched and moving when I step in front of him and Fearless grabs Skiles and pulls him away. It takes some time before I can feed Lopez enough bullshit to cool him off. When Skiles stomps off swearing and clutching the medal, Fearless says "I'll bust your ass if you ever show that fuckin' thing around us again."

I go back to our hut feeling as if I'd come across something mean and rotten. Earl and Caves have just finished playing Monopoly. I tell them what happened, and Caves says "You should have let Lopez have him." Earl hunches his neck deeper into his shoulders as if bracing for a weight, and says "O.K., so granted Skiles is a real jerk and doesn't have the brains he was born with, still I don't see too many geniuses on our crew, and I also don't see how letting him know we're all down on him helps much. Hell, this crossing is taking way too long, and this place especially gives me the creeps. I'll be damn glad when we get to England."

Cavey puts the Monopoly money and pieces back into the box. "That's another twelve thousand you owe me," he says to Earl. "What's your damn hurry about England? You eager for combat? You may think different once you see that flak coming up at you."

Earl thinks that one over and says "That's a piss poor attitude. You want to think positive. The way I see it, the sooner we go in, the sooner we finish up and go home."

"Maybe," Cavey says. "It's going to take a lot more luck than I've had in my young life so far to finish thirty-five missions." He turns to me and asks me how I feel about it.

"How the hell should I know," I say "some of my instructors got through O.K. If they made it, maybe we can too. Anyway, it's not like they're giving us much choice."

Earl pulls twelve bucks from his wallet. "I don't know how you do it, Caveman. You're one lucky bastard." Cavey laughs. He's heard this from Earl before. He says, "Yeah lucky me, that's why I'm here."

We're still in dark dense overcast when we wake next morning, but we're told at breakfast that there's a possibility the system may be breaking up at last. We should be alert for taking off before noon. For once the metro forecast is right, and we catch glimpses of a pale yellow sun poking through the dark gray, steel wool clouds banked above. We're all assembled and ready to go by ten. While waiting for clearance to take off, I write a V-mail letter to Omar thanking him for his advice about the crossing, and also I hope he won't feel too bad but someone here in Iceland swiped Eriksen's camera with the film of the crew pictures we took back there in Labrador.

Six hours later we land in Wales. Nothing any too remarkable about the flight itself, except as we were tooling down the Irish Sea, we saw large white E's etched into the land down off our right wing. We were close to the sacred soil of Eire, and I'd been briefed to steer clear as they were neutrals in the war and those crazy Irish just might shoot to keep us away. As we taxi in after the landing, Caves goes into his kit for a Milky Way. I say, "Don't tell me - I know, Caveman. We're getting closer."

I remember I'd left my letter to Omar in the Operations hut in Iceland. I guess someone will find and mail it. I tape a note on the driftmeter wishing luck to the crew who will get our ship, and feel kind of lost when they wheel her off to the modification center. I'd felt more at home on her than on any of those bareboned bases we stopped at on the way over here. Now even those places don't seem so bad, when it occurs to me that the next time I climb into a B-17, I'll be navigating it to Germany. Round trip, I hope.

As we stand waiting for the train in the early morning fog, Fearless says, "Hey navigator, where the hell are we?" I point to the undecipherable thirty-six letter Welsh railroad sign, mostly W's, L's, and C's, and Earl just has to come up with "Read it and weep, Fearless, I guess we're not in Kansas anymore."

It's a long ride with many stops, but finally we're at the repple depple in Bovingdon where the first thing we hear is don't bother to unpack. We goof off as best we can, talking about sex and passing on all the rumors flying around. Nine days later we're back on another one of those toy trains, this time to the 324th Bomb Squadron, one of four squadrons of the 91st Bomb Group at Bassingbourne. As we bounce around in the crowded compartment, I try to bury those wild rumors. Like Cavey says, at least it ain't the bloody 100th.

SIX

The rumor we'd heard at the repple depple that the 91st Bomb Group at Bassingbourne was an ex-R.A.F. base turns out to be true. A six by six picks us up at the station and drops us off with our gear at one of the old barracks where the Mouse and Earl are to share a double-bunked 7 x 9 foot cell, while Cavey and I are assigned to one a bit smaller. Cavey claims the upper bunk by right of tossing his B-4 bag on it first. He turns over the thin mattress with one hand and says, "This ain't the Waldorf, but it sure beats where the poor bastards in the infantry are sleeping tonight." I fall into my sack and look up at Cavey's big G.I. shoes extending out from the end of his bunk above. The rumor I'd heard about the 91st having been hit hard lately works its way into my mind, fading in and out like an out of range radio signal until I doze off.

I sit up when an announcement squawks tinnily over the Tannoy - all new crews assigned to the 324th Squadron will report to squadron headquarters for a meeting with Captain Hartak at 2000 hours. "That's our invite to the prom," Cavey says. He faces the speaker, throws his hands upward and bows like a Moslem when the message is repeated three more times in the next minute.

After dinner we amble around the local countryside killing time before the meeting. I hear the drone of aircraft and look up to see a long line of over a hundred black R.A.F. Lancaster bombers sharply profiled against a layer of high cumulus. We watch them growing smaller as they fly in trail toward the darkening eastern sky. "Yep, the real thing at last," Caves says, "now just where do you suppose they might be heading tonight, partner?"

We roam through fields in the long summer twilight, coming across B-17's in their dispersal areas close to barns, sheds, and farm houses. Just about every plane we see, the old olive drab painted ships as well as the newer shiny unpainted jobs, is spotted with pieces of sheet metal riveted on like patches on a vaudeville tramp's coat. A piece of bright aluminum about four feet square is outlined against the olive drab right wing of Round Trip II. Cavey whistles and says "Oh man, that ship has seen some action. Reckon we're close enough now."

We join our crew for the meeting inside a room with about thirty classroom chairs, a line of dented and rust spotted steel lockers tilted toward each other against the back wall, and a chalky gray blackboard up front. It all looks much like my high school home room except for the maps of Northern Europe and Germany covering spaces between the grimy windows on the outside wall. The Mouse shows me a list pencilled on the wall where the bottom of a map has been torn off. The scrawled letters are crude as a ransom note and rubbed away in spots, but I can make them out.

Beware The Handwriting On The Wall—
Fog
Fire
Flak
Fighters
Fear
Frost
Flames
Fatigue
Fucking Up
Focke-Wulfs
Foul Weather and this above all
The Five Fickle Fingers of Fate

The crews huddle in bunches like rival tribes, eyeballing each other, all waiting for something to happen. I show the handwriting on the wall to Cavey. He finds a bare spot and pencils in False Friends, Farting, Flogging It. I elbow him to stop when a barrel chested captain about twenty-five or so with a blond crew cut calls out for us to listen up.

The captain announces in a Fort Worth cab driver accent, "No, I'm not Captain Hartak. Relax, boys. I'm Captain Holbrook Yancey Cross. Yep, Holy Cross, exec officer reporting to Captain Hartak and doing my best to keep up with all the endless pokerino details that it takes to run the 324th Squadron of the 91st Bomb Group, Eighth Air Force, U.S. Army, yes sir. I want you all to know that if you have any problems around here, you come see me. I might not be able to help much, but it sure as hell beats crying alone in your beer, or having the chaplain punch your Tough Shit card. T. S. cards will be issued after this meeting."

He licks his lips and waits for his laugh. This is one of his endless pokerino details. Loosening us up. He gets his laughs. The Mouse whispers to me, "This guy's a worm."

Cross lowers his voice as if letting us in on a secret. "Now for some good news. One thing I can assure you right now is that the war's going to be over by the end of the year —" He stops for a beat "— because either us or the Nazeyes are damn sure to run out of paper by then."

Earl tells us to hold it down as Cavey and I groan. Cross raises his arm and calls out, "O.K., now let's hear it loud and clear, any of you boys here from Texas?" A dozen voices shout Abilene, San Antone, Austin, Big D, Corpus, Lubbock, Waco, Houston. Cross looks happy. He has this group under control. I say to Cavey, "How about a vote for ol' Jasper?"

"Yep," he says, "let's go for it."

I call out "Jasper!"

Cavey hollers "Jasper, fuck Jasper!"

He and I fall over each other, sharing our only laugh of the day. Cross and the other crews stare at us, wondering who let these two hyenas out of their cage. Cross then delivers the usual crap about how Texans could probably beat the Luftwaffe all by themselves.

Fearless mutters, "Eat shit, Texans."

More cheers when Cross shifts into anybody here from Chicago, then Brooklyn, Boston, Philly, California, Dixie, etc. He pumps his fist into the air when Dixie gets the rebel yells and hoots.

"Fuckin' degenerate assholes," says Lopez.

Earl says, "Twenty to one he doesn't ask for Wyoming, Caveman."

A corporal comes in and hands Cross a few notes. He reads them and says, "Captain Hartak will be here shortly. Meanwhile if you have any questions, fire away. but for the love of Pete, don't ask me how you can be transferred to the Air Transport Command."

One of the boys asks, "When are we likely to fly our first mission?"

Cross cranks up his phony smile and says, "That's usually the third question. The first two are always where are the girls and when do we go on pass?" Cross waits for his laugh again then continues "— But to answer your question, we break up your crews for the first three or four missions and fly you with veteran crews until you learn the ropes. Ordinarily, we'd have about half of you on for tomorrow, and the rest of you up on our very next mission."

Cavey raises his hand and asks polite as can be, "What do you mean ordinarily, sir?"

Cross breaks off the smile. He doesn't look so friendly or helpful now as his eyes drift from glaring at Cavey to the maps on the wall. He clenches his jaw and inhales deeply before he says, "I really didn't want to get into it at this time, because frankly we've had an unusually bad situation around here the past forty-eight hours, one of our toughest. I know you're going to hear all kinds of rumors about this, if you haven't already, so let me give it to you straight. We've taken a bad hit and we've chalked up a few casualties. Strike that — more than just a few. The fact is that a day before yesterday we sent our usual twelve ship squadron up with the Group. Target — Halle. All went well until halfway between Kassel and Eisenach, where about a hundred Focke-Wulfs jumped our Group. Our squadron took the most damage. Six crews down, half the squadron, sixty of our best boys, and we've had a devil of a time patching up those ships that made it back."

Cross raises his hands to quiet the buzzing. He says "O.K., we take our losses and push on. I put the requisition straight in to Bovingdon, and they came right through. You boys are the replacements. They've flown in new 17's to us, and bet your ass we're working night and day to check them babies out, but that's not the problem. The big problem is right now we just don't have too many veteran crews left around, so it's going to take a few days longer than *ordinarily* —" He gives

Cavey a quick dirty look. "— before we can work you all in, though I wouldn't worry too much about it. We'll keep you busy, and I promise we'll still have enough war left for you."

I can't help thinking of those patched up ships Cavey and I saw earlier. I pull out a cigarette and my hand is not very steady when I light up. "Looks like we're in Dutch with this character," I say.

"Ah, he's nothing but a phony windbag," says Cavey, "Don't let him bother you, what the hell can he do — ground us? Maybe trade us to the Bloody 100th?"

Cross looks around the room. "Any other questions?" he asks. The room is humming with conversation, and about ten hands are up. Someone yells out, "What about Hartak? We've heard all kinds of stories about him."

Cross tacks on the smile again and says, "Yeah, I'll just bet you have. Hartak, well he's tough, but he's fair. One thing for sure, he can't stand fuck-ups, and whatever you do, don't ever use the word impossible around him. He came close to buying the farm on his 19th mission when he crashed into the woods short of our runway. The docs said it would be impossible for him to walk again. Now don't ask me how, but five months later he was back on flying status, and not only that, he signed up for a second tour. He now has forty-nine missions under his belt with everyone telling him that he's really pushing his luck. The brass have tried their best to stop him, but he ignores them and goes up with the squadron every chance he gets. So you can expect to see a lot of him, but as I said, you want to watch yourself when he's around. No fuck-ups, no impossibles."

One of the Texans asks, "How often can we expect to fly missions once we get started."

"Well, of course all kinds of factors enter into that," Cross says, "but once you're checked out and all, you can find yourself flying three or four missions one week, and then two or three the next, or even none at all some weeks. It's kind of complicated, but a simple way to say it is that it's all based on three out of four. So, typically on any given raid our squadron puts up three out of four of our sixteen crews. That's twelve ships. Our Group, the 91st, will put up three of its four squadrons, that comes to thirty six bombers. The Combat Wing will fly three of its four Groups, that's a hundred planes, and we have about a dozen Combat Wings now. So it all adds up to a thousand or so Forts and Liberators carrying ten thousand American terror gangsters on their way to bomb the churches, orphanages, and hospitals of the sacred Fatherland."

Cross pauses to see if he still has our attention. He does. He goes on — "Basically the system is geared to having three crews up and one standing down on each mission. This gives us a shot at patching up and maintaining the equipment." He pats his crotch and says, "That includes the crews' personal equipment." He winks and gets his laugh from the clowns who did all that hooting and shouting before.

He lights up a cigar and says, "You fly unless it's the stand-down day for your crew, squadron, or Group. They often overlap, but when they fall consecutively, and you have no ground school or other duty, you may find you have a three day pass, but again that's not guaranteed. And then of course weather can shove all our plans completely down the drain. Weather over Northern Europe can be our worst enemy, and it has probably destroyed more of our aircraft than the Luftwaffe, but I think I'm getting off the subject here —"

Cross pops to attention when Hartak shows up. Hartak is about five ten, very pale, straight slicked down sandy colored hair, no eyelids over narrow squinty eyes, a thin wire line for a mouth, right angle triangle with broken hypotenuse for a nose, a heavy square jaw — a Dick Tracy profile but not as aligned. One corner of his slash line mouth is pulled down in a permanent scowl, and his eyes are split levelled, as are his shoulders. He walks with a limp, coming down stiffly on his left leg, as if it was bolted to his trunk at the hip, and he grimaces with every step. He snaps his finger and Cross hands him a lighted cigarette. It hangs from his lip while he looks us over as if he tastes and smells something spoiled.

He speaks in a flat, metallic voice much like the robot in the telephone exhibit at the World's Fair. "Greetings. You're now part of the 324th Squadron, and I'll begin by telling you what I tell every new crew. Your hearts may belong to Daddy, and your soul may belong to God almighty, but your balls are in our hands." The tight smile that crosses his face lasts no longer than those 1/100th of a second shots flashed on screen in aircraft recognition classes.

"O.K.," he says, "we're here on serious business, to destroy the enemy. And he is your enemy, as you'll find out damn soon. He has the power, the equipment, and the will to kill you; and the one thing you can count on surer than hell, is that some of you innocents I'm looking at right here in this room are going to be killed. Yesirree bob, I said killed. If that makes you fearful, get used to that idea right now, and it may save your life. I fear the enemy. I fear him every minute I'm up there. I don't mean fright or panic. You panic, your head is up your ass and locked. A dangerous position. You can't perform. You're dead. Fear, on the other hand, is healthy. You sweat, you jump, your adrenaline flows, your heart pumps. You're alive. You can do something. Sure, it may be the wrong thing and you pay the price. I told you this is serious business."

He scans the room, looking into our eyes and shakes his head in disapproval. He nods at Cross who lights another cigarette and hands it to him. Hartak lowers his voice so that he has us all leaning forward, straining to hear him.

"I know some of you are stupid enough to think you're pretty hot. That's not going to last long, believe me, but when you fly your first missions you'd better pay strict attention to what you see and hear from the experienced crews. There are damn good reasons why they're still around. Maybe it's because they're aware of their fear. If you're at all smart, you will be too. I want the 324th to be the most fearful squadron in the whole goddammed 8th Air Force. Don't be ashamed of staining your shorts. Thirty five of those brown badges of honor and your war is over, you can go home. Now if you'll excuse us, Captain Cross and I have some work to do."

He throws us a real good Air Force salute like he was pulling off a wad of chewing gum stuck to his forehead, and limps out with Cross three paces behind. The room stays silent for a moment and then everybody starts jabbering at the same time.

The Mouse says, "I swear if I wasn't scared before, I sure am now."

Earl says, "Boy, he really laid it on the line."

Lopez says, "I wanted to hear more about the last mission and all those guys who went down, instead we got all that talk about crapping your pants. If you ask me, I don't know, I think the guy landed on his head when he smacked into those trees."

Skiles says over his shoulder, "Who the hell asked you, you little filthy Commie rat."

Lopez says, "You're awfully brave in a crowd."

JoJo Cooper and Zibby edge Lopez away and Fearless says to Skiles, "Why don't you pick on a guy your size? Try me once, you twisted son of a bitch."

Caves says to Earl, "We're going to have to do something about Skiles. That guy and his mouth wouldn't last ten minutes in Wyoming."

Earl pulls his old reliable - "Thanks Cowboy, but I guess I don't have to tell you, you're not in Wyoming anymore."

Cavey says "Earl, fuck off."

Eriksen asks, "Was Captain Hartak serious about the shorts?" Zibby says, "Well, I guess there's only one way we're going to find out."

All this takes place in less than a minute, but it seems much longer, like when you run into a period of brief turbulence in the air. I tell Cavey, "We ought to relax. How about shooting some pool."

The Mouse comes along, and we find an empty table where he gives a demonstration of the finer points of controlling a white ball on green cloth. I tell him "Looks like you picked up a thing or two outside Skokie High."

He grins, cleans the table with four great shots in a row, then says "From the school hall to the pool hall is not too far away." He stalks around the table, sizing up his shots quickly. He sings *Off we go into the wild blue yonder — Crash!* after making one hell of a bank shot. It's been a long time since I've seen the boy enjoying himself.

A tall, thin, haggard looking guy holding a skinny brown dog under his arm hangs around near our table watching us. The dog could be part fox terrier but it's mostly mutt, skin and bones. Its owner looks just as scrawny in a uniform that looks like it is holding him up. He has pilot wings on his jacket. I ask him if he'd care to join us, but he says that he'd just as soon watch, maybe learn a thing or two.

I get a kick out of the Mouse strutting his stuff, but I can't help sneaking a few peeks at the guy standing there holding his dog, and I see that his eyes are not on the game but on the Mouse. He's not as thin as the Mouse, nobody is, but he appears emaciated, almost like a convict on a chain gang. And there's something wrong about his movements and the way he checks us out with his very pale, almost milky blue eyes. When he passes near the shaded pool table light, I notice he has no eyebrows and his mouth is twisted so that it looks like he has only half a lower lip.

After a while the Mouse whispers to us, "That spook and his dog give me the creeps, the way they're staring at me, both of them." Then aloud he says, "Look fella, I didn't catch your name, but —"

"Gabor," the guy says stroking the dog, "Willard Gabor. You'll get to know me. I come around to wake you guys for the mission. They call me The Hangman."

I've never seen anyone stroke a dog that way. It makes me queasy. We're quiet until the Mouse says, "Well, whatever they call you, you're one funny guy and we asked you to join us, but if you're not up to it, do us a favor, take your dog and work on somebody else for a while. We've had a long, hard day, and we could use a little easy time now."

"Now isn't that too bad," Gabor says to the dog as he fondles its ass. "We're making Skinny over here nervous."

Cavey chalks his cue and says, "O.K. Gabor, you've had your fun. Now buzz off."

Gabor stares at Cavey under those no eyebrow eyes, then shifts back to the Mouse. He puts the dog down and picks a stick from the rack. He aims it toward the Mouse, shakes his head sadly and says, "You'll never make it."

None of us say a word as he puts the cue back in the rack and walks away with the dog trotting along. The Mouse charges after him and wheels him around by his arm and says, "What kind of shit are you trying to pull here?"

The dog starts barking and jumping all over the Mouse. Gabor spins away, clutches another cue and points it at the Mouse like a bayonet. Cavey and I move toward him. He holds his ground then drops the stick on the table and picks up the dog again. "Down, Flak. Easy there girl," he says, running his hand under her until she is quiet, then turns to face the Mouse. "You heard me," he says. "Deal with it."

The Mouse shoves the guy with his elbow. "Go on, beat it," he says "Scram, you fuckin' loony."

The poolroom is dark except for the low green shaded light over each table. In the shadows Gabor's sunken cheeks take on the gaunt look of a skull. He holds his stare at the Mouse and says, "Yep, it's there. You'll never make it. I can see it in your eyes."

His laugh sounds more like a cackle as he goes off into the darkness with his dog. The Mouse's hand is twitching as he aims his shot and says, "This place is a real booby hatch. Don't they have any normals around here? First, Cross, then Hartak, and now this freak."

He flubs the shot. Cavey runs his palm over the table, pushing the balls aside. He lifts the Mouse by the armpits and seats him on the table rail. He waves a finger at him and says, "Game's over. You know you let that guy make a fool of you, and if you keep this up, you're going to drive us all nuts. He was trying to rattle your cage, and you went for it."

"Yeah, you're certainly not going to pay any attention to that nut," I say. "The guy's whacko. He's got more shit than a blue goose. Like the rumors you hear."

The Mouse looks at me like I'm stupid. "Sure, sure," he says, "Like that real wild one you heard about the Group being hit hard lately."

SEVEN

They issued escape kits to us earlier today. As soon as Cavey and I get back to our room, we peel off the red waterproof tape marked Do Not Open / Emergency Use Only from the four by six inch celluloid packets. Inside we find a small wafer of soap, a threaded needle, thread, a small jack-knife, five hundred deutschmarks in small bills, water purification tablets, a chunk of concentrated chocolate, powdered coffee, a collapsible cup, waterproof matches, a safety razor with three blades, a pocket compass, a fishhook and line, French and German phrase books, I.D. cards certifying us as farm laborers, and a map of Germany, Belgium, Holland and Northern France printed on waterproofed cloth.

The photographer supplied us with civilian clothes for our I.D. picture, but there's not much chance of either of us ever passing for a French laborer. Cavey's picture has him still grinning at my beret, checkered jacket, ill fitting shirt, and paste-on mustache. He's wearing the same get-up and mustache. I pocket the jack-knife and take a bite out of the chunk of concentrated chocolate. One bite is all I take. It is much too rich. Then Cavey shows me a page in the phrase book posing such questions as Wo ist das bahn'-hof, Wo ist das twa'-lette, and most crucial of all Wo ist das ki'-no.

He leaps from his upper bunk acting as if he has just parachuted out of a burning B-17 into the ruins of Dusseldorf, and inquires in Wyoming German, "Wo ist das kino mit Lana Turner und Cary Grant?"

I believe we should go for something a little more practical like "Wo ist das bahnhof auf Bassingbourne?"

We run into Cross outside the main hangar. "Everything all right men?" he says. It's a statement, not a question. We assure him everything is perfectly fine, couldn't be better. "Good," he says, "Good. Hartak has been leaning on everybody up and down the line, and we just could be putting one up tomorrow. You boys might want to check the alert list tonight." He pounds his fist into his open palm and looks at me for my reply.

"Swell," I say.

Cross is not at all sure of how I mean that. He waits for me to say more, then he turns to Cavey who has now become absorbed in gazing at a far off cloud formation. We keep shifting our feet while we stand there in silence. After a while Cross says, "How do you boys like the chow here?", and then without waiting for our answer he shifts into "Lieutenant Gabor informs me he ran into you after our meeting the other night. He was visiting with as many new crews as he could get around to. Part of his job. How'd it go?"

He's pounding his fist into his palm again. Cavey looks at me and sees no help. I'm focussed on his cloud. Cavey shifts his feet and says, "Well, actually we didn't get to spend too much time with him."

Cross isn't about to let us go. He narrows his eyes and says, "I'm sure you'll become better acquainted. He's quite a guy when you get to know him."

Cavey swallows his Adam's apple a couple of times. "Maybe so," he says, "but from what little I've seen of him, I'd say that the guy is either radically nuts or bucking for a discharge. Do you know he calls himself the Hangman?"

Cross thinks that's funny. He laughs. "Yeah, I heard that. Damn if he doesn't look like one, and act like one too for that matter. That ol' Gabor is hot shit, isn't he?"

I want to leave before I say something to get myself in dutch, but Cross establishes eye contact and begins to lecture us. "Ol' Gabor is as good as anyone we've ever had on that duty. Waking you guys for the mission is a damn thankless job, and as you boys can well imagine, a guy takes a lot of abuse on a chore like that, but I'll say this for him, he can take it. The guys have pulled all kinds of crap on him, more than I want to know about. He hasn't a friend on the base except his poor goddam dog, but he doesn't let that make no nevermind to him. We've got the perfect hangman. He's dedicated."

"That's just dandy," Cavey says "but something's loose or missing upstairs. That boy has some serious kind of problem."

Cross jabs his finger at him. "Well, hotshot," he says "maybe you would too if you'd gone through what he has." Cross has been raising his voice, but he lowers it now and says, "Let me tell you wiseasses something. Eight months ago that guy was a damn good pilot with a fine record and no crazier than he had to be with seventeen missions under his belt. Then he developed this ear infection that a lot of the guys pick up from flying high altitude. The docs grounded him, so we had him helping out in the tower until the ear cleared up. He was in the tower on the morning his old crew took off for Leipzig with a new pilot in his seat. As far as we could put together later, they must have lost an engine on takeoff. We watched their ship dive almost in slow motion after it stalled trying to clear the trees beyond the runway. When that 17 hit, the flame was so intense we couldn't get anywhere near it, and then a minute or so later the bomb load exploded one by one, so it was just impossible. No survivors and damn few identifiable remains. I ran up into the tower as soon as I saw the plane going down, and there was Gabor with both hands to his face, staring through his fingers at the flaming wreck, motionless and stiff as if he was paralyzed. He'd seen a few burning 17's before. Nothing unusual about that around here, but these were his buddies in that flaming wreck — his crew. I tried to lead him away, but he wouldn't budge. Then I ducked under a desk when the bombs began blasting off with the detonations shattering every pane of glass in the tower. Gabor stood up stiff there, through all those jagged flying pieces, not moving a muscle. His face was pared open from the shards of glass, like something hung from a hook at the butcher's, and his uniform was soaked with blood. When I tried to lead him to a chair until the medics came, he took a few steps blindly toward the door then fell down and curled up in a corner. All this without a sound out of him. I wiped as much of the blood off his face that I could, then covered him with a blanket and called for an ambulance. When he started moaning, I stuck him with a couple of morphine syrettes I grabbed out of a first aid kit. That quieted him down until the medics came and took him away in a stretcher."

"Oh man," I say, "you'd think they'd send the guy back home after all that."

Cross shrugs. "I dont know, maybe we should have, but what we did do when he came out of the hospital all stitched up with a raw new face sewn on, was pack him off for thirty days R & R at our Flak House down in Torquay. When he came back to us, he seemed calm enough, more like what I'd call subdued. They'd done a fairly decent job sewing up the missing parts of his face except around his mouth. Not much they could do there, as you can see that's still a mess. Also, he had this dog, Flak, that he'd picked up somewhere along the line, and still keeps on a steady diet of peanut butter sandwiches and sweet tea. The docs recommended that we send him to Walter Reed for further treatment, but he couldn't handle going home the way he looked and pleaded with Hartak to let him stay. We didn't want him around either with that awful stitched up face. Bad for morale. But a week later the guy we had waking the crews went over the hill, and Hartak on a hunch figured he'd try Gabor. It turned out he was right, because Gabor took to it right off, like he was born for the job. Hartak is a great believer in following hunches no matter how strange they may seem. Gabor worships the guy, and I've seen those two get along in all kinds of strange ways. That's O.K. with me, because when you get down to it, Hartak doesn't have too many friends around here either. They don't have much to say to each other, but there are times when I think they have a silent code between them that only they understand."

"Yeah," says Cavey, "like planting fear in us."

"Oh yes, that's a given," says Cross.

Cavey, Earl, The Mouse, and I are playing knock rummy after dinner. Six pence a point and the Mouse is cleaning up. He's as good at cards as at the pool table, but always ends up way behind because he gets all screwed up making change. I see the alert list being tacked on the bulletin board by a cute little WAC. She acknowledges my whistle with a wave of her hand, but she doesn't look back. I've no idea what I'd do if she did.

The Mouse sees her too and says "Oh, boy. I'll shit if my name is up there."

"Well, who's going to do the honors?" asks Cavey.

Earl knocks with twelve points and loses to everybody. He stands up and stretches. "I have to take a leak," he says. He slows down as he passes the bulletin board, then goes on to the latrine. We play a hand without him. He sneaks another quick look at the list on the way back.

"Caveman," he says, "you lucky dog. They've got you, me, Lopez, and Fearless on the sheet for tomorrow."

Caves looks at his hand then lays the cards down on the table. "Oh man, oh man, they sure don't waste any time, do they," he says. He picks up his cards and shuffles them over and over, then asks "Did you get a chance to see who we're flying with?"

"We're not together," Earl says. "I'm up with guys I never heard of. The radioman is named Goering believe it or not."

Cavey throws in his cards. "I'm out," he says. "I guess I'll go write a couple of letters before I turn in."

The game is over. I go back with the Caveman, relieved they didn't post me on the alert list. I'm nowhere near ready to fly a mission, but at the same time I don't like the idea of Cavey and the other guys going on without me. Almost like being left out when they choose up sides.

The night sky is clear when we walk back to the room. Cavey asks me to identify some of the stars. I locate his favorite constellation, Scorpio, low in the south and then find Arcturus, Antares, and Polaris for him. He looks up at the sky with me, then he picks up a stone, throws it at a tree about twenty yards away and misses. He grins with satisfaction when he hears it hit on his fourth try.

Back in the room, he wastes no time climbing up in his sack with his Hollywood Starlet Beauty Queens. "I can't put my mind to letters now," he says. I start a letter to Omar for lack of anything better to do. I can't think of anyone else to write to except maybe my mother, and just what the hell could I write now that would make any sense to her. Anyway, she'd only get aggravated all over again if she found out where I am and what I'm doing here. When I first visited to tell her I'd enlisted in the Air Force, she'd gone back to drinking again and didn't take my news any too well. She started throwing things and screaming at me that I was no son of hers, that I was just as heartless as that worthless father of mine, and neither of us ever gave a good goddamn about her feelings. That moron new husband of hers yelled from the other room for us to pipe down, he was trying to catch a little sleep before going on his shift down at the foundry. I told him where he could go as far as I was concerned, then tried to calm my mother down, but I could see it was no use. Right after that I left, and we haven't been in touch since. I hope she's O.K. but I seriously doubt it. I have her down for a twenty percent allotment, but I'm sure most of it goes to the liquor store. Not much I could ever do about that. Cross has her listed as next of kin in my papers, so if I'm unlucky, she's lucky and gets my G.I. insurance. Ten thousand bucks.

Cavey has been silent for a while, and from my bunk below I see his bulky body outlined through the thin G.I. mattress. He seems restless, moving around a lot, and I wonder if maybe he's beating his meat up there again. I'm only a few sentences into my letter to Omar when Caves asks, "O.K. to turn off the light?"

"Yeah," I say "only be sure to wake me if I'm not up when you go. I want to wish you luck." He turns off the light and says, "No way I'll get any sleep tonight." Two minutes later I hear him snoring.

I don't know when I nod off, but next thing I know someone is switching the light rapidly on and off, and saying in a flat voice, "O.K. let's go, Lieutenant Cavey. Breakfast at three, briefing at four. Drop your cock, pick up your socks, you're going to war." It's the hangman, Gabor.

He switches the light on saying "Breakfast at three," then switches it off saying "Briefing at four." He keeps doing that until he sees Cavey sitting up, then he leaves. Cavey stumbles around the room looking for his clothes, and swears how he wants to kill that bastard before anybody else does. He goes off to the latrine and though I want to stay up to wish him luck before he leaves, I soon fall back to sleep.

I wake in what seems like half a minute. It's the Hangman again with his flashlight burning into my eyes. I hear that voice of his saying, "O.K., your turn. Breakfast at three, briefing at four. Come on move it, we're late."

I say, "You got the wrong guy. I'm not on the alert list, and get that fuckin' flashlight out of my eyes before I shove it down your throat."

His voice hits me from out of the darkness. "No, you're the guy I want all right, bright eyes. I never miss."

I sit up fully awake and tell him "This has to be be some kind of mistake. Somebody screwed up."

"No mistakes, no screw-ups. Lieutenant Strong took sick at the briefing and Holy Cross told me to get the next navigator on the roster, which is you, lucky boy. Now drop your feet to the cold concrete. Time's awasting."

I close my eyes in the hope that when I open them he'll be gone. He says "O.K. now, come on, move it, move it."

I drag myself out of the sack, but I'm still not fully awake when I ask, "What the hell time is it?"

"Four twenty. You've missed breakfast. I've got a peanut butter sandwich outside if you want it, and you can forget briefing too. That'll be over by the time we get there. I'm taking you straight out to your ship. You're with Dimple F Fox."

I swear a streak while stumbling around the room throwing on my clothes. I grab my Colt 45 and whatever maps I can find and shove them in my briefcase. Gabor leads me out to his motorcycle, where his dog, Flak, sits in the sidecar munching away on a peanut butter sandwich. "Tough shit," the Hangman says "there goes your breakfast." He scoops Flak up, motions me to get in the sidecar. Flak jumps into my lap.

We stop at the equipment hut just long enough for me to climb into my coveralls, heat suit and boots, and throw my parachute, Mae West, and escape kit into my bag. I go through the motions, doing everything by the numbers, as mindlessly unaware of my next move as any robot. At the moment I am, as far as I know, bewildered beyond any emotion. It is like I'm the person who is supposed to be me in this dream. The hangman holds Flak in the crook of his arm as we speed off into the misty night to Dimple F Fox. I hold on to my hat with one hand, and clutch my gear with the other. He and Flak harmonize howls at the quarter moon, as he takes a turn so hard that the sidecar with me in it leaves the ground.

I've lost track of time. The moon disappears behind a bank of clouds as the hangman drops me off in front of a B-17 half hidden in the cold pre-dawn mist near an abandoned farm storage shed. The ground crew, busy as a pack of scurrying gnomes, are all over the ship carrying out last minute details of their pre-flight tasks. The armorers are halfway through the tussle of loading 500 pound bombs on their racks, waiting until now to avoid the double labor of unloading in the event that the mission is scrubbed.

The machine gun clatter of the hangman's bike hangs in the air after he vanishes into the fog with Flak. It reminds me of my other motorcycle ride, that time with my father in Hackensack. I wonder where he is and what he'd think if he saw me now. I snap out of that when a well built little guy, about five seven, comes over to me and puts out his hand.

"Hi," he says, "I'm Scudellari, Paul Scudellari, the bombardier. You must be the new navigator. Come on, I'll show you around."

EIGHT

The familiar profile of a B-17 emerges from the dark mist, as I walk with Scudellari toward a scrap wood fire burning in an old oil drum. It's early September, but it's down to 40 degrees, and it feels a lot chillier in the damp English fog at four-forty in the morning.

A tall skinny guy chewing on a tooth-pick, and a chunky redhead about five nine carrying his .45 in a shoulder holster outside an old frayed olive drab woolen sweater, huddle over the fire. The redhead calls us over and extends his hand to me.

"Hi cousin," he says, "we been expecting you. I'm Odell Daniels — Odie, your pilot, I see you've already met Paul, and this less than worthless clod over here is Mr. Prescott F. Williams, we call him Ted Williams. He's co-pilot and you'll have to excuse his ways, seeing as how he's from New Mexico and hasn't had proper rearing or much schooling."

Williams bobs his head like a horse and grins, almost pawing the ground. I shake hands, nodding as I say "Odie, Paul, Ted Williams, hi." They expect more, but that's all I can come up with.

Odie says, "I don't think I've seen you around, have I? You must be new." I have to swallow a couple of times before I can say "Brand new, my first mission." Odie doesn't look any too happy to hear this, and Ted Williams sputters but doesn't speak up. Odie says, "Well, everybody has to begin sometime." That's for the benefit of the crew who have now gathered around to inspect their new navigator. I can't hear exactly what they're mumbling, but I want to tell them that I'm none too pleased about the situation either. Ted Williams looks at Odie as if for permission to speak, but Odie turns away and pours me a cup of coffee from his thermos. He gives Williams a warning look, then raises the thermos in a toast and says, "Anyways, to each and every one of us brave warriors of the sky, good luck this fine day."

I say, "I guess I'm going to need more than just luck, like could you tell me where we're going this fine day?"

Odie thinks I'm kidding, and throws back "Stockholm, I hope." That draws a few cheers and applause from the crew. I let him know I'm not kidding, then tell him as best I can, all about how I missed briefing. I hear the crew really bitching now, and I want to run off and hide somewhere, anywhere, anywhere but here.

I ask Odie again for the target. He swishes his coffee to the ground. "Who can drink any of this cold cat piss," he says. The guys in the crew look at him wide eyed. He turns to me and says "Ludwigshafen, back to fuckin' Ludwigshafen."

He might just as well have said Constantinople as far as I'm concerned. I've never heard of Ludwigshafen and Odie picks up on that. He is about to explode, but he turns away from me, then tells the crew "O.K., cousins, party's over. Let's get to our positions now. Gotta get ready for the opera."

Odie reaches into his bag and passes me the notes he had taken at the briefing and a handful of maps and charts. He grabs Scudellari and says, "See what you can do to get him started, Paul. I'll get back to you boys as soon as I can." He pats me on the back. "Not your fault, cousin," he says "nothing personal. You keep a tight asshole and we'll work it out." He walks off into the mist muttering.

I move up close to the fire but it's not much help. I'm shivering. No awaking from this nightmare. I see the gunners pulling and tugging at each other. When I look puzzled, Scudellari says "They're checking each other's parachute harness for security. You don't want to bail out and find yourself slipping out of your harness."

He helps me lift my gear into the plane, and before we climb up to our positions in the nose, I look up toward the sky. No stars. On board, Scudellari says "Let me know if you need anything." What I need is a way out of here, but I ask "How many do you have, Scudellari?"

"Call me Paul. Odie and I have fourteen to go," he says, "the rest of the crew about the same, except for Petersen in the tail who has I think only about four or five left. Did you get Hartak's sermon on fear?"

I nod.

"Well then, you should be happy to know this ship is absolutely crawling with fear. Our navigator took sick at briefing when he saw it was Ludwigshafen again. You can thank him for being with us this morning, lucky boy."

"Well, Paul" I say, "if anyone wants to know, I'm not feeling any too good myself right now."

"Welcome to the club," Paul says and kneels down to help me unfold the maps and charts as best we can in my small area. I'm still chilled to the bone.

He checks his notes and says "Our combat wing of one hundred and eight B-17's is going after the bridge crossing the Rhine between Ludwigshafen and Mannheim. At the same time the other wings, about nine hundred B-17's, will be hitting the I.G. Farben chemical plant on the other side of the bridge in Mannheim. Our squadron of twelve ships with two other squadrons make up the 91st Bomb Group, and we'll be the low Group in the Wing made up of us, the 351st, the 379th, and the 381st Bomb Groups."

I know he is trying to help, and that I can learn more by listening than talking, but my brain has gone dead on me. I interrupt him to ask "With all those planes up there, how am I about to know who's who?"

Paul is patient. He says, "You'll catch on. Look for the letters DF with another letter painted on the side. That will be one of the twelve ships in our squadron. DF is pronounced Dimple, don't ask me why. So we're DF-F, Dimple F Fox, and Hartak leading our squadron is DF-B Baker. Watch out for him. The two other squadrons in our Group are marked OR and LL with letters like OR-X and LL-Y. Also, all three squadrons in our Group, the 91st, have a large white A inside a black triangle on their tail. You can't miss it. Our Group is triangle A, and the three other Groups making up our wing are triangle J, triangle K, and triangle L. You got it?"

I say, "Oh sure, nothing to it. All I know is our squadron is DF and our Group is triangle A, and there'll be a lot of other ships out there with other markings. It's clear as mud." Paul grins and says, "Yep, clear as mud, but it covers the ground. You'll get on to it after a while. Here, let me show you." He draws a rough diagram on the back of a map.

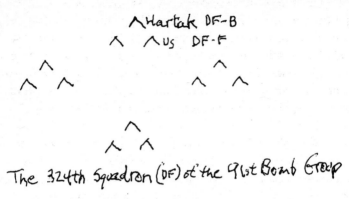

The 324th Squadron (DF) of the 91st Bomb Group

"Does that make it any clearer?" he asks. He looks at Odie's notes again and says "Here, while I'm at it, I'll do the Group for you." He moistens the pencil stub in his mouth, and draws another diagram.

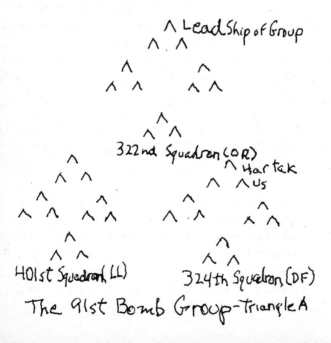

The 91st Bomb Group - Triangle A

Paul hands the rough drawing over to me and says, "You get the picture." He waits to see if I got his little joke. "Of course, we're stacked at different levels," he says, "otherwise we'd be shooting at ourselves which we manage to do often enough anyway. None of our systems are foolproof. We try to keep twenty-five feet elevation between planes, and five hundred between Groups. Sometimes tighter. Any questions?"

"Nope."

"And oh yeah, one more thing. You also may see some planes out there with red and black swastikas. You won't need a diagram for those babies. You'll know them right off."

He returns to his position and I look out at the fog thickening outside the ship, and allow myself the first glimmer of hope that the mission will be cancelled. Odie pokes his head into our area and says, "We just got the word from tower that we're still on as briefed. They're predicting 500 feet visibility at takeoff ha, ha. Maybe they'll scrub this can of worms, or divert us from Ludwigshafen. They really kicked the shit out of us there last time. How you doin' cousin?"

All he gets from me is a bewildered worried look. Paul says, "It's O.K. Odie, he'll be all right."

Odie pats my shoulder and says, "Don't you worry, we're flying No. 2 on Hartak, and I'll stick closer to him than the cheeks on his tight flat bony ass. All you have to do is track our course unless we get cut off for any reason. I'll call you then for a heading and you damn sure better know where the fuck we are, but for now just keep a clear head and listen to the ol' Scooter here. Copy what you need from my notes and get them back to me. Cheers, cousin."

He climbs back up to his seat, where he and Ted Williams run their check list, fiddling with the controls like a pair of piano tuners. One of the ground crew guys makes a last minute adjustment to my oxygen supply valve, then hands me a shiny red apple. I thank him, and he asks, "Would you like me to hold your wallet until you get back?" He too tells me not to worry, everything is going to be O.K. I figure I won't need the wallet where I'm going, and pass it over to him. He pats me again when he leaves, and I hear once more that I'm not to worry.

Paul goes back to check the bombs shackled in the bomb bay. I bend over my table staring at a map without seeing it, not knowing my next move. The ground crew guys are busy as termites as they crawl over the ship with their last minute checking of all radio equipment, topping off fuel tanks, calibrating gun sights, pulling here, tucking there in the darkness. I get morbid and recall a dumb movie I once saw, where the warden and guards were making final adjustments before strapping Humphrey Bogart or somebody into the electric chair.

I force myself to copy Odie's notes, though I hope I won't need them. They can't possibly send us up in this soup. A few seconds later, I see the propeller turn over and hear No. 1 engine cough and sputter to life, zooming to a powerful roar. Then the others kick in one by one until all four are blasting away, and every loose rivet, bolt, and screw on the ship is buzzing, humming, vibrating. It's still dark outside when I mark 0550 Engines Started in my log with an unsteady hand. I'm hot and cold, and my stomach is churning. I wish I could have had breakfast, and pray that I'll be O.K. I bite into the apple that the queer duck on the ground crew had left for me.

We leave our dispersal area for our position in line at the runway. Odie is up there wiping the mist from the side window, peering through the darkness and fog. He taxies carefully down the perimeter track making slow S turns, the only way he can see past the nose of the B-17 pointing skyward blocking his forward vision.

Paul can see ahead from his position, and pastes his face to the plexiglass, as he too stares into the pre-dawn murk prepared to give warning if we come close to any building, tree, or plane out there. We're a rolling explosive mixture of bombs and gasoline, and there are thirty-five other bombers similarly loaded steering in the dark within a few yards of us.

I pray again that they call this off before it's too late. We leave the perimeter and take our place in the long single file of 17's waiting for takeoff, hunkered up nose to tail like a dark gray line of circus elephants. A green Aldis lamp beam slashes through the fog every thirty seconds followed by the roar of four powerful engines racing down the runway with throttles all the way down, straining for power to hoist the explosive load. Each green flash moves us one plane-length closer to the runway, like gumballs in a slot machine.

"Check this," Paul says. He unrolls a condom from its packet and knots a string tightly around its open end, then ties it to a bulkhead and lets the long limp thing hang there. I ask him what the hell that's all about.

"You'll find out," he says. "It's a surprise. Just let it alone for now. Nothing to worry about."

I nod as if it's O.K. I'm on a bombing mission, my first, without briefing, with a crew of strangers, and the bombardier has just strung up an empty condom near my head and told me there's nothing to worry about.

It's still dark and foggy. They'll just have to scrub this mission. We take our place at the head of the runway. Crouched in the plexiglass nose, I see the flash of green. The plane shudders as Odie pushes the throttles forward. The runway moves like a treadmill under the plexiglass slowly accelerating with every passing second. I hear Ted calling off to Odie 30, 40, 50, 60, 70. The four throttle handles are pushed down as far as they can go. We're at maximum power, the only time in the flight when such power is needed. The engines' roar is deafening as we speed down the runway with 6,000 pounds of bombs and 11,000 pounds of high octane gasoline. Any engine failure or pilot error now, and we turn into a greasy black fireball in the newsreels, a letter home from the chaplain, a statistic in a report.

Paul, three feet in front of me, kneels in the very nose of the ship. I look past his shoulder at the dark silhouette of trees at the end of the runway looming closer, growing larger every second. I think of what happened to the hangman's crew. I'm shouting "Come on Odie, lift, lift, LIFT!" The plane takes a bounce, we hit the runway again, I hold my breath, then feel a momentary sensation of floating as I see space appear and grow larger each second between the ship's nose and the rapidly disappearing runway below. Odie doesn't waste much time retracting the wheels. The trees slide under our belly in the darkness, and I make the entry in my log — 0617 Takeoff. It is close to illegible. I remember to breathe.

We climb through the clouds and come out into semi-clearing at 4500 feet. It is still dark and I see the lights of two ships off to the right. We join one of the two planes out there in a climbing turn to the right. Way off on the horizon to the east, the sky displays a long thin band of the palest blue. The blue of the hangman's eyes. I have to steady my right hand by gripping it with my left, as I begin making entries in my log at ten minute intervals. We are now flying in a large circle at 8100 feet. I see the lights of at least twenty other 17's milling around with their bomb-loads near us in the dark.

We keep circling. I flinch each time a 17 trying to catch up with its squadron zips across and through us like a reckless driver cutting across lanes on a crowded highway racing to beat the light. Then out about five miles west, a bright orange ball flashes for a second or two before transforming into thin streaks of flame falling from an ever expanding black cone.

Paul spins around in his seat to face me. He points to the falling streaks. "You see that? Probably never saw each other till too late." I nod.

Odie's voice crackles through the intercom. "O.K. cousins, no use looking out there now. Keep your eyes peeled around here. Call out quick if you see anyone too close, and keep a lookout for the flare from the lead ship."

I hope he's keeping his eyes open and knows what he's doing. I know nothing about this guy. Paul says, "Look out for a 17 with wheels down and shooting red/green flares from the tail. That'll be Hartak's ship, Dimple B Baker. Our squadron will take their slots behind him."

It is lighter now. A bar of garish neon red appears on the pale blue eastern horizon, growing wider and rosier each time I look at it. It is a dazzling sunrise, totally invisible to the earthlings living in the 10/10ths undercast below us. Up here I stand awed at the sight of all these planes in a sky full of every color band in the spectrum. I hear Odie calling out on the interphone, "Eyes open guys. We don't want any contact with all those strays out there this morning looking for their place in the herd." I feel like such a stooge when I'm the only one of the crew to reply Roger.

Our top turret gunner is the first to spot Hartak's ship shooting red/greens. Odie slips us into position, and we settle in off Hartak's right wing twenty yards above and behind him. The other ten ships in our squadron slip and slide their way into formation, and in another fifteen minutes we begin to look very much like Paul's diagram.

The sun is now above the horizon and in the early morning light it's beginning to make some sense to me, as I see the two other squadrons in our Group forming on their leaders firing red/red and yellow/green flares. We keep circling until all three squadrons have formed up, and then we circle some more until the squadrons jockey behind the Group leader flying with his wheels down and flashing a blue light from the Aldis lamp in his tail. When I mark 0653 Group Formation in my log, I notice my writing is less shaky, and that it has taken exactly thirty-seven minutes for the twelve planes in our squadron to get into position with the two other squadrons to form up the 91st Bomb Group.

We stop our circling and move on to take our place with the three other Groups in our Combat Wing. Then we circle again until all Groups are in formation, and our Wing of one hundred B-17's takes its place in the stream of one thousand bombers flying eastward to Germany.

I hope I don't find some way to screw up. I put on my oxygen mask and call the crew on intercom, navigator to crew, navigator to crew. We're at 10000 and climbing. Put on masks and check in.

The intercom comes alive as we hear tail O.K., waist O.K., ball O.K., radio O.K. all around the ship until it gets to Paul who raises his hand for me before checking in. I'm supposed to run this drill every ten minutes until we descend to 10000 feet again on the way home. After Paul puts on his mask, he checks his mike by calling bombardier to navigator. He points to the condom which has blown itself up to the size of a basketball in the thinner air. "Beautiful," he says. "Yeah, super," I say.

Below us are the English coastal towns as we prepare to head out over the North Sea. I kneel down to make entries in the log containing ruled columns like a ledger.

Time	Location	Alt	Temp	True Alt	Indicated AirSpeed	True AirSpeed	Ground Speed
0755	Clacton	16800	-08	17600	152	161	147

Compass	Vari-ation	Devi-ation	True Heading	WIND Dir	Velocity	Drift	True Course	
096	+6	+2	104	068	016	+4	108	Depart English coast

I tell the crew on interphone that we've departed the English coast and call for another oxygen check. No sooner is the check over, when I hear the sharp clatter of machine gun fire. I want to curl up and hide somewhere, but I force myself to my gun position. Paul waves me off. He pulls down his oxygen mask and yells in my ear over the roar of the engines. "It's O.K., just our guys checking out their guns while we're over water."

He adjusts his mask and I go back to my table feeling foolish but relieved. He points to the condom which now has grown to the size of a large watermelon. I've had enough of it, and pop it with the point of my dividers.

We keep climbing over the water and we're at 24000 feet when we cross the coast midway between Dunkerque and Ostend. I'm able to calculate a decent wind and ground speed as we've flown a straight track since departing Clacton. An undercast of about 5/10ths forms below us on my first visit to Europe.

Time	Location	Alt	Temp	True Alt	Indicated AirSpeed	True AirSpeed	Ground Speed
0831	51'06N 02'40E	23650	-34	24200	154	163	145

Compass	Variation	Deviation	True Heading	WIND Dir	Velocity	Drift	True Course	Remarks
089	+6	+2	097	072	20	+6	103	Europe Coast-Dunkirk 3 mi S

I take out my copy of Odie's notes of the briefing. It's a mess of numbers — projected times and coordinates of the turns at each dogleg from the coast to Ludwigshafen and back out again. We are to make four sharp changes on our course to Ludwigshafen in order to keep the German defense forces from identifying our target for as long as possible. I plot and draw these dogleg changes on a Mercator chart I pull from my brief case. I see my .45 in there next to my escape kit, and hope I don't have to use either of them today. I've heard too many reports about what happened to guys who bailed out and were beaten to death or hanged from the nearest lamppost when they fell into the hands of an enraged mob of German civilians.

I try not to dwell on that. I look at the notes again. It occurs to me that Odie hasn't called anyone cousin for quite a while now. The notes show that our position in the bomber stream places us forty minutes behind the first Group over the target, so the doglegs designed to fake out the German defenses will not help our squadron too much. The flak gunners at Ludwigshafen will have plenty time to tune up their radar aiming cannon. We won't be much of a secret after the lead ship goes over, after they drop that first load of bombs. I've seen pictures of burning B-17's in the flak filled skies over the target, and soon I'll be in it for real. I grip an overhead brace with both hands.

NINE

I switch from intercom to the command set and hear Hartak's voice coming over like static. "O.K., tighten up this shitheel formation, we're over Europe now, let's stay alive." I force myself to scan my instruments. This is no place to screw up. We continue on the same heading for twelve minutes after crossing the coast, then swing left on our first dogleg. New compass reading is 078. I check the map and make out Lille six miles ahead and to the right. I keep busy reading my dials and calling for oxygen checks. It's altogether too easy to have a leak in your mask or hose, or anywhere else in the line, and be totally unaware of the problem. Without oxygen at this altitude, you're unconscious in thirty seconds. After two minutes you're dead.

This leg of the mission, about 120 miles according to Odie's notes, should take fifty minutes at our present ground speed of 145 miles per hour. Outside temperature reads minus 33 degrees F. and my heat suit has conked out. I check to see if any of my connections have pulled loose. Wires extend out of me as if I were an oversized puppet. The line connecting my headset to the intercom and radio tangles with the one from my heat suit. Another wire runs from my oxygen mask mike to the intercom, and a flexible hose links my mask like an umbilical cord to the oxygen intake regulator. I'm bogged down with parachute harness and Mae West over a woolen shirt, two sweaters and a heavy sheepskin lined jacket. My movements are as stiff and clumsy as Frankenstein's monster as I lurch around in bulky sheepkin boots in my cramped area. Odie reports that we've blown some fuses.

I feel my insides expanding much like Paul's condom in the thin air at this altitude. My stomach is roiling and I fart off toots lasting fifteen seconds at a time. I hope they're dry. Still an hour and a half to estimated time over target. A wave of confusion and fear sweeps over me. I can't tell if it's part of my last wave or the beginning of my next, as I go through the motions of reading dials and gauges from a crouched position. No seat for the navigator on a B-17. You spend a lot of time on your knees. I keep taking care of business as best I can.

Sparks of light dart off the aluminum and plexiglass of the other squadrons flying all around us. The sun, blinding white with a slim rosy rim, is well above the horizon now, dazzling in a sky of purest blue. I have to squint as I crouch over Paul and look outside for landmarks. He points his gloved hand out past our left wing, where at about fifteen miles off to the north I see a pack of fighter planes closing in on us.

We lumber along at 150 miles per hour as they close in at twice our airspeed. The interphone is busy with chatter from all around the ship. "O.K. guys. Watch 'em," says Odie.

The ball turret gunner says, "They look like Messerschmitts." Their shapes grow larger as they speed toward us. I'm sweating through the cold, staring at them unable to move, like a bird at a snake. Then the top turret gunner calls out on the intercom, "It's O.K., they're ours. Little friends." Twenty seconds later about twenty P-51 Mustangs move into position as our fighter escort, darting beside and above us. They leave S-curved white feathery streaks of frozen exhaust that cross and merge with the long, straight contrails of the slow moving bombers extending ahead and behind us for a hundred miles.

I mark position and time of the fighter rendezvous. The marks are a bit steadier now, and I'm able to grip the pencil and write without removing my double set of gloves. A lot of the stuff they taught us in navigation school seems to be working up here, and I'm beginning to ease up a little. It's like when I first began to make a little sense out of geometry. I want to hold on to this feeling, but it soon slips away.

We plow on at our briefed air speed, 150 miles per hour indicated, altitude 25000 feet. An undercast of five to six tenths altocumulus has developed below us at about 15,000 feet. I peer through breaks in the cloud and see Liege with its huge fortresses plainly visible even from here five miles up. Six minutes later we swing right thirty degrees on a new southerly heading. We are now ten minutes from my first visit to Germany, about one hour from Ludwigshafen, and twenty minutes until the first planes of the lead group cross the target. As of now, the enemy can only guess at our destination. Our present heading would take us right into Mainz or Frankfurt.

Odie calls in to the crew that he's just heard from Hartak that three of the forward groups in our wing are being hit by bandits. Paul points outside, and I see our fighter escort has dwindled down to three Mustangs flying esses above us. He says the rest have gone to join the fight up ahead.

We are over the Black Forest and no enemy fighters or flak yet. Odie calls in. "Stay alert, guys. We just picked up a message that the three forward Groups lost eight ships to Focke-Wulfs before our escort beat them off." A feeling of cold dread snakes its way in and crawls around my mind. How did I get into this? How do I get out? No way out. I'm light headed, woozy. I remember to breathe again. My oxygen indicator blinks with every breath I take.

The Group makes a wide forty degree right turn to take us to our I.P. twenty minutes away. The I.P., the initial point, is where we are to turn and line up for the twelve minute bomb run to the target. Paul points to the cloud bank below now increased to an undercast of 8/10ths. He pulls his oxygen mask away for five seconds at a time and speaks in short bursts.

"No way to see target." Pause. "All bombing by radar in lead ship." Pause. "I'll drop bombs when I see lead ship dropping." Pause. "If anything happens, and I can't drop — " He points to a red switch marked SALVO, and moves his hand as if throwing the switch. "Got it?"

I nod.

"Good," he says. "Oxygen check."

I snap out of it. I hadn't run a check in over fifteen minutes. We turn at the I.P. and Hartak's harsh voice rasps over the command set. "Tighten 'er up. Tighten 'er up. We want a good bombing pattern. We didn't come all this way to drop on their Brussels sprouts." A wave of frigid air races in when Paul opens the bomb bay doors.

Time for flak jackets and steel helmets. Paul told me earlier "I seldom wear them anymore. They're so heavy that they wear you down, and they're no help if your plane is hit." I start putting mine on anyway. The jacket looks like an umpire's chest protector. It's one heavy load, close to forty pounds. Paul helps me haul it on. It's a two man operation. Halfway through giving me a hand with the snaps I can't reach, he decides that maybe he ought to wear his this time. I help him as best I can, and we end up adjusting and checking each other as if we'd rented tuxedos for the prom.

I scan out both side windows before looking ahead. A layer of solid cloud obscures all landmarks below. A tall gray column of smoke pierces the clouds and rises slowly twenty miles dead ahead of us. Paul points to it. Ludwigshafen. Puffs of black and gray pop through the clouds and hang in the air at our altitude up ahead.

Flak.

We head straight toward it as we continue on the bomb run. I stare at each puff exploding hundreds of pieces of jagged steel that can set our oxygen or gas tanks blazing, or stop our engines, or rip the tail or wings off the plane, as easily as it could tear through our bodies. No way to shoot it down, no place to hide. We're on track to the heart of it.

The sky around us is now full of these greasy black and gray explosions. Our ship rocks from blasts of flak above us, and I hear a rough scraping noise as shards of spent shrapnel fall down on our aluminum fuselage. Ahead of us the black barrages are even heavier, thicker, leading us straight into Ludwigshafen. We plow on, steady and level. I scan the instruments: 24,800 feet, 152 miles per hour, minus 26 degrees, but the readings do not register as I force myself to copy them into the log.

Our fighter escort is gone. They can't protect us against flak, and they're as vulnerable to it as we are. You can't shoot flak. Paul is busy flipping switches on a panel to his left. Flak pollutes the sky all around us. A 17 falls out of the squadron on our left spinning down erratically like a falling leaf, its #4 engine on fire. I see its markings — LL-O. Odie shouts over the intercom, "Count chutes! Count chutes!" Lingers O Oboe continues in a flat spin down. There are no chutes.

The flak barrage is heavier now. Every one of those black umbrellas popping open fills our path with blasts of shrapnel. We're going down next. I'm sure of it. My mind is racing. What happens to your body when you fall from 25000 feet? Do you die on the way down, or are you conscious all the time until you slam into the ground?

My map has slid to the floor, crumpled and almost torn apart where I must have stomped on it. I slowly bend to pick it up. It feels like lifting hundred pound weights. I crouch down further, making myself as small as possible. Like a fetus. We continue headlong into the thick of it without evasion, as if we're being reeled in.

We are in the heart of it now. The plane bounces as if riding over railroad tracks when it is lifted by nearby bursts. A large oily black one explodes five yards above us, and I see the orange core followed by the harsh grating sound as the jagged steel rains down on us. A tall trail of smoke rises five miles north, where the preceding Groups went after the chemical plant.

DF-J from our squadron drops out of position. No fire, no spin, nose down and falling, two props feathered on one side, and a shredded wing on the other. I want to scream, but I can't. We're next. I know it. The jagged wing on DF-J bends downwards and then break off as it falls out of sight.

Peterson calls from his tail position. "Dimple T going down! Nine o'clock low." I don't want to see it. I crouch even further with my forearm across my face. Black clouds of flak still popping all around us. Paul checks the clips on his harness. He has one hand on his chest pack chute. I bring mine closer.

Paul turns his attention to the switches on his panel, flipping them quickly now. I see bombs falling as if in slow motion out of Hartak's plane. Our plane jumps twenty feet higher as Paul unloads 6,000 pounds of bombs on invisible Ludwigshafen below the clouds. We continue on this heading for another five seconds until Odie stands the plane on its left wing as the Group formation makes a sharp sixty degree diving turn away from burning Ludwigshafen.

We pull out of the turn and level off in an almost flakless blue sky. The few flak bursts we see are five hundred feet above and behind us. I take smaller gulps of oxygen, and retrieve my log from the floor. It is creased and torn and covered with my boot prints. I mark the log - 1105 Ludwigshafen Bombs Away with a hand shaking as if it had palsy.

Paul turns around to see how I'm doing. I stagger under the load of my flak jacket four steps forward, and lean over him to see the smoke and heavy flak still over the target. We help each other take off our flak jackets. I pull my mask down long enough to ask him if he thinks we hit the bridge. He shrugs. "Beats the shit out of me," he says.

I switch to Command to pick up results of the bomb strike. All I hear is a lot of chatter until Hartak comes on with "O.K. Can it. Bandits in the area. Hitting groups ahead. Shape up now."

Paul points up ahead where we can see the white contrails streaked against the sky from the fighters attacking the groups preceding us. We'll be in that area in two minutes. Our top turret gunner calls out "Fighters - four o'clock high, moving to two!" About fifty blunt nosed black fighters fly past us on the right. Paul clenches his hands above like a winning boxer. They're ours, P-47 Thunderbolts, the second wave of our escort. They soar above us, twisting and turning, sweeping the sky like dragon flies over a pond.

I sag with relief against a bulkhead when we finally leave Germany behind and descend on course over Belgium and northern France. Lille looks better to me heading out than it did going in earlier this morning. We continue our descent and are down to 12,000 feet when I welcome the Channel before us as we pass Calais four miles left. A few minutes later I announce over the intercom "It's O.K., we can remove oxygen masks now."

The crew is way ahead of me. I hear wiseass replies like "Oh really, thanks ever so much," and "Hey, you're really on the ball." I hadn't noticed that Paul had lit up, but now I get a whiff of the cigarette smoke drifting through the plane from tail to nose. Paul flips me one of his. It's a Raleigh, but it's the best smoke I've ever had.

Lots of chatter on the intercom about the heavy flak barrage at Ludwigshafen, and how it was a miracle that we got through, and how lucky we are that the German fighters didn't go after our group. Not a word about our planes that went down.

As we continue our descent over the water, my bladder is sending out some not to be ignored distress calls. I drag myself over to the relief tube, a funnel with rubber hose leading down and out of the ship. My fingers are still numb with cold, and I have a devil of a time unbuttoning and getting through the many layers of clothing. When I finally grope my way to the bottom of things, I find my balls have shrunk to bee-bees, and my dick is a cold shriveled little stump that feels like it's been novocained. I finally manage to line up my apparatus over the funnel, but the attached rubber hose is frozen solid. My frigid fingers start thawing in a most unpleasant way. It all backs up on me as I stand there with a warm wet hand.

Paul is laughing, and throws an oil rag at me to wipe up. The whole crew hears about my accident when the ball turret calls me on the intercom. "Hey, navigator. Let me know next time you want to take a leak, so I can turn my turret around. Right now I can't see out my window covered with your frozen piss."

Odie turns the controls over to Ted Williams, and visits around the plane. The intercom is alive with the guys trading jokes and insults, as if we were on a school bus after a winning ball game, and Odie is back to calling us all cousin again.

I erase and rewrite the most illegible of the shaky entries, and close out the log as the planes peel off from the formation over Bassingbourne. I can't believe it has been only ten hours since the Hangman shook me awake. That all seems as if it happened years ago, like when I was a kid. Paul says "You did pretty good considering it was your first mission." I'm glad he was too busy on the bomb run to see my panic.

"Funny," I say to him, "I never saw any part of Ludwigshafen."

"I wouldn't sweat that too much," he says. "I'm sure you'll have another opportunity."

While waiting at our hardstand in the dispersal area for the truck to take us in, I join Odie and Ted Williams as they walk around the ship looking for damage with the guys from the ground crew. Gashes and ragged holes cover the underside of the wings and fuselage. "I guess we took some hits today," Odie says. "An inch or two either way and we wouldn't have made it." The crew chief hands us each a cigar. Odie thanks him and says "Looks like you poor guys will be patching holes all night."

The crew chief pulls out his Zippo and lights our cigars. "Hell, we have loads of tin," he says, "you fly 'er, we'll patch 'er."

I'm glad to see the guy who held my wallet. "Hey, good luck charm," I say, "I guess I owe you a drink." He clasps his hands behind his back, stands erect and says "My religion forbids alcoholic spirits, but I wouldn't mind if you'd spare me a few shillings."

I pull a pound out of the wallet. I'm no longer surprised by anything I hear around this place. He takes the bill and says, "I asked only for a few shillings. Do you want change?"

I don't know if the guy is jerking me off, or if this is some kind of test, or what. He's staring at me sideways, and in the bright afternoon sunlight, he doesn't look at all like the friendly little guy who tried to cheer me up before dawn. Odie, Ted Williams, and the ground crew guys are laughing about the whole deal, and I wonder if maybe they put him up to it. Odie pats the guy on his back and says to him, "Hell what's the difference, cousin? Our guy doesn't make it, you keep the whole shebang anyway."

I don't see it as particularly humorous, but I'm not about to let him see it bother me. The guy folds the pound carefully, puts it in his pocket, and forces a smile. I don't believe he thinks any of it is the least bit funny either, when he walks away muttering. I figure he's another spooky guy around here. Then I remember that it was an apple he gave me, and I play with the idea that there may be something biblical about that. I shake the thought. You've had a long hard day, I tell myself, be careful you don't start turning weird too.

The truck comes to take us in. We throw our gear and parachutes on after the gunners help each other stow their guns in back. Then we all pile on, pushing and wrestling each other like a pack of cubs. Paul is singing his wild version of In The Mood which comes out as In The Nude. "Ted Williams, you dumb, stupid, filthy sumbitch," Odie roars, "how many do we have now?" Ted's smile is as wide as he can physically make it. He stomps his foot on the truck bed thirteen times. "Fuckin' A!" Odie shouts, "That's my boy! Thirteen to go. Magic number. Thirteen!" Paul stops singing long enough to call out, "Hey, Pete, how many for you?" Peterson, the tail gunner, holds up three fingers. "Third one's always the charm," he says.

Paul says to me, "That's the way to go. Take 'em one at a time." Odie chimes in with "Yeah cousin, that's the only way. Just keep your eye on the magic number." I thank them for their kind words and say, "Thirty-four is my magic number." They all laugh. You'd think I said something funny.

When we climb off the truck, Odie, Ted Williams and two gunners put their arms around each other's shoulders and start singing gospel style. It's hard to pick out all the words, but the finale rings loud and clear — I'm ready Lord, whenever you want me / all I want is just a little more time / Oh, yeeeeeaaas, Lord!

Odie drains the last of the coffee out of his thermos, then turns to me and asks "Are you ready to turn your shorts in to Hartak for mission credit?" I'm loose enough by now to answer, "I would if I could peel it off from all that frozen brown stuff." Paul gooses me when we go into interrogation.

The tape on the intelligence officer's shirt reads 1st Lt. Swan, Thomas. He pours shots from a whiskey bottle for those on our crew who want it. "Nice going guys," says Swan. "How many does that make now?" Half the guys yell their numbers at the same time. Swan turns to me. "I don't believe I've seen you before, you're new, aren't you?" The way he asks, I'm sure he knows the answer to that and a lot more about me. "Yeah," I say, "first one, navigator." My good mood is fading fast. I'm beat. I ask him if I could have another shot.

"Oh sure," he says and pours me a stiff one. "You and I are going to have a lot to talk about. How'd it go for you today?"

"How'd it go for me today? Swell, just peachy."

"His first and he didn't even attend briefing," Odie says. He looks like he's winding up to tell the story, but Swan nods and says, "Yes, I heard."

Odie asks "Do the strike photos show anything?"

"Still a little too soon to tell," Swan says. "Looks like we may have nicked one of the approaches to the bridge, but otherwise not much. Shouldn't be too many fish left in the Rhine though. Early reports indicate the other Groups may have done some damage to the Farben works."

He spreads out a large scale map of Western Germany and asks us to spot the locations where we saw flak. He asks me if I can give him the time and location where Lingers Oboe and Dimple Jig and Tom went down. I check my log and work it out as close as I can.

"Kingston was on Jig, wasn't he?" Paul says.

Swan checks through his papers and says, "Yep, here he

is. Bombardier on Dimple J. Anyone see any chutes?"

"Maybe two or three out of the Lingers ship, but I'm not sure," says Peterson. Another gunner says "I thought I saw two also, but nothing out of Jig or Tom."

"Anyone else?" asks Swan. He gets shrugs. Our little happy time is over.

"Kingston. I went all through training with Kingston. I think this one would have given him twelve to go," says Paul. The deep line cut across his cheekbones made by the edge of his oxygen mask is not the only line on his face. He looks drained, exhausted, like a little old man. He tells Swan, "Let me know if you hear anything about Kingston, and if it's O.K. with you, I'll have another drink now."

Odie falls back into a chair like a boxer who has had a bad round. He says, "Jig was ol' Charley Augustine's crew. I met his family just before we flew over when they visited him in Kearney. He had a real cute kid sister — goddamn!"

It comes to me that I don't know which ships Cavey, Fearless, Lopez, or Earl were on. I don't dare ask if they were on Jig or Tom. "Any more questions," says Swan. Around here, that means exit, end of meeting.

The equipment hut is full of crews dumping their flying gear. I see Hartak a few bins down the aisle. Maybe it's the whiskey, but I can't hold back any longer. "Sir," I say in a cracked voice I don't recognize, "are you aware that I just flew my first mission without attending the briefing?"

It doesn't come out the way I mean it. I get upset when I see six or seven guys gather near us. Hartak doesn't look at me. He rearranges the stuff in his bag. I feel stupid, and sorry I brought up the situation. He zips up the bag slowly before heaving it in the bin. Then he rasps out for the guys hanging around to hear, "No briefing, eh? Tell me, are you bragging or complaining?"

Like the saying goes, I don't know whether to shit or go

blind. I blurt out, "I don't see it as anything to brag about."
Hartak turns toward me. His scowl is hard as an ax. He says,
"Right, complaint noted, soldier." He walks out as fast as he
can on that gimpy leg. Everyone steps aside as he passes.

"Man, you got off easy," says Paul. "For a minute there I
thought for sure he was going to ream you good. Up, down,
across. sideways and diagonal."

Odie says "Yeah, you must lead a charmed life, or maybe
this is just your lucky day, cousin."

"My lucky day," I say. "Lucky I was with you guys. If they
had put me on one of those ships that went down ——" Paul
cuts in with "Yeah *if,* and if the dog didn't stop to take a shit,
he would have caught the rabbit. Man, that's negative thinking. Bad for the old morale."

I heave my bag up in the top bin and try to picture something positive.

TEN

Cavey comes into the equipment hut lugging his gear just as I'm leaving. It sure is good to run into the big guy, but I'm troubled by what I see. His eyes are sunken in a drawn and wrinkled face. He looks exhausted, his back bent and shoulders sagging like he's carrying too heavy a load. He takes my arm and says, "Hey what's wrong partner? You look like hell. Lines under your eyes like you haven't slept for a week. What're you doing here?"

I tell him what I'm doing here, and fill him in on how the Hangman came for me after breakfast this morning. He shakes his big head and blinks, as if he can't absorb what he's hearing. I ask "Have you any idea how the other guys made out?"

He says, "We're lucky. They're O.K. Earl was in the low ship in our element, and I watched them all the way. They landed just before we did and I saw Lopez and Fearless at interrogation."

I'm beginning to feel better as we walk down the road to our room. Two old buddies swapping stories about the mission. We take turns telling about the times when we were most scared. Each story hairier than the one before. Caves wins when he tells me what happened when his bombs wouldn't release over Ludwigshafen. "I hit every switch on my panel," he says "and nothing happened. I couldn't move because we're in that diving turn off the target, but soon as we levelled out, I plugged in a portable oxygen bottle and crawled back to the bomb rack to see what was wrong. Scared shitless. The wind blitzing through the open bomb bay doors. I was still shaking from all the flak, and I didn't dare get too close to the edge of the open bay. There I was looking down at five miles of open air between me and the ground without a clue what to do other than to tug at a few wires and fiddle around blindly with the shackles. I leaned over the open bay as far as I dared trying to reach behind each bomb. My hands were numb and fingers frozen stiff, but I yanked every wire I could reach. Then suddenly I heard a rumbling and pulled myself back just in time. I watched each of those bombs drop, all but one son of a bitch dangling on end, hung up on a shackle. I stretched out and managed to kick it loose, but I was so wobbly that I almost went down with it. It took all I had to drag my ass back. Then after all that, we found we couldn't close the bomb bay doors. They were jammed, and we couldn't even hand crank them shut. We flew all the way back with those doors hanging open, freezing our ass. I don't think I'll ever thaw out. After we landed, one of the ground crew guys found a five inch chunk of flak wedged in there behind a hinge. A couple of inches one way or the other would have put it square in our bombload, and there would have been nothing left of us but little pieces drifting down over the Fatherland."

Cavey lowers his voice. "You know partner, I really fucked up. I haven't a clue where our bombs hit when I kicked them out. Probably an old folks home or orphanage. We should have brought them back, or dumped them in the sea, but we just had to get rid of those fuckers hanging the way they were. By the time we went into interrogation, the navigator and pilot had cooked up a story reporting that we dropped on a cluster of industrial buildings outside Kaiserslautern as a target of opportunity. Damn, I hope what we hit was industrial."

I can't come close to matching that one. The best I can come up with is my experience with the relief tube. Caves remembers that the same thing happened to him. He says, "Soon as these shorts thaw out, I'm going to peel them off and turn them into Hartak. This super size combination load should qualify for double credit."

As soon as I get through the door to our room, I collapse into my little sack, too far gone to even take off my shoes. It's been almost twelve hours since the Hangman came for us. I'm bushed, and weak with hunger. I'd skipped the coffee and doughnuts at interrogation, because I was way too nervous to be able to keep them down, and then there was all that booze I tossed down. Other than this morning's apple, I haven't had a thing to eat since dinner last night. I should have snatched that peanut butter sandwich away from the hangman's dog.

It's a tossup whether I'm too tired to eat, or too hungry to sleep. Sleep wins. I close my eyes and ease into it as if it was a warm bath. When I wake three hours later, I have no idea where I am for a while. I hear Cavey snoring in his bunk above me and it all comes back. It takes a few heavy shakes to bring Cavey back among the living.

"Come on, Caves," I say, "up and at 'em. Eighteen thirty, chow time. Let's go. I can eat a horse."

We're halfway through devouring the usual unidentifiable stew, when the Hangman, Gabor, drops on to the bench facing us. We pay no attention to him. He spoons out a chunk of peanut butter from the G.I. can on the long table, spreads it on a slice of bread, and tosses it to his dog who scarfs it down in two bites. When he asks us to pass the ketchup, I slide it over without looking at him. "Hey, you guys aren't sore at me," he says. "What the hell, I'm just doing my job."

"Yeah, well do it somewhere away from us, creep," I say.

I can't tell what he mutters when he moves down the bench to the end of the table. Cavey says "Man, that guy is loco, touched in the head. We'd best be for ignoring that loon."

We study the stew while Cavey speculates on the breed of furry critter which might be found at the bottom of the pot. "I wonder," he says "if that's the same dog that Gabor had yesterday." I tell him he's barking up the wrong tree.

Gabor passes us on his way out and says, "Catch you guys later. Pleasant dreams." Cavey puts his mess tray on the floor, and the dog licks it clean. He reaches down to pet the dog and says, "It's a dog eat dog world, isn't it Flak ol' girl, remember to steer clear of this kitchen." Gabor pulls the dog away. He flashes the V for victory sign at us, then pulls back his index finger. I'm at the point where I'm not going to take any more shit from him when I get a look at his gaunt patched up mask of a face, and I begin to feel sorry for him. The feeling doesn't last long. He waves his extended middle finger at us.

Cavey half rises from the bench, his right hand clenched into a fist. "Damn," he says "if I wanted shit, I'd squeeze your head. Now get the fuck away from us before I bust you one."

Gabor blinks his spooky eyes and the dog growls at us. He picks up the dog, fondles him, then as he slowly walks off says over his shoulder "I'll catch you guys later."

We sit silently for a while, then Cavey goes back for seconds on the stew. He comes back with a loaded plate saying, "The K.P.'s claim it's mutton. Probably the part that goes over the fence last. Did you hear that turd say he'd catch us later?"

My mind has been on nothing else. I clench my teeth when we scan the alert list posted on the mess hut door. I'm up with Odie again. Trapped. Cavey sees his name too. "I just had another taste of that mutton, or whatever it was," he says. It's still twilight when we walk slowly back across the fields to the room.

Cavey is up in his bunk writing a letter home. Our little radio with its cracked case of yellow brown bakelite is tuned to Radio Hamburg with Jack Teagarden fading in and out with *Muskrat Ramble.* I'm in my sack trying to read a book of stories that Omar stuffed in my bag back at Goose Bay. They're damn good by a writer called Ring Lardner, but I can't stay with it. The announcer comes on the radio rattling off something in rapid fire German. "Turn that shit off," Cavey says.

I stare around the room at the wooden chair, the little radio on top of the beat up four drawer bureau, the bare light bulb dangling from the ceiling, our clothes in wire hangers suspended from the pipe extending across the end of the room, our foot-lockers, and the two page picture of Betty Grable in a white one piece bathing suit taped on the wall. It was there when we moved in, and some sick pervert had drawn a huge cock pointed right up the crack in her ass. I'd take it down if I didn't think it might screw up my luck somehow. The walls are painted halfway up in a dark industrial green. The upper half, an ivory shade turned grimy, is smudged over with scribbled names, dates, home towns, and the usual basic sexual messages and drawings.

I see up near the top, scrawled in red pencilled block letters * * * 2nd Lt Barney Cotton * * * Pride of Chicopee, Mass. * * *. Under his name is a line of bombs drawn about four inches high, with dates and German cities labelled above the fins. There are nine bombs. The last one is tagged Wiesbaden 11 Aug 44, just a few days before we moved in here.

I shudder when I think of that poor bastard Cotton lying

in this very bunk just a few weeks ago, drawing his bombs on the wall after each mission, keeping score. I can see the Hangman shining his damn flashlight in his eyes to wake him for his last mission. I can't sleep in this bunk. I want to talk to Cavey about it, but he has fallen asleep with his clothes on, his fountain pen still in his fingers only a line and a half into his letter. I peel his shoes off and put a blanket over him before switching off the light. I crawl back into my sack and lie there too worried, and maybe too tired to sleep. I feel I'm doing Cotton wrong when I move the Betty Grable pin-up to cover his bombs.

I doze off, but wake every half hour or so to look at my watch. Cavey tosses, turns, and mumbles in his sleep. I try not to think about Cotton by focussing on the pinup, but I keep seeing the flak over Ludwigshafen with DF-J falling from the formation with its engine on fire, the other one spinning in as its wing breaks off, the guys dropping from the planes. I wonder again if they were conscious and screaming all the way down. Cavey sounds like he's having a real bad dream, maybe a nightmare. I push at his mattress above me. He groans as he shifts around. It's almost twelve thirty and I'm wide awake.

I'm deep in sleep when the Hangman flashes his light in my recoiling eyes. He stands there flicking the light switch, until he sees me plant my feet on that cold cement floor. "All right, both you guys, breakfast at three, briefing at four. Both of you," he repeats. I pick up a shoe, throw it at him and say "O.K., O.K., I hear you, now get the fuck out of here." I look at my watch again. It is 0254 hours.

Cavey bumps around the room swearing loud and clear as he searches for something. I take it as long as I can, then I say, "What the hell's wrong with you?" He doesn't answer, but goes on searching, bumping, and swearing. He crawls around the room on his hands and knees. I finally figure out what he's looking for, and retrieve his shoe from out in the hall where it landed when I missed the Hangman. He snatches it from my hand without a word.

I put on two pairs of long johns, two pairs of wool socks, G.I. pants and shirt, and a sweater. Cavey stares at me as if I've gone flak happy when I tie a string around my dick. He breaks silence with "Tell me I didn't just see you tie a string around your dick."

"Yep," I say "that's what you saw all right. I want to be able to find the goddam thing this time when I feel the urge to purge."

"Mine got so numb," he says "I'd need barbed wire." He slams his fist into his mattress and starts swearing again. He has a peculiar look in his eyes. I ask, "Now what the hell's the matter?"

He speaks slowly pronouncing each syllable as if talking to a child. "Matter? Nothing's the matter. Nothing at all. What the hell could be the matter? We're in like Flynn. Shit, we get through this one and we have only thirty-three to go."

We eat our breakfast in a hurry. K.P.'s heap the powdered eggs, burnt toast, vaselined sausages, bacon, and grits on to our trays. I drown it all with gobs of ketchup, and wolf the eggs down with maybe four cups of scalding black coffee. I push the sausages and most of the grits aside when I recall yesterday's jumbo fifteen second farts. Caves takes my grits and sausages and washes them down with the canned grapefruit juice that he calls battery acid. Neither of us have much to say through breakfast nor on our way to briefing. A few guys stop to ask me if I know I have a string sticking out of my fly.

The briefing takes place in one of those sliced barrel Nissen huts. We step from the quiet dark night through the blackout curtain into the noisy, brightly lit room, crowded with benches for the crews of the three squadrons that the 91st Bomb Group is putting up on the mission today. Thirty-six benches, one crew to each bench. A center aisle separates them into two rows. Up front is a platform with a large map of northern Europe covering the entire wall. Our route to today's target is marked on the map. A black cloth covers the section over Germany.

The hut is filling rapidly with crew members. Most are heavy smokers, and they're chain smoking now. Some of the boys chomp on one inch cigar butts, trying to look tough. The place smells like a dirty ashtray, with a thick layer of smoke hovering like cumulus under the low arched ceiling. The crews greet each other with smacks on the back and punches on the arm, everyone wearing their own idea of uniform for comfort and warmth. It's almost like a motorcycle gang. The noise builds to such a level that if I wanted to talk to anyone here, I would have to shout to be heard over all the chatter. I don't want to talk to anyone here.

I go to the bench where Odie, Ted Williams, Paul and the rest of the crew are huddled together. They make room for me. "Morning, cousin. Glad you could make briefing this morning," Odie says. His eye catches the string hanging from my fly, but before he can say anything about it, Paul pulls me aside and says "I don't know what you've got going down there, but whatever it is, it looks like it's coming loose."

I explain about the string. He laughs and passes the word on to Odie, who wastes no time letting the crew in on it. They gather around me making cracks about not letting it get caught in a propeller, and what if the string fell into the wrong hands. I go along with the kidding. It makes me feel less like an outsider with these guys whom I've known only since yesterday. I ask Odie "What's the deal on your regular navigator?"

"Oh, they checked him over, but couldn't find anything wrong. They're shipping him out and I don't know where. I'm sure nowhere pretty. He wasn't much use to us the past few missions. Meanwhile, I guess you're Lucky Pierre."

I wave at Earl and Fearless talking together on the other side of the room. It seems like all of our old crew are up today. I look around the hut, and through the smoke I see JoJo, Lopez, Eriksen, Skiles, and Zibby. Eriksen is sitting on the same bench as Cavey. The Mouse is only a few rows behind me. He comes over to me, and I see his pimply face is flushed and his eyes are bloodshot.

"I know I'm going to fuck up," he says as he clutches my sleeve. "Right now I can't tell my ass from my elbow. Why did they pick me? I never could handle this aircraft." He bites his lower lip. I'm afraid he's going to cry.

"It's O.K.," I say. "I know how you feel. Nobody feels ready for their first. You're going to do fine once you're up there." I don't know what else to tell him so I keep on feeding him shit like that until I find myself turning angry.

What the hell does he expect from me? Comfort? Kind words? Hell, I'm in bad shape myself. How can I tell him what he's facing? I've been trying to keep it down, but now an iron band draws tighter inside me, and my mouth turns sour with the same metallic taste that I had over the target yesterday. A touch of nausea hits me as I see the black flak bursting, and our planes going down yesterday over Ludwigshafen.

The Mouse is repeating "I'm going to fuck up bad, I know it. I can't —" His jaw drops when I cut him short. "O.K. Mouse, come on, that's enough now. No shit, you're going to be O.K. I'll see you later." He grabs my arm again and starts to say something, but I pull away. I can't breathe. I rush outside the hut for some air.

I lean against a tree in the darkness. My fingers tremble as I raise a cigarette to my lips. I want to run away from here, but I know I won't, or can't. It's my old nightmare come true, where I'm on top of this big red bus growing lopsidedly taller and taller as it speeds faster and faster down a narrow road and there's nothing I can do to stop it from toppling over.

A guy moves slowly on the path to the briefing hut. He's taking his time, as if he wants to be alone, or the last one in. As he comes closer, I can tell by that gimpy walk of his that it's Hartak. He hits me for a cigarette. When I give him a light, he recognizes me and says, "Time to go in, soldier. You don't want to miss today's briefing."

"No sir." I gulp and follow him back into the noisy hut. I check my string to make sure it's secure but not too tight.

ELEVEN

I step through the blackout curtain back into the briefing hut. A continual rattle of coughing ricochets around the smoke filled room along with the chatter of a hundred voices trying to be heard all at the same time. I make my way through the crowd to Odie and the crew. Odie stands with one leg up on our bench. He's talking a blue streak to Paul, stopping only to take swigs of coffee from his thermos and doesn't notice that neither Paul or anybody else at the moment is paying too much attention to him. Ted Williams still looks out at the world with his fixed grin, not saying a word, and the rest of the crew horse around as if they were all waiting for a ball game to start.

They go from griping about the food at the base to making wild guesses about the possible target for today, then they all get into a hot debate on where's the best place in Cambridge to pick up girls. The Green Man, The Bull, and The English Speaking Union are nominated, but the consensus is that for real sure fire nooky, the Sunday afternoon tea dance at the Regent can't be beaten. I've never been into Cambridge, and it looks like there's a damn good chance that I never will. All I can think of is Ludwigshafen. I glance up front and Hartak seems to be having a perfectly wonderful time laughing it up with the Hangman. I sit down on our bench feeling more trapped than ever.

The cigarette smoke hovering above under the arched ceiling has turned thick as a blue-gray thunderhead, and the whole place sounds and smells like an Oklahoma truck stop. It is now 0356. The hubbub increases, bouncing off the walls.

"You O.K.?" Paul asks.

I shout to make myself heard. "Oh sure, fine, just swell. Top of the world. Tell me, is it always like this before briefing?"

He pushes his cap back and says "No, now that you mention it, it is kind of quiet this morning." Then someone behind us yells Tan-hut, and the commotion cuts out abruptly as if turned off by a switch.

Colonel Close, the Group's commanding officer, strides swiftly down the aisle like a man late for a train. It's four o'clock, right on the hack. The crews stand up, a few of them stiffly at attention, until the colonel bounds up on the platform and gives us at ease.

We sit down and wait for him to give the signal to draw back the curtain covering the map. He nods his head, the curtain falls away and we see a line of red twine that runs straight across the North Sea into Holland, then zigs once and zags twice, passing just north of the Ruhr valley.

I can't tell what the target is yet, but a spell of groaning rises when Close touches his pointer to the map and says, "Target for today, gentlemen, is the vital complex of railroad marshalling yards north of Hamm. Half of Germany's rolling stock switches through here on their way in and out of the Ruhr. Our latest recon photos show the yards jammed with freight cars loaded with coal and ore en route to the Krupp steel works at nearby Essen. A successful attack on today's target should deal a severe blow to the enemy's transport system, and put Krupp out of business for a long time." Close pauses a moment and the chatter in the hut starts up again. He peers around the room until the noise level tails off. He raises his arm in a loose kind of Hitler salute and says "Good luck men and happy hunting." He hops off the platform and strides out as swiftly as he came in.

"Anyway," says Odie "I'm glad he didn't pull the old one about laying eggs on Hamm."

I hope I don't seem too stupid when I ask Odie "Is Hamm a bad one? I've never heard of the place."

He shrugs and says "I can think of a few places I'd rather go to this morning. It's right next to the Ruhr, Happy Valley, land of no return. Say your prayers we don't drift too damn close, cousin."

"The Ruhr, the fucken Ruhr," Scudellari says. "Flak Center. Last time we went there we lost about forty ships —"

"Forty-two," Odie says.

Holy Cross is now up on the platform acting as briefing officer. He asks for lights out and shows us slides of yesterday's photos of the rail yards around Hamm taken by a P-51 recon ship from our bombing altitude of twenty-five thousand feet. He goes on to give us our position in the bomber stream among the twenty Groups totalling over seven hundred B-17's that we expect to put over Hamm today. He lights a cigarette as he waits for us to mark that down in our notes.

"As a diversionary effort," he says "a three group combat wing of a hundred bombers will be hitting the ordnance depot at Osnabruck fifteen minutes before we fly over target. If conditions prevent us from bombing Hamm, the secondary target is the railroad yards at Munster. Failing that, our target of opportunity will be any known industrial installation in Germany. The 324th squadron will lead our Group today, Captain Hartak in command. Engines at 0540, take-off 0610."

I write down as much of it as I can on my clipboard. Odie pats me on the back, and nods his approval. I guess he knows that I'm doing it to keep busy, to cover my jitters. It takes all I have to hold my pencil steady. I diagram our position in the Group, then show it to Paul. He pencils in DF-C for Hartak's plane and says we want to keep an eye on that baby. I mark the slots for all the guys of my old crew.

The weather officer talks way too fast for me to get much of his forecast. The gist of it is that we should have a clear view of the target, and favorable landing conditions upon return. Nobody believes a word of it. Most of what he says is greeted by hoots and Bronx cheers by the crews. Ted Williams gets into the act, stamping his feet and whistling through his fingers.

"He always has favorable landing conditions forecast, pure propaganda," says Paul, "but he's been lucky lately about the rest of his forecast. That's bad news he's giving us over target. If he's right, we'll be bucking a head wind all the way in from the I.P. A flock of sitting ducks."

The Group navigator tells us, "We depart England from Harwich at 11000 feet, climbing on course until we reach bombing altitude of 25000 just before crossing the Dutch coast south of The Hague. Our course to target takes us across Holland until our first dogleg at Gouda 5201 North 0443 East. We then head northeast making two more doglegs to take us around the Ruhr to the I.P. at Dulmen, twenty miles northwest of the target Hamm.

I write it all down, even the bomb load. We're carrying a 1000 pound GP, six 500 pound GP's, and four M17 incendiaries. Paul tells me GP stands for General Purpose. One ship in each squadron will carry GP's armed with one, two, and six hour delay fuses; and one ship in the Group, called Nickels, will drop bombs fused to explode at one thousand feet releasing thousands of leaflets that urge the German people to overthrow their evil leaders who have brought this devastation to their homeland. Over Ludwigshafen yesterday, Nickels dropped counterfeits of ration books and deutschmarks. The Nickels ship today will be DF-E, Dimple Easy. I remember Mouse is flying as co-pilot on that ship, and I turn to wave at him. He stares at me, then closes his eyes and doesn't wave back.

A bald communications officer, who looks like he has to be the oldest 2nd Lieutenant in the army, rattles off today's radio data. A scouting force of three P-51's, Buckeye Red, will precede us by a half hour, and pass on weather information en route. Two other 51's, Buckeye Blue, will send weather over target twenty minutes ahead of the lead ship. One B-17 will circle over the North Sea at 20000 feet to relay any messages. Fighter to bomber communication will be on VHF channels 724 and 746. The call sign for fighters is Peacock 1, bombers are Vernon. Authentication code is Sour Pickle, ground control is Silkworm. Of course, all communication should be limited to absolute minimum. The old cooter asks if there are any questions. He brushes the dandruff off his shoulder. There are no questions.

Holy Cross stands up at the platform to give us the time check. It is almost quiet as he calls off "Fahv, fo, three, tew, one, hack. It is now 0434." The briefing is finished.

The Mouse is sweating when he comes over to me. "Look at me," he says. "I'm shaking like a leaf, fucked up beyond all recall now. My brain feels like mush, and all this gobbledygook they were dishing out, were you able to follow any of that?"

"Hell no, not very much," I say "but I got a lot of it down here. What do you need to know?"

He rolls his eyes. "Shit, I don't even know where to begin."

I tap him with my clipboard. "Don't worry, you're goin' to be O.K. You're off our right wing, one element over. I'll keep an eye on you. No big deal. Remember you're Mighty Mouse."

"Yeah, sure I am. Tell it to this sad sack of shit over here," Mouse says loudly for the Hangman to hear as we pass him on our way out. The Hangman hears him all right. He points a bony index finger like a pistol at the Mouse, then shakes his head slowly from side to side.

I hustle Mouse out of the hut before he can start anything. "Don't mess with him," I say, "that's just what he's looking for. You don't need that now. You're going to be busier than hell, and I want you to take care of yourself, ol' Mouse. Keep your eyes open and your asshole shut, and I'll catch you after the mission. Drinks on me."

I start to sing the Mighty Mouse song, *Here I Come To Save The Day*, but trail off when he doesn't join in. He looks miserable when we shake hands and say goodbye. His hand is cold, moist, and trembling more than mine.

I pick up the maps for the mission at the navigator's briefing held in a room packed with the thirty-six navigators from our Group. We chart out our planned course, marking the checkpoints en route, and the estimated times and location of each dogleg and fighter rendezvous. We are told that the first wave of fighter escort, P-51 Mustangs, is scheduled to pick us up at the Dutch coast, and stay with us to the I.P. The second wave, Mustangs and P-47 Thunderbolts, meet us right after target. That's a great plan if it works. I hope they are the only fighter planes we see today.

After drawing my flying gear and escape kit from the equipment hut, I join up with Odie and the crew to ride out on the truck with our stuff to the plane. I see Dimple F Fox emerging from the early morning mist just like yesterday. I recall what we went through at Ludwigshafen. I'd tried to keep it at a distance with all the busy work at briefing, and doing what I could to buck up the Mouse with that line of crap, which after a while I almost went for myself. Well, forget it, brother, play time is over.

One of the ground crew guys lends a hand as I toss my bag up into the plane. It's the guy who held my wallet yesterday. "Good morning, I hope you're well," he says, cheerful as a bird. I tell him I'm pretty good, considering. I hand him my wallet. Maybe he's my good luck charm, my mascot.

"Whatever you did yesterday, do again today," I say. "Come to think of it, I don't even know your name."

"Tevis, sir. Paul Tevis, T/5." He slips the wallet into a pocket in his fatigues. "This is in good hands. I'll see you get it as soon as you return." I shake his hand, then climb up to my little area on the 17. I recall how weird he acted yesterday after the mission, and I wonder whether this business of the wallet is such a good idea after all, then I see the new shiny red apple he dropped inside my parachute bag.

We start engines on schedule, and join the elephant parade of 17's taxiing around the perimeter track to the runway. I sweat out every second of our takeoff, as our ship hurtles down the runway. A few minutes later, as our squadron tools around assembling over Bassingbourn, DF-P, Earl's ship, radioes in to Hartak that they've found a stowaway on board.

The guy they found is a clerk at Group headquarters, and definitely not in his right mind. Messages go back and forth, until Hartak tells them to rustle up a spare oxygen mask, wrap him in any blankets or clothes they can find so he won't freeze, make sure he stays out of the way, and keep an eye on him.

It's taking longer for the Groups and Wings to assemble today, with all the layers of stratus around us. We press our heads to the rain-stained plexiglass, nervously ready to call out any planes crossing our path as we go round and round. We break into the clear at 12000 feet, but it takes an hour and forty minutes before all eight hundred bombers are in position, minus a few who crashed on take-off or collided during assembly.

Right after we depart the coast over Harwich at 0814. I'm startled by the sound of our guns until I realize that it's our gunners checking their guns over the water. We make our landfall over the Dutch coast south of The Hague as briefed at 0904 and continue on to our turning point at Gouda. I call for an oxygen check.

Far off in the southwest I see the welcome white contrails of our fighter escort, eight squadrons of Mustangs. They meet us and swarm above, sweeping the sky in lazy S turns. The mission is on schedule, proceeding as briefed. We make the turn at Gouda, and Hartak's voice cracks through the static over the radio. "Tighten 'er up. Bandit country."

Peterson in the tail shouts over the intercom, "I think I saw someone jump. Out of P behind us." I switch to the command set and hear, "Dimple P Peter to Dimple Charley Leader. Dimple Charley, we've lost our passenger. Jumped. No chute."

"Roger," says Hartak, "tighten the formation, goddamit."

I catch glimpses of land through holes in the cloud bank below, but they become fewer and further between. By the time we turn on our final leg to the I.P., it's about an 8/10ths undercast of slate gray stratus based at 12 to 15000 feet over layers of low cumulus. Up here though, the sun is a blinding yellowish white in a dazzling blue sky speckled with Mustangs zipping back and forth above our bomber stream. I wonder about the guy who jumped out of Earl's ship, why he did it, and what went through his mind on the way down, and for how long.

We can't see the river through the undercast, but I inform the crew when I figure we've cross the Rhine. Spotty puffs of flak pop up through the clouds from time to time. They're sparse and nowhere near us. I know that situation is bound to change soon.

"No German fighters yet," I say to Paul.

"Not yet. Keep your fingers crossed," he says. He points at the solid undercast, almost 10/10ths now. "Looks like we're using Mickey today," he says. Mickey is short for Magic Eye, the radar equipment in the lead ship which can perceive land shapes on the scope through heavy cloud.

"Pilot to navigator." It's Odie on the intercom. "What's our wind?"

I check my log for the wind I'd marked after our last turn on to our present heading. "One twenty eight at thirty-three, that's 1, 2, 8 at 3, 3," I say.

"I thought it was something like that," Odie says. "Shit, bucking a headwind all the way in from the I.P. We'll be crawling in to Hamm."

We've made our turn and are now between the I.P. and target. Hartak's voice rasps angrily over the command set, "Goddam sunvabitch, tighten 'er up! Tighten 'er, you bastards!" I look out at the planes ahead and to the right in our element. We're tucked in so closely, that our wings overlap. Paul hits the switch opening our bomb bay doors.

The bomb run from I.P. to target is usually supposed to take between twelve and fifteen minutes. We've been on this run against the wind for ten minutes with a ground speed of only 114 miles per hour, and we're not close to target yet. The Group before us sails slowly through a heavy line of flak that leads straight into Hamm somewhere under the layer of cloud below us. Ten miles ahead, I see large, box shaped, black areas of flak.

"Fuckin' barrage flak, tracking flak. They've got it all," Paul says, "and this headwind's a real bitch. We'll be in flak forever." He helps me put on my weighty, unwieldy flak jacket. I enter my readings into the log with a shaky hand. We've run into the flak now. A straight line of heavy dark gray patches lies outside our plexiglass nose, exploding before us, leading us right into what looks like large black crates of bursting flak.

The German radar gunners below have us tuned in. They know we cannot take any evasive action on the bomb run and they know by now our speed, our altitude, and our track. We're the blips floating in a straight line across their scopes. It's simple. They send up a barrage of flak in our path. We fly through it. Most of us will get through. Some won't.

We're bouncing over the railroad tracks of flak bursts. The ball turret gunner calls out, "Dimple S is hit! Explosion in nose. Smoke."

"Count chutes," says Odie. I look out down to our right and see DF-S spinning down for a second before it disappears. "Four chutes," says the ball turret gunner. "Six," says Peterson in the tail. I try to recall if any of the boys from my old crew were on Dimple S. The flak bursts increase around us as we head directly toward a large black barrage flak area. My guts knot up.

Paul crouches near his switches, his eyes locked on the lead ship. I have the shakes as I wait with him for the bombs to drop from Hartak's ship. The flak bursts continue all around. and there's nothing, absolutely nothing I can do but stare at them. Our plane is rocked by large bursts of black and gray flak on both sides, then I see the bomb bay doors slowly swing shut on Hartak's ship. I know for sure I saw no bombs drop from that ship. Paul slams his gloved fist into a bulkhead, before hitting the switch closing the bomb bay doors on our ship. Our Group turns away from the heavy flak before us, and goes into a diving turn to the right.

"What's going on?" I ask Paul.

"Shit. Either we're going to the secondary, or it's a 360."

Odie's voice comes over the interphone. "Bad news. We're going around again. Hartak called a 360."

I switch to the command set. Hartak's rough voice comes over in a controlled monotone. "Piss poor fuckin' bomb run." We're out of the flak area now, and our air speed has picked up quite a bit from our diving turn. We pull out of the dive, climb back to our bombing altitude, and head back in a wide sweeping turn to the I.P. where we'll start another bomb run.

A cold lump, hard as stone, forms inside me at the thought of going through this bomb run all over again. There must be some mistake. And why are we turning to the right? We'll be passing close to the Ruhr this way. I'm too scared and confused to say or do a damn thing other than pray Hartak knows what he's doing

"Keep your eyes peeled for bandits," Odie calls out over the intercom. We're the lone group up here. There are no groups ahead, behind, or near us now, as we continue our broad circle back to the I.P. Hartak has taken the 91st out on his own. None of the other groups chose to follow. I see large boxes of barrage flak ahead. Our group climbs and banks sharply for 30 seconds left, then right, as we follow Hartak's ship in evasive action. We're way clear of Hamm, but the flak is coming up thicker now. Paul turns around and says, "That's goddam heavy stuff. Where's it coming from?" I work out our position as near as I can figure from my log. Through a break in the undercast, I see a large city about six miles west. "Looks like Dortmund out there," I say.

Paul is furious. "That bastard Hartak! He's fucked up good this time. He turned to the right on his damn 360, and we head smack into the Ruhr!"

The flak is intense now, as we speed back to the I.P. at Dulmen. The wind is behind us, almost a tailwind on this heading, giving us a ground speed of 179 miles per hour. We follow Hartak through evasive action turns. It doesn't fool the German flak gunners, as the barrages increase now and explode in clusters closer to us.

An enormous black cloud of flak bursts just off our left wing. A 17 from the element above us falls out of control from the formation, missing us by less than ten feet. It veers and collides with DF-E. Locked together, they drop for a few seconds. Then an engine fire spreads along DF-E's wing, followed by an explosion which separates them, and both fall from sight in fragments. No one even suggests checking for chutes. My knees buckle and I grab a bulkhead to keep from caving in completely. The Mouse was on DF-E.

He's dead! I try to think of what I'm supposed to be doing now. We stagger clear of the flak and make another large sweeping turn to rejoin the bomber stream at the I.P. I force myself to enter the readings into the log, but my hand is quivering, and I press so hard that I break the pencil point. It's a struggle, but I manage to open my jack-knife to sharpen the pencil. I stare at the blood when I cut my finger. I must not think about the Mouse sitting in the plane as it sets fire and explodes. I must not think about the Mouse.

Paul shakes me and points to the intercom. I don't move. He switches it on for me. I become aware of Odie shouting, "Get on the ball, navigator! Oxygen check, goddamit." We've taken hits all over the aircraft, especially around #2 engine. Everyone calls in O.K. on the oxygen check. Odie feathers #2. We're running on only three engines against the wind through an incredibly blue sky. I see the flak rising ahead through the gray scud of clouds below. No place to take cover as we begin our slow bomb run on Hamm for the second time.

The Mouse is dead!

I must not think about the Mouse.

TWELVE

The 91st Bomb Group with the big black triangle A on their rudders circles around the I.P. following Hartak in DF-C, while our squadron re-forms to make up for the three ships that we lost. The gaps are filled, and we now are flying three elements, instead of four, of three ships each in our squadron. I can see that the other two squadrons of the 91st are missing planes too. Twenty-nine B-17's of the thirty-six that took off from Bassingbourn a few hours ago, tooling around up here five miles over Germany.

We keep circling until Hartak finds a break in the seven hundred ship bomber stream, and maneuvers our group back into the formation. We are in position for another bomb run on Hamm. Rectangular patches of tan, brown, and green fields can now be seen through breaks in the cloud below. We're still bucking a head wind, but the undercast has reduced to about 5/10ths. Black and gray flak explosions form a line like an arrow pointing our way to Hamm. We follow the line.

Paul opens our bomb bay doors again. "Looks like we'll bomb visual on this run," he says. For the second time today I see the volleys of flak increase. We're five minutes from the column of smoke rising from the rail yards at Hamm that have been hit by the groups preceding us. All we'll accomplish at most, is to add fuel to a fire out of control. We plow on.

A heavy black barrage explodes under our right wing, yanking us up ten feet. I want to shut my eyes, but I can't. I stare at another burst close to the dead propeller, motionless on #2 engine. I hear the coarse scraping sound of fragments and splinters of spent flak shells raining down on our aluminum fuselage. I shrink at each nearby burst, and go numb.

The plane jumps up fifteen feet when Paul releases our bombs. We follow Hartak in a diving turn, this time to the left. Paul looks back at Hamm and grabs my arm. "Did you see it?" he shouts. "Did you see that pattern? Those flak gunners had us square in their scopes this time."

I hadn't seen anything but a load of flak and the tower of smoke piercing the clouds, climbing ten thousand feet from the city burning five miles below us. What I did notice was that Hartak went left when we turned away from Hamm this time. "Hartak is not taking us through the Ruhr again," I say.

Paul claps his gloved hands together. "Damn right," he says. "The sonvabitch would be flying alone if he screwed up like before."

We breathe easier when we confirm that the fighter planes up ahead are our escort. Four squadrons of P-47 Thunderbolts. They hover overhead as we fly almost due north now, passing east of Munster toward our briefed turning point. From there we'll head west on a straight line out of Germany to Holland, then descend over the North Sea back to our base at Bassingbourn.

We receive reports of the groups ahead being attacked by German fighter planes, but we make it through unopposed. Just before we come to the islands off the Dutch coast, I notice the #4 engine running rough and coughing. I call Odie, and he says yep, manifold pressure is down on that engine, and our hydraulic system is just about gone. A few minutes later, Odie feathers #4. With #2 out also, we're now flying on only two engines. We hear from the engineer that we've lost all the gas out of the damaged right wing tank.

Our two remaining engines labor to pull us forward, but we're losing air speed and altitude. We can't keep up with the formation. We're alone up here, except for two welcome Thunderbolts zigging and zagging above, covering us until we limp back to the North Sea. We're over the water at 10500 feet, but losing altitude fast.

Odie calls in again. "Homing in on Manston. Give me an ETA." I work out our estimated time of arrival at Manston to be 13:50, forty-two minutes away. Manston is an emergency base on the English coast with an extra long runway of 6000 feet. We're going to need every inch of it, that is if Odie can manage to get us there without going into the drink.

"We're shaving it thin," he says. "Losing 500 feet a minute. Dump the heavy stuff." We toss flak helmets and jackets, guns and ammunition out through the hatches. I see the wake of a few boats in the sea ahead. Odie announces "We're in contact with Air Sea Rescue. We may not make it to Manston. Not much gas left. Flying on fumes."

Paul and I look for our chutes, but we don't clip them on. We're over water. I check my altimeter. 2100 feet. Running out of altitude fast. Paul looks down anxiously at the water coming up closer to us every second. Off to the left, the white cliffs of Dover suddenly rise from the sea. We skim over them at 600 feet. I can just make out the runway at Manston up ahead, and pray that we can reach it before we run out of gas. Or altitude. Odie takes us straight on in, no pattern, landing in a cross wind on the nearest runway. We touch down, tipped over on one wheel, bounce a couple of times, then just when it appears that we're going to flip over, we level off and taxi forever down the long runway. While we're rolling, Paul yanks off his helmet and slams it down. He bends over, covering his face with his hands. He looks up at me and gasps out hoarsely as if they were his last words, "Hartak, that fuckin' Hartak." He brings his forearm to his eyes, wiping them with his sleeve.

I stand over him, not knowing what to do or say. The Mouse is dead and I should be grieving, but as far as I can tell, I have run out of emotion. Totally drained. I am mute, aware only of a gnawing sense of relief. After going through all this, I'm still alive. They didn't get me.

I close out my log without realizing that I've been whistling, until Paul says, "Cut it out, godammit." I know he's right, but it doesn't keep me from replying, "Up yours." I feel the blood rising in my cheeks. A vein in my forehead throbs. I no longer feel empty. I feel like dirt.

The crew gathers around Odie outside the plane. Peterson says "I don't know how the hell we walked away from this one. That cross wind one wheel landing was the scariest I've ever been through. Looked like we we were sure going ass over teakettle on that second bounce." Everyone begins talking at once, just like in the briefing, but not as lively. They want Odie to know that it was a super effort, considering the conditions. Next thing you know, we're having a Town Hall discussion on what was really the scariest part of today's mission. There's a lot of talk about Hartak and the 360, then a couple of the guys mention the three ships that went down from our squadron. The conversation drops off. It's nothing like the hi-jinks after yesterday's mission. I go off into the bushes, loosen up the string, and let it pour. It was so hectic up there today, I never gave it a thought.

While waiting for a truck to come out to bring us in, we walk around the plane inspecting the damage. I see a large slash in the rear of the fuselage where the aluminum has been torn back like an old poster on a tattered billboard. The rest of the ship is riddled with jagged, fist sized holes punched through the skin, especially up and around the wing near the engines. Ted Williams and Odie dig chunks of flak metal out of the holes, and pass them out for souvenirs.

Most of the talk on the truck taking us in is about how lucky we were to make it here to Manston after taking so many hits. It turns quiet for a while, until Paul says, "I hope they nail that bastard Hartak next time. Nobody wanted that 360 but him. We had to be the only Group in the whole goddam 8th Air Force stupid enough to follow that fuckin' nut."

"Yep," says Peterson, "ol' 360 Hartak. He's done it before and he'll do it again. He loves that shit." Odie isn't comfortable with the drift of this conversation. He turns to Ted Williams and asks, "What's the magic number now, professor?"

I'm surprised when I hear Ted speak. His voice is low but clear. "Still a long way to go, Odell. A dozen. Twelve big ones." You can almost hear each guy on the truck working their own numbers. I think about the thirty-three ahead of me. It's all so hopeless.

The Mouse. None ahead for him.

They haul our ship away for repairs, and put us through a short interrogation, before returning us to Bassingbourn in the bucket seats of a beat-up B-26. A half hour later, we're back at the 91st, two hours after the Group returned from Hamm. A heavy blanket of fatigue settles over me. All I want is to crawl in my sack, and wake up when the war is over.

After dropping our gear at the equipment hut, Odie and I snag a lift in a station wagon going to squadron headquarters. I still have to turn in my log of the mission, and Odie has to file his Form 1 and damage report. Paul and Ted Williams tag along to pick up their mail at the squadron office. We turn in our papers to the clerk, and are on our way out, when Holy Cross sees us and calls from his office. "Hey guys, come

on in. Have a little kickapoo joy juice." He points to the Old
Overholt bottle on his desk. He works up his pasted on smile.
"Well, how'd you guys do today? I heard from the folks at
Manston that you had a kind of rough one." He chuckles and
pats Odie on the back, as if bucking him up after losing a
tight ball game. Odie moves away from him. Ted Williams
frowns, and turns toward the window. "Son of a bitch," he
mutters.

Paul looks as dark as a storm, like he's about to explode,
but Odie heads him off. "Yeah," he says, "it was rough all right.
I guess you can say that. It's about as close a call as we've ever
had. Coming in on two engines with no fuel and half our
controls shot out, I thought we'd had it this time for sure."
The clerk brings in four coffee mugs on a tray. Cross pours
the whiskey almost to the brim, then raises his cup in a toast.
The smile never leaves his face. "To absent friends," he says.

I take a quick gulp, then another. I shake my head to get
rid of the picture of the Mouse leaning over the pool table to
wrangle with the Hangman just the other night, while the
Hangman stares into his eyes and tells him that he'll never
make it. I hold the mug in both hands as it clatters against my
teeth.

Odie and Cross swap stories about previous missions
they'd been on together before Cross finished his tour. They're
trying to make like it was great times. I'm dog-ass weary and
downcast, but the Overholt braces me up. Ted Williams helps
himself to a refill. He looks directly at Cross. "Consider this
my report sir," he says. "We caught hell from flak over the
target, but I've never seen worse than what they threw up at
us from the Ruhr when Hartak took us on that 360. I consider
that turning to the right was mighty poor judgment, especially as it took us close to that big city off our left wing."

"Dortmund," I say.

Cross pours the last of the whiskey into our mugs. He

pulls another bottle out of his desk drawer. He says "Yeah, well thanks for the report, Williams. Just make sure you don't put it in writing, O.K.? I sure got an earfull at interrogation. All the boys pissing and moaning about that 360. One thing I can tell you for damn sure, Ol' Hartak had his own good reasons for it, and though you won't get any alibis, I guess his ears are still burning."

Paul slams his mug down so hard that it sloshes over. He glares at Cross and says "His ears are burning? May his soul burn in hell. He may be your buddy, but I hope the bastard has his fuckin' head blown off next time out."

Cross stands up. The smile has dropped off his face. He says, "Watch your mouth Mussolini, you're not around your dago gangster pals now."

Paul lunges across the desk, grabs a handfull of Cross' shirt and tie in his left fist, then hammers his right, square into Cross' open mouth.

Odie tries to pull him back, and yells "Give me a hand with this guy!" I help him grab Paul just in time to feel Cross's fist whiz by my ear and catch Paul right under his eye. Paul tears himself out of our grip, but Ted Williams tackles him as he lunges again at Cross. The three of us struggle to drag him out of the office. Cross is yelling, "Get that wop bastard out of here before I kill him."

Odie goes back into the office to cool Cross down. The clerk comes over to give us a hand with Paul. After a while Paul settles down. "Let me go," he says. "Get your hands off. I'm OK now."

The clerk says to him, "Easy there, Lieutenant Scudellari. Don't try to push it any further. This one you can't win. If Cross presses charges, you're in truly deep shit. I'll try to reason with him, let him know there are four witnesses to say he provoked you. He's going to have it in for you, but he may not push it much further. It's not like we have too many crews left around here. Meanwhile try to put this shit behind you. Forget the whole thing."

"I'd listen to this guy if I were you," Ted Williams says.

Paul rubs the welt rising on his cheekbone. He shakes his head and says, "That fuckin' Cross, that son of a bitch."

The clerk pulls out his jackknife and presses the flat of the blade down hard on the bump above Paul's cheekbone. "Hey, no question about it," he says, "but he sure isn't worth ten years mopping latrines and chopping rock."

I think about the flak filled sky over Germany. "Oh I don't know," I say, "I can think of worse duty." Ted Williams smiles and Paul nods. They know what I mean.

Earl is lying in my sack, talking to Cavey in the upper bunk, when I make it back to the room. I fall like a collapsed balloon on to the thin mattress. Earl gets up just in time to avoid me landing on him. I'm famished and exhausted, completely worn out, but just being here, lying in my good old dependable sack is all I want to do for the rest of my life. I stretch and yawn like an ape in a zoo.

"What the hell happened to you guys?" asks Cavey. "You really had us worried. When your ship dropped out of formation, we were sure you were gone too, until they told us at interrogation that you made it to Manston. You O.K. now?"

I'm eager to tell the whole story, but I catch myself. "Any word on the Mouse?" I ask. "Did they see any chutes?"

"Zip," says Earl. "We were just talking about that. You couldn't expect much the way those two ships slammed into each other, and when we came down, we found out that JoJo Moore was on the ship that rammed into the Mouse."

I hit my head on the upper bunk when I sit up abruptly. "Oh no, not JoJo too, I didn't know." I hold my head in my hands. I don't want this to be happening, but I don't know what to say or do. I think I want to scream, but I don't. I fall back in the sack.

Caves leans up on one elbow in his bunk and says, "It's sure going to be hell when the Western Union boy stops his bike at their folks' doorsteps. Man, I wouldn't want to be there for that."

Earl's head sinks further into his neck. The lines of his frown grow deeper. "I remember the Mouse's dad, so proud of him, and how they looked so much alike, when he came to say good bye back in Kearney."

We're quiet for a while, staring at the walls. I figure Earl and Caves are thinking about how their folks would react if the telegram was about them. I picture my mom slumped at the soiled kitchen table, letting the telegram slip out of her fingers, and using it as an excuse to drink herself blotto.

I don't know how long we sit like that. Cavey breaks silence saying, "You didn't finish telling us what happened to you guys after you dropped out of formation." I fill in the details as best I can including Paul's run-in with Holy Cross. When I finish, we gab about Hartak and the 360. Earl says "Let's face it, he got us in and he got us out."

"Not all of us he didn't," Cavey says, "I think we left a few back there."

"Well," Earl says "maybe you've got to accentuate the positive. Only thirty-three to go for us." We turn quiet again. Earl breaks into singing accentuate the positive, eliminate the negative. He gets as far as latch on to the affirmative, but he can't carry the tune and fades off when we don't join in. I'm all worn out, but I feel jumpy. I check my watch. Five after five. Still an hour to dinner. I ask Earl about that loony stowaway on his ship.

Earl says "I actually don't know too much about it. We didn't know he was on board until after we took off. We were well under way when one of the gunners found the guy buried under the life rafts near the radio compartment. We checked with Hartak who told us to keep an eye on him, and keep him warm. All the guy had on was his Class A uniform, pressed neatly like he was going on a weekend pass. We told him to lie down, stay quiet, and covered him with what blankets we had. Lucky we had a spare oxygen mask. He was pretty good about it, did what he was told, until just before we crossed over into Germany. When we were all busy, he gets up and starts talking to our waist gunner. According to the gunner, the poor bastard was jabbering about peace and love and salvation, not making any sense at all, and before he could make him go back and lie down, the guy had one leg outside the open gun hatch, and a second later he was gone. When we came down, the gunner said he's never going to forget the look in the guy's eyes during that last second. We've heard some rumors why he did it, but all I know for sure is it was one hell of a long step down."

Cavey coughs loudly, trying to cover the sound of one of his super farts. Earl sniffs. "Who the hell cut the cheese?" he asks. "Goddam, Caveman, where were you brought up - in a barn? That last one made my eyes burn." Earl makes a big show about opening the window and says "I heard some talk around that the guy jumped on account of his pal, a co-pilot who didn't come back from Ludwigshafen yesterday. They say that those two were close. Mighty damn close. A couple of the guys even said they were in love."

"What's going on?" I ask. "Did I hear you say in love?"

Earl snickers. "Yeah, I said love, L-O-V-E, glorious love."

This makes little sense to me. I've heard some talk about stuff like that, but I've never actually run across any guys like that and besides I never could figure out the mechanics of it all. I say, "How do you you mean love? Hell, they were guys." Earl grins like he knows something I don't. He does, but I'm not about to give that wiseass the satisfaction of asking any more about it.

We kid around on our way down to dinner, until we see

our names on the alert list posted on the mess hall door. That brings us down in a hurry. We talk about the Mouse and JoJo and some of the other guys we knew who went down with them today, while we wolf down army sausages, cabbage, and potatoes in the cold mess hut.

I'm more depressed than ever and see no way out, but it doesn't keep me from going back for seconds with Earl and Caves. We attack the food, really packing it in while we keep talking about the Mouse and JoJo, We bring up details about what happened when their two ships crashed into each other. I've never been so hungry in my life. Caves had a bird's eye view of the ship after it broke away and describes how it dropped like a rock for about 500 feet, flames crawling along its wing before it exploded. We're talking loud and fast, and eating non-stop as if we're in some kind of eating contest at a fair. The K.P.'s look at us as if we're nuts when we keep coming back for more.

We finally push away our mess trays. Earl has taken to smoking cigars lately, and hands us one of his King Edwards. They're smelly things. We lean back and puff smoke at each other. "Damn," Cavey says, "we gobbled that swill like a pack of hogs. I swear, it's like the worse I feel, the more I eat. I guess it must have been seeing that damn alert list."

"I felt like shit long before I saw the list," I say. "Did you guys see how spooked the Mouse was at briefing? Like he knew he wasn't going to make it. He kept telling me that over and over, and I, like a damn fool, tried to talk him out of it."

Cavey leans back, puffs on the cigar and says, "Hell, don't blame yourself partner. Nothing you could do about it anyway. Look, I don't believe that I'm going to make it either, why don't you try to talk me out of it?"

Earl chomps on his cigar, and hooks his thumbs in his suspenders like Edward G. Robinson. He says, "Makes no damn difference whether you think you're going to make it or not.

Me, I'm absolutely positive I am going to make it, still I know that the damn flak doesn't know or care what I or any of us believe. A split fraction of a second either way makes the difference between having your balls shot off or coming out O.K. And for what it's worth, JoJo was all excited to be going on his first mission, and nobody tried to talk him out of it."

Cavey gazes at the lit end of his cigar as if it was a crystal ball and says, "This is one fine smoke. You know you just can't beat a real good war. I think I'll head on down to the PX and get me a box of these stogies."

He asks me to lend him a couple of pounds, which reminds me about good old T/5 Paul Tevis and my wallet. I'd forgotten all about that. Just a few more hours until the Hangman comes, and I'll be seeing Tevis soon enough in the morning. The sausages begin to repeat on me.

THIRTEEN

I'm only half asleep when the Hangman comes around and blinks that goddam light in my eyes. Cavey climbs down from his bunk and shoves him out of the room saying "O.K. scram, shithead, we're up." He slams the door and leans against it breathing hard.

I know that I can't go on another mission. I've had it. Cavey extends his hand. I grip it and he yanks me clear out from under my pile of blankets. He switches on our little radio set, twiddling the dial trying to pick out a station. Nothing but static until he finds a station fading in and out with the news in Welsh followed by a Scripture reading. It's the only sound in the room as we get dressed, neither of us saying a word as we tug on our layers of clothing.

A steady bone-chilling rain falls as we drag through the darkness to breakfast. We hope the weather will turn worse, so they'll call off the damn mission. We're both bushed, and Caves looks drained. His big mitts are trembling as he pulls out a cigarette. I'm none too steady either when I light us up. I can't stop thinking about the Mouse, all kinds of shit, like whether he was killed right off or wounded, or if he froze at the controls unable to maneuver his ship when that other plane closed in on him, or if he ever saw it. I must be getting flak happy. I don't know if I'm talking to myself or to Cavey when I say "I can't get it through my head that he's dead."

"Oh, he's dead all right," Cavey says.

We keep walking without much talking. I've been forcing myself to reject pictures of the Mouse that buzz around in my mind, but I can't shake the image of the two planes wrapped together before they exploded, nor can I escape the misery of wondering whether he was killed right off or if he was conscious all the way down. I try to dump it as only so much morbid brooding, but what comes up is that it could just as easily be the Mouse walking here through the pre-dawn murk thinking these thoughts about me.

I stop to look up at the sky just before entering the briefing hut. Nothing but low overcast above us. "They're not going to let us fly in this shit," I say. Cavey pats me on my shoulder and says "You must be new around here."

He looks overdrawn and weary in the sudden harsh light when we step inside. We pass by the curtained map and I say, "Maybe we'll have an easy one this time."

"I don't give a fuck any more," he says. "They're all easy when you come back." I'm too far gone to answer anything but "Ain't that the truth, see you later, pal." Soon as I say it, I remember that was my parting shot to the Mouse.

I find Odie and the crew at the bench waiting for the start of briefing. Odie tells me "We're flying in a ship borrowed from the 322nd squadron who are standing down today. Old Dimple F is still under repairs at Manston."

Target for today is the shipyards, docks, and warehouses in Hamburg. Paul says, "Same place we went a month ago, but I'm sure we won't go today in this weather." The weather officer steps up to the platform and blames the present rain on a weak occluded front that should dissipate by engine time.

He predicts clear conditions at takeoff and over the target, and we should be back well before an expected cold front moves in tonight. He flashes his weather maps with their squiggly lines on the screen. Again nobody believes a word he says.

It is still raining an hour later at 0540, when the truck takes us out to Lady Be Good (DF-R), the ship we're flying today. She's an old timer and has seen her share of flak, judging by the aluminum patches spotted all over the original olive drab fuselage. A picture of the torso of a bathing beauty painted with Lady Be on the olive drab nose section has Good and her legs on a shiny aluminum patch next to it.

Odie and Ted Williams walk around outside inspecting the plane with her ground crew. Paul and I check things out up in the nose. It's just another B-17, but we'd all feel better about it if we were back with Dimple-F Fox. Each ship has its own ground crew and I find myself missing strange ol' Tevis with his apple. We just don't like changes. Call it superstition or ignorance or whatever, but nearly all the guys wear the same shirt, or socks, or underwear that they wore on their first mission, as well as carrying some weird thing or other for good luck. I still carry my lucky nickel, the one my dad flipped me from the change when he bought hot dogs the day he took me on that motorcycle ride.

The ground crew guys move slowly in the rain through their pre-flight rituals. They're convinced that this mission will be called off. The bomb loaders stow the smaller incendiaries in the bomb bay, but sit in a group on top of the big 500 pounders. They don't want to go through the labor of winching them up, only to bring them down again.

I hear the clatter of a motorcycle. It's the Hangman with Flak perched dripping wet on the sidecar. O.K. guys, back to the sack, he says, we're scrubbed. Paul and I smile and shake hands. A day without flak can't be all bad.

After dropping our gear at the equipment hut, Paul and

I go back for a second breakfast. We're lingering over our coffee. He reaches for his lighter, and what looks like an empty medicine bottle slips out of his pocket.

"See him?" He holds the bottle to the light. "My lucky roach. Isn't he a beauty?"

Sure enough, I see a fair sized cockroach mooching around in there. As far as I can tell, it's a fine looking animal with a glossy brown coat, but no better than many specimens I've seen scurrying for a corner when you turn on the light in a dark kitchen.

"Meet my mascot, Lucky Pierre," he says. "He's been with me on every mission since my sixth, when I first saw him crawling across the plexiglass right after we crossed over into Belgium. I slapped at him, but missed the little bastard. I wondered what the hell he was doing on the plane and how he got there, but then things started happening. It was a rough one to Dusseldorf and I forgot all about him until we were over the water on our way back. I was stowing my oxygen mask back in my bag, and there he was again, this little brown thing near the bottom of the bag — fat, dumb, and happy, chomping on a chocolate bar I'd started on earlier."

"Lucky Pierre," I say.

"Yeah, lucky all right. Lucky I didn't mash him right then and there, but I was feeling way too good about us making it back, and it didn't seem right somehow to kill him. After all, he'd made it back too, which made me think maybe the little bugger was good luck. I remembered something from school about what happened to the Ancient Mariner after he killed the albatross, so I carefully dropped an oil rag over him and knotted it up so he couldn't get out. Later, after we landed, I slipped him into this bottle, and he's been in it ever since."

Inside the bottle Pierre seems healthy and frisky enough, though a bit nervous like most roaches. I invert the bottle but Pierre keeps his footing. I ask "How do you keep him going?" Paul looks proud and happy that I'm taking an interest.

"Oh, a few bread crumbs once in a while, and a couple of drops of water every day. Water is important."

The roach waves his long antennae lazily at me. "Is it such a good idea keeping her in solitary on bread and water?"

Paul corrects me. "Him," he says, "I've been trying to get him a mate, but though there's a ton of them around here, it's not as easy to catch a live one as you might think, and then it has to be female."

"Maybe if you're a roach it doesn't matter. They probably get the job done one way or another." Paul looks disappointed in me. "I make sure to drop a little sugar in for him once in a while, though it's probably not good for him."

For a while I don't know if he's talking to me or the roach when he holds the bottle up to the light and says, "You might think I'm nuts, but do you know what was going on in my mind when we were catching all that shit out of Dortmund on that 360 yesterday?" He pats the bottle, slides it back in his pocket and turns to me. "When it was at its worst, and I was sure we were going down next, I thought of opening the bottle and turning him loose. These little guys have survived for millions of years, and though we'd be nothing but bits and pieces after we crashed, Lucky Pierre would have been able to dust himself off and go about his business. Who knows how long he'd been on the plane before I found him. He's probably got more missions than Hartak."

On our way out I say "It takes a big man with lots of heart to truly love a roach. Do you ever intend to give Lucky Pierre his freedom?"

"Oh sure. Right after my last mission. I go home, Lucky Pierre goes home."

"Well, better be careful where you turn him loose. I've stepped on quite a few of these lucky little guys in my day."

I dive into the sack when I get back to the room. Cavey has a head start, snoring away full blast in the upper bunk. It doesn't take long for me to catch up. I'm out cold in less than a minute. Cavey's stomping around the room wakes me.

I see a touch of fog outside, but the rain has stopped. He turns up the volume on the radio set, and I hear the announcer rattle off a stream of words in what I take to be German or maybe Dutch. All I can make out is Radio Antwerp before some guy plays "Don't Fence Me In" with a polka beat on a tinny accordion. I yell at Cavey to turn the damn thing down, but he plops down on the edge of my bunk and says, "Boy, are you ever going to move your ass out of this sack? I've been to dinner and back, and you're still in here. I tried to wake you, but you were out cold like you been drugged. You stay in that sack much longer, you'll develop bed sores."

I turn to the wall for more sleep, but my growling stomach sends me a message. I hustle over to the mess hall for dinner. Later, I catch up with Cavey at his spot at the bar. He's slouched over his drink like the other guys, turning the glass slowly in his hand. It's early in the night, and not much conversation going on. We've lost a load of steady customers in the past few days.

Most of the guys stare blankly at the carved Swiss clock over the bar, where every fifteen minutes, Hansel and Gretel pop out to perform unmentionable acts on each other for exactly thirty seconds. The place is quiet as church on Tuesday, and if anybody is drunk, they're damn well covering it up. Caveman and I have had three shots each without much to show for it that we can tell. We're not talking much either. I see Hansel strutting out of his box, and I check my watch. He's sixteen seconds late at 2100 hours. Way overdue for us to check the alert list.

We pass a large table off in a corner where the only noise in the place is coming from. I see Earl, Odie and Ted Williams along with a few other guys we know sitting with Hartak, Holy Cross, and the Hangman. Earl calls us over.

I look at the Hangman, Cross and Hartak. I make some excuse about checking the alert list. I'd as soon sit down with Hitler and his cronies. Odie reaches out his long arm and pulls me in. "Don't bother," he says. "I've checked. They can't fight this goddam war without us. We're up." He scans the table. "From what I see here I'd say we're all up, right, Holy?"

Cross has that halfassed smile plastered on his face when he waves his arm around the table, and says, "But of course, the cream of the crop, the chosen few."

Cavey mutters "fucken bullshit artist" and stands up to face Cross. I yank him down and tell him to stifle it. Odie turns to Hartak. "What's the matter with those jerks at Division? Can't they count? Can't you tell them anything?" Everybody starts talking at the same time except Hartak, who takes another pull out of his bottle. It's hard to make out what each guy is saying, but the general drift is we've about had it. We jaw at each other another ten minutes or so, until we run out of steam and it turns quiet again. Ted Williams is glassy eyed, and I'm sure half looped, when he, of all people, stands up and says to Hartak, "I just want to say, Captain." He loses his grip on the table and stumbles a bit, but he goes on, "I just want to say, Captain, O.K., you don't seem to give a shit one way or another. O.K. That's O.K. with you, that's O.K. with me, but that doesn't mean —" Ted gets lost and looks around the table for a little help. None of his trusted buddies back him up. He plows ahead. He tries to focus on Hartak and says, "They keep this up and you won't have nobody left to push around." He looks pleased with himself, as he lets go of the table and topples into his chair.

I'm glad to see that Hartak's eyes are closed, and he's either passed out or sleeping it off, so he probably didn't hear Ted Williams popping off. I'm wrong. Hartak shakes his head like a dog tossing off water. He pounds the table and says, "Ted Williams, your ass is sucking wind, and you're fucked up beyond all recognition, but let me lay out for you your basic problem." Hartak stands up and I wish that Caves and I had never come to this damn table. It looks like we're going to get a speech.

Hartak looks around the table, his eyes blazing as he waves his bottle at us and says, "You see, like Ted Williams here, all you guys make the same fuckin' mistake. You still have some shit-ass notion that you're hot shots because they made you lieutenants, gave you spiffy uniforms and more money than you know what to do with plus flight pay. You went out and bought cars, drinks, pussy, the works, and then to top it off they even gave you a brand new big aeroplane to fly over here. Yeah, you're hot shots all right. In a pig's ass you are." Hartak takes a pull out of the bottle. "Well, chumps, you've been screwed, blued, and tattooed. Better believe it. You pay a price for all you get in this life. Fuckin' well told you do, and now they've presented the bill, and you realize you've been stiffed. Tough shit!" He pounds the table again, and looks around at all of us, challenging us, looking for a fight. Nobody takes him up on it. He hitches up his pants, unbuttons his collar and loosens his tie.

"Yeah, it was going to be a nice little game you could play with leather jackets, silk scarves, and loving broads, and now it's turned out to be shitting your pants surrounded by terror, hard labor, and boredom. That shiny toy they gave you to fly is nothing but four engines mounted on a great big piece of tin that can explode into flames at any minute. They're cranking them out by the thousands, and they have more than enough twenty year old punks like you, ready, willing, and eager to take your place. Sure, they dress you up and let you strut around acting like fuckin' heroes, but you know damn well by now you're no heroes, and that this is not a game. Well, you're wrong, it is a game, but you poor saps don't know the fuckin' rules."

Holy Cross stands up, pats Hartak on the shoulder, and tries to make him sit down. Hartak shoves him aside and says, "Shit, you shouldn't need me or anybody else to tell you that in a game like this, you're bound to lose quite a few of these toys, but what the fuck, everybody knows we have a lot more where they come from. You're worried sick that you'll be next, aren't you? Well, for damn sure some of you are absolutely fuckin' A right for the first time in your dumbass brief lives."

He pulls a fat cigar from his shirt pocket, and takes about four matches before he gets it lit. Cross tries to help with his Zippo, but Hartak shoves him aside again. Hartak points his cigar at us and says hoarsely, "Boys, the fact is I pity you, but that's all I can do, and before you start feeling sorry for yourselves, remember every mother's son of you volunteered for this shit."

He looks around the table again with that challenging glare, then stares at the bottle in his hand, as if wondering how it got there. He puts the bottle carefully on the table, draws his sleeve over his mouth and says "Come on Hangman, let's get the fuck out of here, away from these poor bleeding hearts. We've got some serious drinking to do." He walks away dragging his left leg stiffly in that gimpy walk of his. The Hangman gives us his sick grin and the finger, as they go off together. Neither of them turn around when Ted Williams smashes Hartak's bottle on the table.

Hansel pops out to bugger Gretel again at ten thirty. "Time we were shoving off, partner," says Cavey. On our way back I ask him what he made of Hartak's little speech. We walk in silence for a while before he says "Hell, that was just part two of his welcome speech to new crews. Who gives a shit. It doesn't change a thing. What it all boils down to is we still have twenty-eight to go."

No mission today. Another day of cold rain and sleet. I wonder what's going on when I get a message to report to squadron headquarters. A guy from the Red Cross is waiting there for me. He tells me "Sit down, son. I'm afraid we have some bad news for you."

I try to figure what could fall into the category of bad news around this place. It turns out that my mother was one of the thirty-four victims of that fluke ferryboat accident in Chester, Pa. last week. The Red Cross guy is uncomfortable when I don't speak. "If there is anything I can do for you," he says "do you have any questions, would you like to have me speak to your commanding officer, perhaps get you some time off."

"No, thanks," I say "it's O.K." I feel disappointed. I had half hoped that if I made it through here, I'd find some way to straighten things out with her, maybe help her cut back on the booze, but forget that now. I know I should feel mournful, but nothing comes up. Maybe I just haven't thought of people being killed elsewhere.

I wonder what she was doing in Chester, Pa.

FOURTEEN

It's a squadron stand-down day. Cavey is not making much progress teaching me to play chess, when we hear Holy Cross squawking over the Tannoy that all crews of the 324th are to report to squadron headquarters at 1330. I groan and Caves agrees wholeheartedly.

"You didn't hear any announcement, did you?" he asks.

"What announcement?"

We don't waste any time. Ten minutes later, we're off the base at the bus shelter, waiting for a ride into Royston. The driver of a lorry stops to offer us a lift. She looks like she might be in her late forties, a stocky woman, with salt and pepper hair cut very short, florid, beet-red cheeks, and Orphan Annie round blue eyes. A large brown woolen sweater covering a gray one is buttoned up front with sleeves rolled back above a pair of Popeye sized forearms, and her work pants are tucked into a pair of muddy boots which stink from being deep into a load of more than just mud.

It takes her a full five seconds before she breaks through her British reserve to tell us she is Vivian L-e-a, not l-e-i-g-h like the cinema star, and she manages as best she can her son's dairy farm up near Caxton's Gibbet while he's off in the service in Burma, and how do you Yanks like this country.

Before we Yanks can reply, she delivers a lecture about how Churchill has bungled the war through his fear of the Rooskies. Frequent finger gestures for Winston and the rest of that Tory lot punctuate her speech. "I have nothing but scorn," she says "for Anthony Eden who could have perhaps saved England, but discarded his principles to serve his vaunted ambition." She's revving up and taking off on Lord Beaverbrook's horrible newspapers when we roll into Royston. When we say goodbye and thank her for the lift, she says it was her pleasure and we're welcome to visit her at the farm whenever we have free time.

Caves and I wander around the narrow sidewalks of the town, looking in store windows and loading up on fish and chips. The pubs are closed until five, so we drop into the local movie house. It's a real exciting picture with Gene Tierney called Laura. After the show, Cavey says "I sure feel like fucking her again." Like a dumb stooge, I challenge him. "Are you nuts? When the hell did you ever fuck Gene Tierney?"

"Never, but hell, I often feel like fucking her."

The pubs are still not open, so we mooch around town again. We stop at a bike shop, and Caves comes up with the idea that a bike might come in handy. Next thing you know, he's bought himself a used bike. Me too.

Being in uniform and on a bike makes me feel self conscious at first, but I get over it quickly. I put my cap in the basket and enjoy the wind running through my hair. Caves and I sprint down the road racing each other. It's like being a kid again. He tells me to tighten up the damn formation when we cycle as close to each other as possible without touching. We yell as we bike past open fields, our hands off the handlebars and arms folded across our chest. We keep cruising around until the pubs open. We try The Green Man, and I see our new friend, Vivian Lea, drinking beer at a table alone. We ask if we can join her, and she insists on buying the first round. It's called Bitter for damn good reason. She sees that I'm not too keen on the stuff, and suggests that I might prefer the Mild. I try that and it's even more bitter, but after knocking down a couple of them, it doesn't matter much anyhow.

Vivian sucks us into a game of darts, which is a lot more complicated than it looks. She's really good at it. We play for drinks, and after paying for the first round, Vivian is home free. We stop Cavey just in time from flipping a few darts at the house cat drunkenly weaving its way through the pub licking all the empty glasses in sight. Caves may not be too far off when he says, "That's their way of cleaning glasses here."

Vivian asks him if that's the way he behaves at home, and then goes absolutely nutso when she hears where Caves is from. She takes his hand and says "I've had an absolute fascination with your Wyoming since childhood, when I first learned that the territory had granted the vote to women in 1869 fully fifty years before they were given that right in your Constitution. I believe it was your very first state to do so."

She is almost breathless when she says "It's been my dream to visit the Yellowstone some day and cast my eyes on the great mountains and rivers." Cavey nudges me. The guy is beaming as if they've found gold on his claim.

He has one long arm around Vivian, she has one of those Popeye arms on my shoulder, and we're rocking when Caves proclaims, "Soon as this damn war's over, you'll be my guests in God's country." We drink to that. Although I've done my share of drinking, I've hardly ever spent any time in bars at home, three or four times at the most, but I feel at home in The Green Man.

Vivian is of the opinion that we two Yanks are a pair of good chaps, not too unlike her son, a prisoner of the Japanese in Burma, from whom she hasn't heard in quite a while now. We don't know how to handle that, and for a moment there's a lull at the table until she turns to Cavey and says softly, "Tell me, is the Belle Fourche as lovely as its name?"

"It sure as hell is," says Cavey.

She shakes hands with the grip of a blacksmith when she gets up to leave, and repeats her invitation that we absolutely must visit when we have a bit of time. We thank her for the invite as well as for her offer of a ride back to the base, but we have our own transport tonight.

Even with a fairly bright moon, Caves and I have trouble holding the road as we pedal the six miles back to Bassingbourn. We help each other out of the ditch a dozen times, and toward the end are ready to chuck the damn bikes, but we finally make it back and salute smartly as we pedal in tight formation past the M.P. gate.

We find our room packed high with canvas mail bags, a present from Hartak. A memo from Holy Cross stapled to one of the bags states that in addition to our regular duties and responsibilities we are assigned to one week of mail censor duty for skipping today's squadron meeting and lecture on customs and behavior governing U.S. military personnel and British civilians.

Another stand-down day. Tomorrow marks a month to the day since we broke our cherry. Twenty-six to go. We've flown enough to have our old crew back together again, though I sweat each of them just as I did the first one

It's not exactly the same old crew. To replace the Mouse at co-pilot, Holy Cross gave us Ted Williams who was without a crew after Hartak had transferred Odie and Paul to lead crew status. By and large Odie's crew, especially Paul, were pretty decent to me, and they taught me a lot on how to stay healthy over here, but it's good to be back with Earl and Cavey and the rest of the boys of our crew. Nobody says a word about it, but we all feel better with Ted Williams as co-pilot, especially Earl. With the Mouse in the right hand seat, Earl would get arm weary from jockeying those old heaps for eight or nine hours at a stretch with no break. Nothing against the Mouse, but he couldn't handle the position, though of course none of us ever wanted him replaced the hard way.

For our first mission together, Cross assigns us an experienced engineer, twenty-two missions, for the top turret. Skiles is moved from that position back to the waist gun, JoJo's old spot. He has been pissing and moaning about that ever since briefing. Target is the Focke-Wulf engine plant at Frankfurt, and by the time we reach the group assembly point, we're all damn well fed up with his bellyaching. We're high over the North Sea when Fearless tells Skiles to button it up, and they're about to slug it out right there, when Cavey tells them to either can it or step outside and settle it.

The flak is not as heavy as we had expected over Frankfurt, but what there is comes awfully close. Our top turret gunner says "They must have their instructors manning the flak cannon down there." We catch enough to put our ball turret out of commission, and though Lopez is unhurt down there, he's in real deep shit. We've taken some flak which jammed the mechanism so that he can't rotate the turret to align it with his exit hatch back into the plane. We have to find a way to get him out of there, as any kind of rough landing with him still in the ball would flatten him like a pancake. The engineer and Skiles have worked on the turret for two hours, trying everything in the book, even hand cranking the turret but it just won't budge.

Earl gets on the intercom. "Hey, Comrade, you still with us?"

Lopez comes through with "Nobody here but us chickens, boss."

"Here's the scoop, Conrad." Earl says "When we get back,

we circle over base at 10,000, you kick away your emergency hatch and bale out. Got it?"

"Bale out, forget it," says Lopez. "No way."

"You've got your chute in there, haven't you?"

"Yep, but that's for emergency."

"You dumbass stupid jerk, what the fuck do you think we have here now, the junior prom?"

"I ain't jumping. Not unless this bucket sets on fire."

Earl doesn't want to mess with him anymore. "You'll jump all right. That's an order."

"Fuck you, lieutenant." Lopez has heard our Jasper story over and over again.

Earl laughs. "That's fuck you sir, you goldbricking yardbird son of a bitch. You know you can't be in there when we land. One bounce and you're mashed pig shit."

"Then maybe this time you bring her in nice and easy. I'm not jumping. That's it, over and out."

We circle the base when we get back to Bassingbourn while the rest of the squadron lands. All of us have taken turns pleading, bribing and threatening the stubborn little bastard. He's still in there. Eriksen receives a radio message from Hartak who has landed. He reads it off in that schoolboy voice of his. Sergeant Lopez. Jump. This is a direct order. Hartak.

"Fuck him too," says Lopez.

We keep circling. Colonel Close radioes up that Lopez faces a court martial if he doesn't jump. "That'll be real tough shit," Lopez says. "No missions for six months. Who's he kidding?"

We're all pissed at him as we go around for another half hour. "That little fella is giving me the red ass," says Cavey. The engineer reports we're running low on gas. There's no way we're going to get Lopez out of that ball unless he bales out.

"Last chance, Conrad," says Earl. "One more go round and I'm taking her in." Lopez doesn't answer.

We turn into final approach, Ted Williams tells Lopez "There's a good chance we took flak in the tires. If they're flat, your turret won't clear the runway. They'll wash you out with a hose, man."

Still no answer from Lopez. We won't know if the tires are good until we touch down. "You're lucky Ted Williams thought of that in time," Earl says to Lopez. "It's your ass on two landings now 'cause I'm just going to skim the runway then take off again, touching down on those tires just long enough to check if they'll hold. Only you can see them, Conrad. If they're damaged, you're jumping. goddammit."

"Take her down," says Lopez.

We're lined up with the runway. I see a crowd down below with an ambulance standing by. Earl brings the ship in on a flatter glide path than usual, and much faster. We're going to need maximum power to go up again once we find out if the tires are shot or not. Our engines have been toiling to pull this old bucket for seven hours, and now they're going to be forced to a surge of every ounce of power remaining. If any of the four engines weaken under the stress, we're all gone, or if Earl brings her in too fast, slow, or low, it's goodbye Lopez. I sure wouldn't want to be him now, crouched in the ball, staring at that black runway coming up faster and faster.

We hear the hard squeal of the tires on the asphalt. Then our cheers are drowned out by the roar of the engines, as Earl pushes all four throttles down to the bottom. The engines respond. Lopez' gamble has paid off.

Earl calls down to him, "You lucky dumb bastard. I'm beat, and shaking like a pup. Ted Williams has the wheel now."

Lopez says, "Nice going Earl, and thanks."

Ted Williams is still pissed at him. "Save your thanks. We still have to land. A crosswind, downdraft or any of the five fickle fingers when we come in, and the chaplain will be filling in your name on that form letter to your mother. You can still jump."

We circle around one more time, Lopez stays in the ball, and we do have to fight a cross wind. I think our luck has run out when the plane tips so far over that we land on one wheel, but Ted Williams somehow steadies the ship enough for a landing without a bounce. It's not pretty, but we can all walk away from it.

We taxi in to the hardstand without the usual after mission horsing around. The crowd and the meatwagon are long gone. No muss, no fuss. Just another mission. Twenty-six to go. The ground crew guys poke around looking for holes.

FIFTEEN

It must have been Ted Williams who first had the idea, but we finally cook up a story that Lopez couldn't jump because his older brother's chute didn't open when he jumped with the Airborne into Anzio. We hope they'll buy it. Not at all likely they'll check it out, but even if they should, they're bound to find a dead Lopez somewhere around Anzio.

One more mission under our belt. By the time we pile into the truck taking us in, none of us are sore at Lopez any more. We're all beat, but that doesn't stop us from cavorting around. Zibby cracks us up when he says "I've heard of guys sticking to their guns but this was ridiculous." It's like we'd somehow pulled out a last minute win in a game we figured was lost. "I must admit you have balls, Conrad," says Earl who then gets all tangled up trying to make a joke about balls and the ball turret. We laugh anyway and we're all loose as a goose at interrogation where Swan sets out glasses and a bottle on the table and wants to know just what the hell went on up there with Lopez.

Earl feeds him the line about the brother in the Airborne and all. Swan gives him a fishy look, but there's not much he can do about it. We're each going to give him the same story and he knows it. He switches to asking details on the mission; places and times. I read off what he needs to know from my log. "Anybody see anything unusual," he asks.

We make up all kinds of shit just to keep him pouring. I say "I think I sighted the contrails of an enemy jet." You get their full attention when you say jet. "No," Zibby says, "I think it was more like a V2." Fearless says, "It was definitely a pair of rockets." We go on like that until Swan gets wise, pours us one more, then sighs as he puts the bottle away. Cavey says, "Don't you want to hear about the missile site I'm sure I saw outside Antwerp?" Ted Williams says "Yeah, I saw it too." Swan says, "I wish you guys would quit trying to jerk me off. That I can do very well by myself." He puts the cork back on the bottle. End of interrogation, back on the table.

Only twenty-four left to go now. I'm about half crocked, as Caves and I weave our way back to our room. The mail Cross sent over for us to censor is in three mailbags filling up our room, and we stumble climbing over them. "Partner, I reckon it's about time we checked up on some of this fan mail from our adoring public," Cavey says. We tug at the bags and have a devil of a time before we manage to open one.

He grabs a handfull of letters and scribbles A. B. Cavey, 2nd Lt. AUS across the corners of the unsealed envelopes and inside the V-Mail. After the first few letters, he shortens his signature to A. B. C. I fill my fountain pen and join in. We must have knocked off close to fifty apiece when Caves stops singing the third verse of Home On The Range for the fourth time and says, "Hey partner, maybe I'm wrong, but don't you think that we ought to read at least a few of them?"

I keep scribbling away. "Come on, Caveman," I say, "there's got to be a ton in these bags. Let's just move this load. We're not about to catch any Nazi spies here." Caves looks up from the pile of letters and says, "Hey, no kidding, some of these are fuckin' whizzbangs."

He reads me one out of a square blue envelope. It's from a guy who can't wait for the war to end, so he can go home and give it to Dearest Thelma over and over again their special way. A few minutes later Caves finds another square blue envelope from this guy wanting to give it to Dearest Gladys their special way. We rummage through the bag for square blue envelopes. We find four more. Dearest Patsy, Dearest Violet, Dearest Dorothy. and then jackpot— To My Darling Wife Harriet.

"This guy's one of our great national resources," Cavey says. "A gal at every base. Check out these addresses and you can just about follow his training program."

I don't know who who thinks of it first, but we're completely in synch when Caves says, "What do you say? Are you thinking what I'm thinking, partner?"

Serves the bastard right. We switch the letters around into different envelopes. We don't read any more of them, just scribble away until we finally clean out one bag. It's been a long day.

"I sure wish we could see his return letter from ol' Harriet," says Cavey.

Target today is the rail yards at Cologne. Twenty-one to go after this one. I draw my gear at the equipment hut, and though I don't see him, I can sure hear Hartak cursing over in the next row of bins. There's no mistaking that metallic voice, like the robot at the telephone exhibit at the World's Fair. Ordinarily, I try to steer clear of him, but he sounds as if he's in pain. When I get to him, he's having a hard time, struggling with the snaps on his heat suit. His eyes are red rimmed and watery. He stinks of cigars and booze, and his clothes reek from having been near vomit recently. I try to help him with the heat suit, but he has it all turned around bassackwards with the bib in the back.

He yells at me. "Get the hell away from me. I can damn fuckin' well handle this myself." I watch him fiddle with the heat suit flaps, until he gives it up as a bad job. He continues swearing, but simmers down after a while, and I'm able to tug the suit off and put it back on the right way. "I'm O.K. now," he says, "hand me my mask."

I reach into his bag and pull out his oxygen mask. He clips it into a walk-around oxygen bottle and says, "Works every time. Like Popeye and spinach. My shot in the arm." He presses the mask to his face and inhales deeply. "You didn't see this," he says.

"My lips are sealed." This reminds me of the mail, so I ask "How about letting us off the censor detail?"

A deep scowl forms in the corner of his mouth. A network of thin purple veins like a relief map of the Mississippi River Basin develops in his flushed red face. He glares at me through heavy lidded bloodshot eyes as if I'd stuck them with a hot pointed stick.

He snarls. "Who the fuck do you think you're talking to, soldier? Stand at attention when you address a superior officer. How dare you dicker with me? Now march your ass out of here, you cheap, conniving bastard. You're ten minutes late."

Earl is talking things over with Ted Williams in the pre-dawn darkness when I get out to the ship. He asks, "What the hell was keeping you?" I slam my bag down hard on the ground. "Nothing," I say, "not a goddam thing". I stomp around for a while and then say to them, "Know your enemy."

"Well, in case you forgot, your enemy today is Cologne," Ted Williams says. I kick my bag. Earl looks at me, then figures he has to boost my morale with a display of his rare sense of humor. He says, "Target today is the perfume factory. The perfume factory at Cologne. Get it?" He pats me on the back. I want to hit him. I want to hit somebody. I turn my back on him, walk away and hear him say, "Well fuck you too," as I throw my bag into the plane and climb up into my position.

The 8th Air Force is sending 1,156 heavy bombers to Cologne today. Our Group is part of a Wing of 108 B-17's going after the railroad marshalling yards. Six Wings of 17's and B-24 Liberators are hitting the Ford/Opel Tiger tank assembly plant north of town, and three wings of 24's are to bomb the railroad terminal in the heart of the city once more. We and the R.A.F. have clobbered the terminal a dozen times, until there's not a brick left standing, but the damn thing is still in operation only a hundred yards across the square from the great twin spired cathedral. It's truly a holy miracle that none of our thousands of bombs have damaged the cathedral so far. God must be on our side. Those majestic twin spires jutting into the sky make a perfect navigational landmark for us.

As usual, we lose five or six of our 1,156 due to engine failure and collision during assembly before we cross into Europe over the islands in the estuary south of Rotterdam. I keep an eye on DF-C, Hartak's ship, the Group leader. Odie is his pilot today, while Hartak commands the group from his usual co-pilot seat, probably taking deep snorts from his oxygen mask to clear his head right now. I try not to think about how many lives, ours and the enemy's, depend on that bastard's hangover.

Paul showed up at briefing today, even though he wasn't slated to fly. He hasn't flown a mission in over a month, ever since they put him on lead status. He swears that Cross is trying to keep him from finishing his tour, and is saving him for one of our real tough missions, like Berlin maybe. I didn't tell him so, but I'm sure he's not just whistling Dixie. That would be the way a prick like Cross would try to settle his grudge.

Skiles is in the top turret, back in his regular position with us. That ought to cut down a lot of his bitching. I told him that he could run the oxygen check today, and he just ate it up. He actually does a good job in that turret, if only he didn't insist on the whole world knowing it.

I enter the instrument readings into my log as the formation turns southeast. We're north of Eindhoven on our dogleg to the I.P. Skiles is up in his turret calling for an oxygen check, when he interrupts himself to call out "Damn, shit, bandits, three miles out, ten o'clock high, closing fast!" My pencil snaps in my hand. Maybe it's our fighter escort who've recently left us for some reason after picking us up at the coast. That hope doesn't last long. Cavey points to them. That iron band tightens in my gut as I see these fighters are painted black with yellow markings and red swastikas. About fifty of them. Me109's, Focke-Wulf 90's, even a few Heinkels thrown in, a mixed bag. Six or seven of their brown Me262 jet jobs zip around one hundred feet above them.

Skiles warns Fearless, Zibby, and Lopez to get ready. For now, they can't see the enemy from their positions. The fighters line up and pounce on us. I see the orange streaks of their tracers flash toward us. Our ship vibrates as Cavey and Skiles fire back from their turrets. The enemy fighters dive down sharply, dropping out of sight. Lopez calls out, "I see 'em now!"

Ted Williams says, "Watch 'em. They'll be coming back."

"Right," Lopez says. "Shit, they're climbing back now!"

Fearless calls out, "I see our 51's. Heading our way."

Zibby says, "Careful, might be more bandits."

I look at my watch. A minute and forty seconds have passed since Skiles first sighted the damn Luftwaffe fighter planes. I haven't moved an inch from my spot and force myself back on the job trying to recall the routine. I clutch the broken pencil and focus on the blunt point writing quivering letters and numbers across the log.

Part of our escort returns. Tracers zip by as the Mustangs

and the enemy Messerschmitts and Focke-Wulfs twist and dive through our bomber stream of hundreds of B-17's. The bright blue sky is stained with black smoke and orange flames of German and American fighter planes and B-17's going down. For an instant my senses seize up in a vision of it all as if it was a picture in a magazine. We plow on. A minute later and it's all behind us. Earl calls on the intercom, everybody O.K.? Skiles calls for an oxygen check.

Lopez says "We lost three." Fearless saw a load of chutes come out of DF-P. Lopez says, "One of the chutes was on fire. I counted six total. "War's over for them the hard way," says Skiles. "Yeah," says Zibby, "if they don't get lynched by a mob of Krauts."

The chatter stops when I croak out in an odd voice, forty-five minutes to target. We close up the formation to make up for the three ships we lost. A half hour later, we turn at the I.P. for the bomb run on Cologne. I call back to Eriksen to release the chaff, hundreds of thin strips of tin foil carried in each plane that are supposed to screw up the enemy radar by appearing as so many confusing lines on his scope. They say it helps.

A gray black column of smoke rises from burning Cologne ten miles ahead. I flinch at the sight of the first black stains smirching the sky. The flak comes up thick and heavy, but the bursts are nowhere near us, about five hundred feet below and way off to the left. Maybe the chaff is working after all, or maybe it's atmospheric conditions, or maybe the German gunners are just having an off day, or whatever. I want to cheer. I recall that Churchill once said something about experiencing no emotion more exhilarating than to know you've been shot at and the bastards have missed.

We drop our bombs, and seven seconds later the whole Group dives in a sharp descending turn to the left, as we get the hell out of Cologne fast as we can. The twin spires of the cathedral still stand. No further trouble on our way back to Bassingbourne.

Twenty-one to go.

Cavey, Ted Williams, Earl and I stare at the clock where Hansel is buggering Gretel one more time, while we half listen to the news on Armed Forces Radio about Roosevelt's campaign for a fourth term, and the Cardinals winning their fourth game from the Browns in the World Series. Earl pounds the bar and says "That son of a bitch has been in the White House since I was in second grade." He and Cavey get into a fight about unions and politics. I try to break it up when Earl calls Cavey a Red, but the fight is over because Cavey is laughing out loud. They almost start up again when Cavey says to Earl, "You stupid little prick, if shit were electricity, you'd be a powerhouse." I'm relieved when right after that Holy Cross and about four other guys join us and we can change the subject. Later, Earl and Cavey shake hands and buy each other a round.

I hear Cross say, "I hope the squadron breaks out of this lousy spell of bad luck we've been having lately." One of the guys pulls out his rabbit's foot and says, "This is magic, it never fails." Cavey tosses down his drink and says "I don't know, it sure was no help for that ol' rabbit and he had three more." Another guy pulls the old one about if it wasn't for bad luck he'd have no luck at all. We all launch into a competition of bad luck stories. Cross says "the guy with the worst luck had to be this co-pilot from the 322nd Squadron who was the only guy on his crew able to bail out of their burning ship before it exploded over Paris. This co-pilot, drifting down alone in his chute through heavy cloud probably thinking how very lucky he was to get out of the burning ship alive, ran out of luck when one of our B-26's flew right through him."

Cavey says to me "That mean little sonvabitch got a kick out of telling us that fuckin' story." We drink some more and later Ted Williams proposes that we award the 91st Bomb Group Tough Shit Medal with Oak Leaf Cluster posthumous to that poor-ass unlucky co-pilot. We all agree on the medal, but Cavey and I would hold off on the Oak Leaf Cluster. One of the guys, I don't know who, calls us a couple of lowlife stupid narrow minded bastards. He's looking for a fight, but nothing comes of it because Cavey says "Oh shit, give that man a box of Milky Ways," and I can't stand up straight.

SIXTEEN

The mission for today is scrubbed before briefing due to weather over the continent. That gives us two days off, as tomorrow is our squadron's stand-down day. Cavey and Earl grab a forty-eight hour pass, get all spiffed up and head straight for London.

I don't go. Last time I went in, it was not what you might call a happy experience. I dragged around to the British Museum, and Westminster Abbey, and Buckingham Palace, and the rest of it. They were impressive, but I found myself gazing skyward a lot. I could be in Piccadilly or checking my watch once more against Big Ben, when images of flak coming up from the cathedral at Cologne or over the steel plant at Essen would worm its way into my mind. I remember thinking while I was looking at the dinosaurs, that probably some poor bastards at that very moment were going down after running into a staffel of Focke-Wulfs.

I went to three movies and walked out before the ending each time, then wound up falling down drunk in Hyde Park and throwing up twice, once on one of those double decker buses, and the other time on some poor girl trying to give me directions on Euston Street. A couple of G.I.'s had the good sense to pour me on to the train at King's Cross and tell the conductor to drop my carcass off at Royston. My hangover lasted longer than my leave.

After Earl and Cavey take off, I skip breakfast and submerge into my beloved sack wanting little more than to remain there undisturbed forever. Man's best friend is his sack. It's like pulling out of quicksand when I finally drag my ass out around noon. My growling stomach insists on being fed.

The sun has burnt through the fog, and I hop on my bike after lunch, pedalling around back roads and lanes until I come across a small crossroad with wooden arrows pointing to Caxton's Gibbet 5 mi, Biggleswade 6 mi, and Bishop's Stortford 8 mi. I recall Vivian Lea telling us that her farm was at Caxton's Gibbet, so I bike in that direction knowing I probably won't find it anyway.

It's a little after four, and not a soul to be seen anywhere in Caxton's Gibbet. At this hour the pubs are closed, but I see a woman in one of those big red phone booths at the side of the road. I wait for her to come out, then ask her for directions to the Lea farm. She's most helpful, telling me to go to the top of the road and deny myself two turnings then bear left to the heath where the third row of hedge leads to the path behind the vicarage which should take me to the the old west road for about a half mile past the forge, and there you are, you really cahn't miss it.

I don't know how but after a few dry runs, I come across Vivian Lea's lorry parked outside an old farmhouse. She's out in a pasture wearing a man's jacket and a worn mustard color sweater over those Popeye arms and doing something with a cow when I wheel up the path to her barn. She's surprised and seems genuinely happy to see me again and right off asks about that splendid chap from Wyoming.

Vivian turns the cow loose and leads me to the house

where she excuses herself and comes back in a few minutes wearing a clean housedress. She shows me around the house, which is larger than it looks from the outside, having at least six bedrooms. Vivian is most proud of the bathroom which was made out of a large corner room and completed just before the war started. It is the biggest bathroom with the largest tub I've ever seen. She runs her hand along the white porcelain finish then says "If I had any sense at all, I would never have put in anything so frivolous."

She takes me into the dining room where a tall, big boned woman pours tea for us. The woman is about thirty and plain as rocks, with large dark eyes, a pocked complexion and black hair pulled back in a tight bun. Her name sounds something like Martha. She's Dutch, from a village near Utrecht, and has been here on the farm helping Vivian since the men went off in the early months of the war. Vivian says that Martha hasn't heard from her family since the Germans moved in. I ask Vivian about her son in Burma. She says "I recently received a letter from the Red Cross informing me that his name had appeared on a list of prisoners shipped by the Japanese five months ago for construction work on the island of Morotai. I've had no word from him in over a year and I fear the worst." She bites her lip and says "I believe it's time for tea."

Martha goes to the kitchen and comes back with a teapot, a tray of cheese, cucumber sandwiches, scones, and jam. She sits with us at the round oak table. I ask them about the farmhouse, and they both have all kinds of questions about America which I answer as best I can except I have to plead ignorance to Vivian's questions about Wyoming. I say, "you know far more about the place than I do." Martha wants to know all about Chicago.

After a while I tell them I must leave. I may be a navigator but I know I'll have a problem finding my way back to

Bassingbourn in the dark. I haven't been qualified for night biking. Vivian asks if I could possibly stay the night, and I can't come up with a single reason why not.

She's sure I could use a good hot bath before retiring. I'd like that. I haven't been in a tub since I was a kid. I try to cover up when Martha comes to take my clothes for laundering while I soak in the large tub. She returns in a few minutes, and before I know it, she's scrubbing my back with a hard, stiff brush. I try to act natural, not say anything. For all I know, it may be an old Dutch custom. If it's O.K. with her, it's O.K. with me. She doesn't say a word either, like she's washing a horse. After the scrub, she gives my shoulders a rubdown. I lean back and go with it, though her hands are as hard and roughened as weathered two by fours.

I don't even say anything later when I'm in bed, and she brings in a couple of extra blankets. She tucks in one of the blankets around me. I wave my arm to thank her, and she lifts my hand to her mouth and kisses my fingers. I'm amazed. I don't know what else to do but sit up and put my arms around her flannel nightgowned waist. She pulls my head to her tits and kisses the top of my head for a while then lifts the blankets and climbs into bed with me. She smells of laundry soap.

Two thoughts come to me at about the same time. One has to do with wait till Cavey hears about this. The other is about how it looks like I'm going to get layed at last. The most I've ever had is dry humping twice in back of a car with the sister of a guy I used to work with in Buffalo, and once in the basement at her sweet sixteen party, but I've never been close to actually being in bed with anyone. Martha and I hug and kiss. I'm getting hard in a hurry.

She grips my dick and I can feel it grow in her hand. Her other hand clasps mine, moving it back and forth around her muff. Softer, she says. I ease up on the pressure and she slips my finger inside. We kiss more and deeper. She makes sounds like she's catching her breath as I move my finger inside her. I hear a long sigh as she arches her back then twists around until she's on top of me.

She kneels between my legs, and I reach up to fondle her tits which are harder than I thought they'd be. She leans back, squatting like a frog, with her ass on my thighs and knees at my hips. Then she bends forward and lets me suck on those heavy globes until her nipples are as hard and erect as I am. I feel the roughness of her hand on my dick as she strokes it then she raises herself up on her knees and guides it inside her.

She leans over me, bouncing her tits hard against my cheeks. I reach up for them, and my head goes side to side as I suck on those firm nipples. I thrust up three or four times as she sways above me. I feel a surge, then I explode inside her. Aaaahh, she says as she rocks back and forth over me until the end of my dick feels raw and painful. No, no, she says as I slide out of her. She takes two fingers of mine and puts them softly inside her.

I sense the strength of this woman as she throws her body against mine over and over until she stiffens as if in a seizure. She falls back on to her pillow, breathing hard and trembling. When I kiss her, I taste the salt of her tears.

We lie quietly in each other's arms for a while. Then she kisses my fingers again before climbing out of the bed. I hear her running water in the bathroom down the hall. She returns with a couple of hot wash cloths and wipes me down all over. She smiles and asks, "ah, do you not feel good now?" I kiss her and tell her it's all in the way she handles those wash cloths.

She gets back into the bed, and I nod off with her nestled close to me, her hand cupped around my crotch. It can't be more than a few minutes before I awake. "Ah ya, what do we have here?" she says. She throws back the blankets and we both look at my hard on. "Oh, it's nothing," I say. She strokes it slowly and says "Ah sir, surely this is not nothing."

We do it again. This time she comes while I'm still in her. She cries out "Ah, Anton, Anton, Anton!", and bites my hand when I put it over her mouth to keep her from waking Vivian. She settles down, then takes my hand and leads me to the bathroom. I sit back feeling proud when she draws a hot bath for me, soaps me down, then climbs into the big tub with me. Later when we get back in the bed, we suck each other off. I fall asleep wondering about Anton, and what Cavey is going to say when he hears about all this.

I'm back in my sack at Bassingbourn waiting for Cavey to return from London. I hope he comes back in halfway decent shape. The party's over. They posted the alert list an hour ago and our crew is up again. I try reading a couple of old magazines lying around, but all I do is turn pages. There's nothing on the radio but a gardening talk and a very unfunny comedian on the BBC stations, and I'm not in the mood for the tinny dance music coming through static from Bremen and Hamburg.

I think of Martha back there with Vivian in Caxton's Gibbet. If it weren't for the eggs in the dish towel on top of our chest of drawers, I'd find it hard to believe it all happened. When I woke this morning, it took a while for me to figure out just where the hell I was until I saw my clothes folded and pressed on a chair near the bed. By the time I got my ass in gear, Vivian and Martha were having breakfast after feeding the chickens and milking the cows. Vivian made a fuss over me, insisting I eat all the kippers, eggs, buttered toast and jam she piled in my plate. I made her stop although the only eggs I'd seen in England up to then came in a yellow white powder out of a gallon can. There were no eggs, kippers or jam on their plates.

Martha was proper and courteous to me in front of Vivian, and I took my cue from her. She excused herself before I finished my breakfast, saying she had work to do, and wished me good bye and the best of luck. After that, I didn't have much more to say to Vivian. She too wished me luck, and hoped I would come back soon, perhaps with my friend from Wyoming. She placed a dozen eggs wrapped in straw and a dish towel in the basket of my bike. When I told her that it was far more than I could accept, she told me that I must share them with my mates.

Martha was swinging a scythe in the pasture when I stopped to say goodbye. She put the scythe down and walked up to the fence. I bent over to kiss her goodbye, but she turned away. She gripped both my hands so hard that I almost flinched. She held them to her cheek, but wouldn't look at my face. She released my hands slowly. "Please, please be careful", she said, then turned away and went back to her work. I biked down the path and waved goodbye but she didn't look up.

Cavey and Earl bounce into the room. Earl is singing *Yank My Doodle It's A Dandy*. He's way out of tune as usual. He and Cavey smell of booze and look happy, but they don't look anywhere near as spiffy as when they left. The breast pocket on Cavey's jacket is torn open, and Earl is holding up his pants because his belt is missing. Basically, they're O.K. Not as good as I hoped, but nowhere near as bad as I feared.

Cavey hops up into his sack and stretches out. "Oh, partner, it's good to be back. There's no place like home," he says, "be it ever so humble." Earl offers me a cigar. I pass. He takes his own sweet time, making a big deal out of lighting one with his Zippo.

Cavey starts to peel off his clothes and throw them down from the upper bunk. "A cold shower and I'll be good as new," he says. Then he announces as if I didn't know, "We're up tomorrow, good buddies."

Earl throws his cigar down and crunches it with his heel. "Yeah, I saw the good news when we came in. Hell, I hope it's an easy one. I know for damn sure that one of our crack pilots is in piss poor shape right now." He pulls out another cigar and says pip pip old chaps as he goes out the door.

When Cavey comes back from his shower, I ask "How'd you guys make out?"

"Like Jesse James at the bank. You should have been with us, partner, you really missed out on the time of your life. It was a goddam joyride from the start and it kept getting better. When we arrived in London, we ran into Skiles who had been on our train. He told us about a great hotel near Marble Arch where he'd stayed before, so we figured what the hell, may as well. We hit a few pubs on our way there, then while walking down Oxford Street, Earl notices this pretty gal, hell of a figure, walking along and keeping pace with us, stopping each time we stop to look in a store window. Finally, Earl saunters up to her and asks her if she's following us. She's bold as can be, and says that it all depends where we're going. I figure we might as well go for it, and tell her we're on our way to check in at a hotel, would she like to follow us there. She looks us up and down, then tells us no need for a hotel, for ten pounds each, she'll call her friend with a charming flat in Kensington, where we could all stay and have a party. Skiles pops off that's twice as much as the hotel charges, and the gal says she and her friend would provide us with all the amenities, what we Yanks call room service. That settles it. She tells us we can call her Annabelle. I tell her that I'm Ben Franklin, and these are my good companions John Quincy Adams and Patrick Henry. We hail a cab, and all pile in with Skiles still bitching about the price. The flat is on the fourth floor of a big apartment house near Harrod's. When we stopped for breath on the third landing, Annabelle collects our ten pounds each, lifts her dress giving us a flash at the goods, and puts the money in her stocking.

"Tell me again. How'd she look?" I say.

"Oh man, like your favorite wet dream. Long black hair, sparkling blue eyes, and built like a brick shithouse with all the bricks in place. About the only thing you'd say was wrong with her was bad teeth. She'd keep her lips together when she smiled so it wouldn't show, but she was a cheerful gal. I really liked her. Anyway we follow her into the flat where we're greeted by her friend Dorene, who's not what you'd call as cute as Annabelle. She's older, maybe about twenty-six or seven, but we have ourselves a lot of woman here, with a figure like Mae West. Dorene sets drinks out for us, and puts an Artie Shaw record on the phonograph. Earl and I start dancing with the girls, but Skiles acts like a real horse's ass saying he didn't lay out ten pounds for dancing. He wants to know when he's going to see some action. I pull him aside and ask him about his clap. He says it's all gone now, that pencil medicine is a fuckin' miracle, he's clean as a whistle, then he starts shooting off his mouth about how he paid for pussy and he wants it now.

The girls try to calm him down, but he's smashed and nasty, and insists on getting his action now. Finally Dorene shrugs her shoulders and goes into the bedroom. Annabelle tells Earl and me that we can watch if we'd like to, but we'll have to be quiet. She takes us into the next bedroom where they have a peephole in the door and one in the wall. I'd never seen a guy actually in the saddle before, and let me tell you partner, that's one funny sight to behold. Skiles is lying on the bed with his clothes on. The stupid shit is yanking his wang while waiting for Dorene to come out of the john. She comes out wearing a shiny green kimono and one of those white feathered shawls. When she slides out of the robe, let me tell you boy, this is one fine hunk of woman standing there. She parades around the bed for a minute and I get hard just looking at her from the peephole. Skiles takes off his pants and shoes, and when Dorene lies down on the bed, he climbs right on top of her. It's not easy to keep from laughing out loud as I watch that broad pink orang-outang ass of his bobbing up and down a couple of times, but it's over before I know it. I doubt if he had time to get it in. The son of a bitch didn't even take off his shirt and socks. That was the end of the party for him. Dorene went off to take a quick bath. When she came out, she ignored him, like as if he wasn't there.

Neither of the girls said a word to him after that, but there was nothing they wouldn't do for Earl and me. We did it all kinds of ways in all kinds of combinations. Half the time I didn't know who I was into. I hope it wasn't Earl. Skiles started bitching about being left out, but Earl told him to go fuck himself. We all thought that was pretty funny considering the situation. He disappeared soon after that, and we didn't see him again until we boarded the train coming back tonight, but that sad sack of shit made believe he didn't see us."

Caves jumps up on his bunk and says "You know there's no way you can beat a real good war. Yep, you missed out on one hell of a good party. What the hell did you find to do around here the past couple of days anyway?"

"Oh, not too much. I biked around a lot and got up to Caxton's Gibbet to visit Vivian Lea one day." That doesn't make too big an impression on him. I remember how eager I'd been to tell him about all that went on, but after hearing about his goings on in London, I just don't feel much like talking about Martha now. "Let's can the chatter. Get some sleep," I say "another big day ahead." I turn out the light. Our cigarettes glow orange dots in the mirror above the dozen eggs on our chest of drawers.

Cavey shifts his bulk around in his sack above me. "And one more thing," he says "I don't know if I should tell you this, but it's just between us partner. It's about something that happened the next morning before we left the girls. Dorene had cooked up a swell breakfast for us and we were all sitting around talking, when Annabelle excuses herself from the table, then taps me on the shoulder to follow her back into the bedroom. I hear Earl and Dorene laughing behind us with Dorene calling out one for the road ducks as Annabelle shuts the bedroom door behind us.

Sure enough Annabelle throws her arms around me and hits me with a kiss that I feel clear down to my socks. Before I can follow up on that, she says I want you to have this. It will bring you luck and protect you. She puts a small thin religious medal in my hand, closes my fingers around it then brings my hand up and holds it close to her mouth while she says some kind of prayer which I can't make out. Carry this with you as a blessing, she says, it will protect you.

I thank her for her kind wishes and I slip a ten pound note in her stocking. Some cards fall out of my wallet and she helps me pick them up. She sees my freshman I.D. from Wyoming and asks if she can have it. It's hers. I know for damn sure I won't be needing that anymore. She takes a necklace from her purse and places it around her neck, then pulls out some fingernail scissors and cuts my picture out of the I.D. She trims the picture down to fit in a locket on the necklace and kisses me again when she snaps it in place. She says you'll be safe now. We're holding hands when we leave the bedroom. Man, that was a quickie, Earl says. I let it slide. No way I can explain to him what went on in that bed room."

Cavey leans over from his bunk above. He asks, "You still awake?"

"No, I'm in never never land."

"No shit partner, you come along with us next time. We told them about our pal Grover Cleveland, and they're awfully keen to meet you. Dorene gave us her number, and we're to ring her up next time we're in town. She just doesn't want us to bring that bloody awful Patrick Henry ever again."

"Good deal. It's good to know you're thinking of your buddy."

"Well, fuck you and sweet dreams."

I wake up when I hear the Hangman rousing guys down the hall. He opens our door and calls in. "O.K., come on you guys, breakfast at three thirty, briefing four thirty." No blinking lights, no flashlight in our eyes. He's quit pulling that shit on us. He saves that for the newer guys. I bump against the chest of drawers in the darkness and hear the unmistakable sound of eggs hitting a cement floor.

"What the hell was that?" asks Cavey.

"Don't ask. I don't think you'll like the answer and besides it's a long sad story."

SEVENTEEN

I see Scudellari at briefing, up in the front bench with the squadron lead crew. He waves me over and says, "First mission that bastard Cross has put me on in over a month. I told you he was saving me for a real rough one. Look out, cover your ass, this is bound to be a beauty."

No sense in letting him know he's probably right. Cross is not about to forget the fight they had in his office, and he sure is prick enough to stick it to him any way he can. I say, "Come on Paul, accentuate the positive. You've got it beat. Hell, you're up there in the same ship as Hartak. You know damn well nothing bad ever happens to bad guys."

It doesn't go down right. I even sound phony to myself. He gives me a long look then says "Thanks pal, thanks a lot."

What the hell does he expect from me? He's been around longer than I have and should know the score by now. Damn it, I don't pick the targets and I sure as hell don't need to hear any of his shit about how rough it's going to be. It doesn't help that we're only a few steps away from the spot where I tried to buck up the Mouse that time.

I point to the .45 in Paul's shoulder holster. "Keep an eye on Hartak," I say. "Shoot the bastard if he even hints at a 360." I slap him on the back, wish him luck, and head for our crew's bench. I feel clammy and short of breath. He calls out as I walk away, "Remember what I said, watch your ass today buddy."

Fifteen minutes later we find out the target today is the Leuna synthetic oil refinery two miles south of Merseberg, Hitler's largest oil refinery, deep in the heart of the Fatherland near Leipzig and Germany's most heavily defended target with over seven hundred flak cannon and four fighter bases close by. We went there three weeks ago on November 2nd, a black day. Thirteen of our Group's thirty-six ships went down, nine out of twelve from one squadron alone. Total loss for all groups was forty-three bombers, and the damn refinery is still in operation. That's why we're going back there today. The guys are quiet. They call it Murdersberg.

Our squadron was lucky enough not to go with our group on that last show, as it was our stand-down day. I remember dinner at the group that night with all those empty places, and Hartak saying to Holy Cross loud enough for all to hear, "Damn, if only we'd been there instead of sitting home on our dead ass. I swear those Krauts will pay and pay hard for each crew we lost today. We're going back, that's for damn sure, and I'll see to it that our squadron leads the Group. We'll pulverize the bastards to nothing but ashes. They'll be crawling around in caves by the time we're through with them, and I pray that it's soon."

It may have come out like a speech, but none of us who heard him doubted he meant every word of it. Hartak arrived at briefing this morning, late as always, but sober for a change with a tight smile of satisfaction instead of his usual scowl. He's getting his wish. He's taking us back to Merseberg with our squadron leading the Group today, and our group leading the Wing. That fuckin' Hartak is at the head of four groups today, one hundred forty four bombers. He can't wait for take-off. He talks it up with his crew and others around him. I've never seen him so high spirited. The guy is eager for Merseberg. I look around at the rest of the guys. You don't need a crystal ball to know how they feel.

No horsing around at this briefing. The guys are quiet even for the weather forecast, where we have a brief glimmer of hope that the mission may be scrubbed when the weather officer says that heavy cloud over the continent may call for higher than normal flight altitude. Standard operational bombing altitude is 25000 feet plus or minus 500. At higher altitudes we're at less risk from flak, but bombing accuracy is decreased. At lower altitudes our accuracy increases, but we're sitting ducks for flak. It's a rough compromise. At 25000 feet it all balances out. Both sides have equal opportunity.

It's an hour after briefing, 21 November 44, 0525 hours, cold and dark, as we wait out on the hard-stand near our ship. The Hangman came out ten minutes ago to say "The forecast over Europe is still bad, everything is moved down an hour."

"Move it down a year," Zibby says.

Our crew huddles around the fire in the oil drum trying to keep warm before climbing into Mah Ideel DF-E, an old patched up bucket of bolts which has been good to us so far. We wait for the good word out here in the countryside with the fire casting strange shadows dancing on the old farm house twenty yards away. I wish I could curl up in the nearby shed and hide out until all this shit is over.

The chill and the uncertain waiting is beginning to get to us. Zibby gets into an argument with one of the ground crew guys over all the boxes of ammo he's carrying on this mission. Lopez and Skiles are yammering at each other as always. Ted Williams shuts them down when he says, "Knock it off. Murdersberg is bad enough without having to listen to you two jerks. You both talk like you've got rocks in your heads."

Earl goes into his morale building act. "Hey guys," he says "how far can a boy walk into the woods?."

"Come on, Earl, cut out the kid stuff," says Cavey. "Yeah," says Ted Williams, "that's real stale." Eriksen pipes up "I know that one. Halfway, after that you're walking out." The kid beams when Earl says "Right on the button. That's my boy who said that." I'm just pissed off enough to say "Whoopee, so what? Last I heard this isn't going to be what you'd call a walk in the woods."

Earl lets that pass and turns to the crew with that sad shit eating grin of his, like when he thinks he knows something we don't. "Think about it," he says, "once we make it back, we have only seventeen to go, that's better than halfway to our 35, and that's what I call walking out of the woods instead of going in."

I'm about to say "Golly gee Earl, thanks for those words of inspiration" when I look up at the rest of the guys who'd been huddling mute as cattle in the cold darkness. They're all talking again like they're really buying Earl's line. Eriksen chimes in with "Sure, guys, you have to look at the bright side."

Zibby is smiling now. He says "Have you guys heard about how a new radio operator in the 322nd tossed out the whole goddam unopened box when he was told it was time to release the chaff." Lopez says, "Maybe it landed on a fuckin' flak gunner's head." Fearless says "I've brought a can-opener along in case ol' Lopez here is stuck in the ball again." Eriksen comes up with "Hey do you guys know that a day after tomorrow is Thanksgiving?"

That stops us. Thanksgiving. The kid looks around and says "Did I say something wrong?" Zibby says "You know kid, you're a real ray of sunshine, aren't you." Then Earl is drowned with Bronx cheers when he repeats his old riddle about what the midget said to the undertaker — I'll have a short bier.

Skiles says "I just have to tell how I had this babe Annabelle just begging for more on my last trip to London." Cavey and Earl jab their elbows into me while Skiles goes on with "She told me she'll do it for free next time."

Fearless says "That dame is either blind or fuckin' stupid, probably both."

Skiles isn't about to tangle with Fearless. He says "I'll bet I can get you and the whole damn crew fixed up by her on our next pass to London."

Ted Williams says. "You really are one horny bastard. Why don't you save some of that until you find the right girl?" The guys howl at that.

"Hell, I am saving it. Got damn near a quart by now," Skiles says. Snickers and moans come from the crew, but now they're revved up again, shoving and pounding away at each other through their heavy layers of clothing.

It's still dark at 0615 when the morning fog crawls in. We can hardly see the trees fifty feet away. This is one mission they'll damn sure have to scrub. I move near the fire and flop down on my equipment bag. Maybe I'll take the bike up to Caxton's Gibbet later. I hear the phone ring in the ground crew's tent. The crew chief comes out. "Just got the good word," he says, "you guys are on." I join our crew in the general bitching session then I check my watch. Engine time in eight minutes. Tevis slinks over to wish me luck. I hand him my wallet and pull myself up into Mah Ideel. We're off on the road to Merseberg.

The weather is B-A-D bad. We have to climb to 14000 feet before we find it halfway clear enough to assemble. We're way behind schedule when Hartak leads us toward Lowestoft on the coast before the Group is fully assembled. It's one ragged formation and the three other Groups that make up our Wing are in worse position, but Hartak won't wait for them to shape up. He doesn't want to miss the rendezvous with our fighter escort. Even he won't go to goddam Murdersberg without fighter cover.

It's still a muddle with the sky full of B-17's crossing over each other's contrails, working to get into position, when we reach the North Sea. Our group makes a slow S turn to allow last minute stragglers to get into their slots. Hartak finally has the Wing in a halfway decent formation when I peer through the clouds and spot the familiar lighthouse way down below as we cross the enemy coastline at the town of Den Helder at 52'57N.

Up ahead and above us I'm relieved to see the contrails of our escort, over a hundred P-51 Mustangs as they zig and zag sweeping the skies before us. Hartak has made our rendezvous. He gave us orders at briefing — "Shoot at any ship that pointed its nose at us." That gave us a jolt even though we know the Germans have rebuilt quite a number of crashed Mustangs. They paint them up with our markings, and when they slip into our bomber formations it can turn into a slaughter. They've caught all too many crews with their pants down.

"Well, the bastards are not going to get any of us," Hartak said. "You see any of them pointing their nose at the formation, I don't care what their markings are, give 'em a burst, blast them. Our boys have all been warned to fly their fighters alongside our bomber stream, to never under any circumstances fly at us nose first. They make any mistakes, it's plain tough shit. That's it. Any questions?" There were no questions.

We cross the Zuider Zee. Thirty minutes later, the cloud layer is so high that we're forced to climb to 29000 feet, but we can't keep formation in all this cloud, nor can we bomb with any effective results from this altitude. If this weather continues, we'll have to divert to the secondary at Magdeburg, or find a target of opportunity. No chance of Hartak going for either of those choices. He wants Merseberg. He'll have to come up with something soon. We're fifteen minutes from the I.P.

The clouds are thick now, even at this altitude. Hartak takes us down to 22000, searching for a break in the clouds. but it's much thicker down here. You try to fly formation in this stuff, you're sure to see some fireballs from our bombers running into each other. We follow Hartak as he continues his descent. We're down to 19400 now. Lopez calls from the ball, "The other groups have turned off. We're alone! The only group up here."

Ten seconds later we break through the cloud cover, and I see the brown and green rectangles of German farms below us. We're at the I.P., and when I check the altimeter, I see this damn lunatic Hartak has taken our Group down to 16800 feet alone, 28 miles and twelve minutes from Merseberg.

I look ahead, but fail to see the usual black tower of smoke rising from a bombed city. Then I remember that it hasn't been hit yet. We are leading the pack, the first group over Merseberg today. Down to the left I see the fake oil refinery five miles long that the Nazis have built out of plywood, painting it to look more genuine than the real one fourteen miles north. I hate to think how often we've been sucked into bombing the fake refinery.

Cavey opens the bomb bay doors. My guts knot up as usual when the first heavy black box barrages of Merseberg flak start coming up. They're right on our track, and would blast us out of the sky if they were at our level. The large black puffs are exploding directly above us. I hear the spent metal pieces scratching on our aluminum as they rain down on us. I yell at Eriksen over the intercom to release the chaff. I pray that it's of some use, and that we can drop our bombs and get the hell out of here, before the flak gunners determine our true altitude. Nobody comes to Merseberg at 16000 feet.

They probably couldn't trust their instrument readings at first, but they must be adjusting now that we're in sight as we come up over the outskirts of the real refinery. I can make out many of the flak batteries in their sandbagged emplacements below. It all looks so clear at this altitude.

The flak barrages are thicker and more frequent, and too many are at our level now. I see chutes coming out of DF-T as it drops nose down away from the squadron. The flak is all around us now — thick, black, and greasy. Oh, Lord get us out of here! I see the bombs drop out of Hartak's ship. Our ship hops upward as Cavey releases our bombs. We hold our track for six seconds more, then Hartak's ship makes a sharp banking turn to the left, and the 91st Bomb group follows him as we try to escape from Merseberg.

The heavy cloud cover above has partially thinned out by now as we head back west climbing up to a safer 24000 feet. We run into some more tracking flak. It comes damn close, but is not as heavy as at the target. When I take my readings, the instruments seem out of focus, and I feel a strange heavy weariness. I blink my eyes trying to stay awake.

The next thing I know Skiles is gripping my shoulders. I have no idea what the hell he's doing here or what he's up to. Maybe that dose of clap has finally got to his brain. He looks directly into my eyes as he holds up an oxygen mask, then points to my mask and pantomimes falling asleep. He repeats this a few more times until I finally get it. Something had gone wrong with my mask, either a leak or a blockage, and I had collapsed from lack of oxygen. Skiles had come down from his position in the top turret behind me and replaced my mask with a spare he had in his bag.

I grasp him with both hands and acknowledge my thanks. He pats me on the back and shuffles back to his position. He's about to climb up into his turret when I hear a loud pop and see the white dust of shattered plexiglass raining down on him in the hatchway behind me. Ted Williams yells over the interphone "We're O.K., we're O.K. Plexiglass in top turret hit by flak. No one hurt."

Skiles stands motionless, wide eyed, dazed. He puts his arm around my shoulder for support. I brush pieces of plexiglass off his helmet and flight jacket, then help him pull the mask hose out of his little green walk-around oxygen bottle and plug it into a regulator behind me. He pulls down his mask long enough to say "Shit, this is a fuckin' mess. Looks like I'll have to hang out down here for a while."

"Squeeze in," I say. He lies down on the floor and it's damn tight quarters as I go back to work.

When we go off oxygen on our descent over the North Sea, Skiles fills me in on what happened. It started when Earl had to feather our damaged No. 2 engine, and called down to me for a heading in case we had to leave the formation. After calling twice with no reply, he called Cavey to see what was wrong. Cavey turned around and saw me slumped down on my knees, out cold. He didn't see any blood on me and couldn't figure it out. He tried to revive me, then yelled on the intercom for help. Skiles was down from his turret in two seconds and knew right off that it had to be my oxygen mask. Checking around, he found where a piece of flak had cut my hose. Lucky for me he carried a spare in his bag.

Skiles has carried a spare mask since learning back in Alex that without oxygen at 25000 feet you become unconscious in fifteen seconds. In ninety seconds you become very dead. "Yep partner," Cavey says "if it wasn't for ol' Skiles here, you'd be past all need of oxygen."

Cavey turns to Skiles and says "You're damn lucky I screwed up and didn't know what the hell to do when he passed out. If you hadn't come down when I called for help, that chunk of flak in our turret would have blown your head clear off along with the plexiglass."

Skiles stands up and gives Caves a dirty look. "So what are you saying — that you saved my life? I knew you guys would pull some kind of shit like that trying to take the credit." He goes to the piss tube, holds up the funnel and says, "Now don't tell me this is for officers only."

"No," Cavey says, "I reckon it takes all kinds of pricks." Skiles slams the frozen relief tube down in disgust when it backs up on his hand. He swears at it, the Air Force, and the world in general. Cavey smiles when he gives Skiles a rag to wipe his hand.

Word about what happened to me has passed on through the crew by the time we land. They all want to know what it felt like. Skiles has put out the story that I was dead when he first reached me, and he had brought me back. I do my best to convince them that I never died. Eriksen seems disappointed. He asks, "How can you be sure?"

"Yeah you're right," I say, "maybe I'm a zombie. I know I sure feel like one."

After that most of the talk is about how that maniac Hartak took us in alone over Merseberg at 16000 feet. "Jesus," Earl says, "he'd have taken us even lower if that cloud layer hadn't broken up. That stubborn old bastard was determined." We're all agreed that he'd have followed that cloud right into the ground before turning back. Ted Williams says "This was worse than his 360's, but we sure had those flak gunners flummoxed for a while. They didn't know where the fuck we were."

"It didn't take them long to figure us out," says Fearless. "They must have thought we were lunatics. Anyway, who gives a damn what they think?"

Skiles and the rest of the gunners are stowing the guns on the truck. I catch him looking at me a few times, but I steer clear of him until we get to Interrogation. Swan puts out the bottle for us, and I make sure the whole crew hears me when I raise my glass to Skiles and say, "Thanks friend. Thanks a million." We shake hands, and for once the guy doesn't have anything to say.

Swan wants to know what this is all about. Earl tells him, but before he's halfway through, Skiles fills in what he thinks Earl is leaving out. Earl shrugs and lets Skiles finish it his way. Skiles takes another drink and raises his glass to me. "Here's to hoping you don't ever have to pay me back," he says. I know what he's trying to say, but he makes it sound like a debt he's holding over me. Swan asks us to get back to more details on the mission, and we give him an earfull on Hartak and his going into Merseberg at 16000 feet. He takes it all down in his notebook.

"O.K., get it all out," he says "let's hear it." We go on for another ten minutes. He looks surprised. We hardly ever give him anything. Usually, we just jerk him around for drinks. "Thanks for your cooperation, boys," he says "now permit me to tell you what happened to the 398th, who was supposed to be right behind you guys. When you got down to 20000, their group leader decided he'd had enough. He wasn't about to follow Hartak through the undercast down to God knows where. He figured they'd be better off above the cloud layer. He split his group off and climbed up through the overcast and couldn't get into the clear until they hit 29000. And up there tooling around in the blue waiting for him to pop out, was a staffel of Focke-Wulfs, who jumped them out of the sun and shot down six of his crews in twenty seconds. He was one of the six."

That's something for us to think about, and it slows us down for a while. Then Ted Williams says, "Yeah, real tough shit for them. but that still doesn't make Hartak right."

"Maybe not," Swan says, "but it doesn't make him wrong either. For all we know, that group leader of the 398th may have been the one who was right as rain, but you are the guys walking around." Swan closes his notebook, and then tells us they've just received the damndest Telex about an infantry patrol in Belgium coming across a B-17 sitting in a corn field with nobody in it. According to the markings, it was DF-T from our squadron, a ship we lost at Merseberg today. The way they figure it, the pilot must have put the ship on auto-pilot before he and the crew bailed out, and the ship flew until it ran out of gas before gliding in for an unassisted wheels up belly landing in that snowy corn field.

We wonder how many of that crew made it down to a German prison camp. Swan puts his bottle away after pouring one more round. I'm kind of groggy when we leave the hut. Earl puts his arm around my shoulder. He says "I told you pal, we're coming out of the woods. Only seventeen to go now." The afternoon sun is warming, as I walk with Cavey and Earl to the Red Cross tent for coffee and doughnuts. "I hate to admit it Earl," I say "but after getting through today's shit, you may be right. Seventeen almost sounds like a manageable number."

I'm not sure how to deal with Skiles coming to my rescue. I wish it had been Cavey, or anyone else on the crew for that matter. Skiles, that jerk —of all guys! A bright guy like Cavey, my closest friend, was unable to do much more than let me lie there and die, while a jackass like Skiles took action and saved me.

I laugh and Earl asks me what's going on. "Oh nothing," I say "I just happened to think that any son of a bitch who saves your life can't be all bad." When I go to pick up my wallet, the boys in the ground crew tell me to forget it, kiss it goodbye. My good man Tevis has gone over the hill.

EIGHTEEN

We've been alerted for three days now, only to have the mission scrubbed before briefing each time due to a massive cold front lingering over the British Isles and northern Europe. Cavey and I spend most of the time horizontal in our bunks. We can't stray too far from the base when we're on alert every night. Not much incentive to leave anyway. Nothing but cold and dreary gray out there, and sheets of cold rain and sleet. I'm almost at the point of believing I've caught up on all my lost sack time, and there can't be a girly book left on the base that Cavey hasn't rummaged through at least two or three times.

Cavey's voice drifts down from the bunk above me. "You're going to have a bad case of bedsores if you don't stir your flat ass out of that raggedy sack."

"Great, maybe they'll ground me. E."

Cavey thinks it over. "U", he says. "Come on partner, move it. You're converting into a real zombie."

I say, "G."

Caves scratches his head. "Did I hear you say G?"

This is our fourth game of Ghost in the past half hour.

He blows a blockbuster fart that even he can't stand. He stretches a long arm and opens the window an inch without leaving his sack. I pull the blanket over my nose.

I think I've got him. We're nearly up to the one minute limit and he's coming up blank, Then just before time's up, he blurts out R.

"E-U-G-R? Man, you've been sniffing too much oxygen. It's softened your brain."

Caves comes down from his sack, picks up the girly books strewn all around the room, looks me straight in the eye and nods slowly. "E-U-G-R," he repeats firmly. He places the girly books in a neat pile on the table, as if he had nothing else on his mind, and now I know I have him. He sings along with Sinatra crooning *I'll Never Smile Again* on the radio. Absolute positive sure fire proof that he's bluffing.

"O.K., Mr. Shitforbrains," I say. "I challenge E-U-G-R."

He looks astonished, as if I've gone completely out of my mind. "What? You challenge E-U-G-R? Surely you jest."

This is going to be good. "Bet your ass, I challenge it, you big fake. Do you think you can pull that shit on me? O.K., come on now, dickhead, what's your word?"

He slowly unwraps a Milky Way and turns up the volume on the radio. He shakes his head, pitying me for being such an illiterate dunce. "What's my word? Why, you poor dumbass mistrusting bastard, the word is eugre, E-U-G-R-E - eugre - a small mouselike mammal, native to the Northern Plains of Western United States. Considered an omen of good fortune by the Shoshones and rarely observed because of their lengthy period of hibernation." He rattles all that off without looking at me.

He's so bad that I can't help laughing. "Eugre! You phony baloney, what do you take me for?" I kick off my blanket and point to my crotch. "Eugre this, you big faking pile of Wyoming bullshit."

"Man," he says, "you're uncouth. You really ought to watch your fuckin' language."

I still hold back on telling Cavey about Martha. There's no way I can tell it right. It may be foolish, but I know my man Cavey, and if he ever saw her and knew about what happened, he'd never let up on me, and I can't say that I'd blame him much. I know what went through my mind when I stopped near the pasture to say goodbye to her. How plain she looked, and old, like one of my high school teachers. Still, I can't forget how nice and kind she was to me, like nobody ever treated me before, and I don't mean only the sex part. And of course, there's good old Vivian Lea. They are both good, decent women, and it makes me feel good to know there are still people like that in this crazy world. I'll bike up there again for a visit on our next stand-down day.

The weather finally breaks. Cavey and I aren't flying together today. He, Eriksen, and Fearless are assigned to another crew, while we break in a bombardier, radio man, and waist gunner, all flying their first mission.

I can't say I'm any too well disposed to having someone other than Cavey up in that glass nose with me, especially some green kid on his first mission, but I know there's damn little I can do about it. I meet the new bombardier at briefing. We shake hands and I ask him where he's from and where he took his training, and all that shit, but I don't give him much more. We're going to Cologne again, and I'm occupied with my own problems as I look up at the dark sky from the truck taking us out to the plane.

His name is Archer Bishop, and I answer his questions with yep, nope, maybe, and a couple of you'll find outs. He's polite, and thanks me each time I answer, even throwing in a few sirs from time to time. Coming from him, it seems natural, not military, My guess is that it's the way he talks at home.

Home for him is some small town in Virginia, near Roanoke, and he hopes I'll pardon his poor dumb hillbilly ways. By the time we reach the plane, I've begun to warm up to him a little.

Something about the way he walks alone around our 17 in the darkness reminds me of my first mission back with Odie and Paul. Damn, that seems like a century ago. I recall how Paul helped me out and I feel like such a jerk for being so rough on Bishop.

I advise him to be sure to take a leak before we climb on board. Then I tell him about the frozen piss tube on my first mission, and how I had missed the briefing. I help him get set up in his position in the nose turret. He thanks me but I can see that he's nervous.

He turns and says, "Last night I ran into somebody who calls himself the Hangman. Is he completely right in the head?"

"Not even for a minute," I say. He nods as if that confirms his suspicions, then he asks "What kind of guy is Hartak?" I pat him on the back and say, "You'll find that out for yourself soon enough. Don't worry about him, we have a party to go to now."

The mission to Cologne turns out to be one of our easy ones. We took a few flak holes in the wing fairly close to our No. 3 engine, but nothing serious. Our group didn't lose a single plane, but it was pretty goddam cold up there today. Sixty below zero Fahrenheit all the way, so there must have been more than a few fingers and toes lost out there. Ice formed and grew outside our oxygen masks as our exhaled breath froze. I kept reminding Bishop to break off the ice before it built up too much. At times he looked like a hulking walrus.

We may have had an easy time of it this time, but other groups weren't so lucky. Swan tells us at interrogation that the 445th group, following us by fifteen minutes, were almost totally wiped out. Only nine of their thirty-six returned to the base after they were hit by two sturmgruppen of F-W 190's just before they turned at the I.P.

"Holy shit," Ted Williams says, "I remember worrying when we got there how it was a perfect setup for an ambush with us sandwiched in the clear between a thick layer of cloud above us, and an almost solid 10/10ths below. Those Focke-Wulfs could easily have jumped us from above, without us catching sight of them until too late, and then escaped by diving into the undercast. Probably the way they hit the 445th. We're damn lucky it wasn't us."

The new radio man says, "I guess it can always be us. Maybe next time."

We look at him as if he's said fuck in church. Hell, we all carry that thought around inside. Some dwell on it more than others, but still saying maybe next time when referring to your buddies, and I know this may be another stupid superstition, is altogether too much like jinxing us.

Swan says "This is as good a time as any to tell you about last week's thousand plane raid against Coblenz when we didn't lose a single plane. The really weird thing about that easy one, is that a radio operator in the Bloody 100th on his thirty-first mission caught one piece of flak right in his heart. He died in a few minutes, and no one else in any of those thousand planes received so much as a scratch."

Not much we can say about that. Caves looks around to see if anyone else is going to reply. No one speaks, so he says it. "Well then it wasn't such an easy one for that poor bastard."

I can tell by Bishop's strained smile, that this conversation isn't doing too much for his morale. It's certainly not helping mine. I interrupt Swan who is preaching another sermon now, by signalling him to pour the kid a drink.

The strike photos show that our bomb drop was fairly close to target, but the Nazis will round up a few thousand slave laborers from their concentration camps to lay down new tracks and fill in the craters, and they'll have trains running through the yards again before too long. Then we'll have to go back and make more holes. It's like when we bomb the oil works at Merseberg. We put a good part of the refinery out of commission, but they have twenty thousand prisoners working night and day patching up the pipes and putting the buildings back together, and less than a week later they're back in business. We've bombed the shit out of that place a dozen times, but they're still going strong, and we keep on going back.

For a while, our primary target was their fighter plane assembly plants and engine works. We bombed every aircraft factory in Germany until there wasn't a wall left standing. So they rounded up another forty or fifty thousand prisoners, and moved all their aircraft works underground and in caves. Our intelligence reports show that last month was a record month for German fighter plane production, and they now have more fighter aircraft than ever. It makes you wonder what would happen if we hadn't been bombing them.

Sixteen to go.

Cavey and I bike down after dinner to the Rose and Thorn in Bassingbourn. Odie and Paul are there with some new guys we haven't met. The new guys look kind of lost, but Odie and Paul act like it's one big happy party. Odie tells us his magic number is now only one. Paul's is three. We put our arms around each other like in a football huddle. Cavey says, "Odie, I hope you're as lucky on your big one as we were today."

Odie lifts his glass and says "Luck, it's all luck. I don't buy that shit about a flak shell or bullet out there with your name on it. It's all a matter of being in the right place at the right time. The right place at the wrong time, or the wrong place at the right time and you're done for. And I'm talking about only an eighth of an inch this way or that, or a fraction of a second sooner or later."

He orders another round of drinks for us, then goes on. "Like, for instance, you're floating up there at 25000 feet, five miles above the Fatherland, and you show up as a nice fat blip on Oberleutnant Ludwig von Flakmeister's scope. He tracks your altitude, speed, and course, calculates the wind and the proper lead. Then the blips line up, he hits a few toggle switches, and sixteen flak cannon send up a slew of 88 and 105 millimeter flak shells homing in straight for your asshole. Now of course you don't know any of this. You're staring at flak already up there exploding all over the sky, and you're scared shitless, praying that you can get through somehow. What you should keep in mind though is that the flak you see is not what's going to get you. That stuff is gone, exploded past you. It's the flak you never see that hits you. Ol' Ludwig has pushed his switches. His guns have fired, the flak shells are on the way up, and you've already bought the farm, if the laws of the universe and physics still are in force. You're very dead, only you don't know it yet."

Paul has heard all this from Odie over and over again. He says to the new guys, "Don't worry boys, there's still hope. Poppa Odie is only warming up."

"My boy," Odie says, "you tell 'em Scooter. Drink up, I have to get rid of some of this used beer." He goes outside to unload against the piss wall.

Paul says to the new guys, "What Odie was trying to get across and what you want to keep in mind is that it takes a while for that flak to climb five miles against gravity up to our altitude. And in that time, hell, anything can happen. The wind may shift, the fuses may be set wrong or it may be a batch of bum shells, or they may hit the formation below you, or you may veer to keep from running into another ship, any goddam thing. Hell, guys have bent to scratch their ass just as a burst of flak whizzed past where their head was a second ago. Of course, you may also veer right into it, or bend down at the wrong time in the wrong direction and have your head blown off. Face it, they're the hunters, we're the ducks, and the hunters always bag a few ducks. What you want to keep in mind is that most of the ducks get away."

The new guys don't have much to say when Paul finishes. I look around at them and see mostly eyes. They may not be talking, but you don't have to be a genius to guess what they're thinking. Cavey says to me "The big difference between us and these new guys is they fear the unknown, while we fear the known. Hartak should be proud of us."

We stop to scan the alert list after dinner. Bishop is our bombardier again instead of Cavey who is flying in the deputy lead ship. Zibby and Eriksen are replaced by two guys I never heard of. I figure they have to be new. "Hey cowboy," I say, "looks like they're grooming you for the big time. Next thing you know you'll be up in there with Hartak."

Cavey picks up a handfull of stones and starts tossing them one at a time at a tree. "That son of a bitch Cross," he says, "what the hell's he trying to do? I came over with you guys and I'm going back with you. You can bet that's going to be squared away real soon." It takes about ten tosses before he finally hits the tree this time.

He doesn't stay sore very long. Once we get back to the room, he climbs up into his bunk and pulls out a couple of his girlie books for a last look before we hit the sack for the night. He stares in adoration at Jane Russell lying bare shouldered in a hayloft. "Oh man, how I'd love to be rolling around in the hay with her some fine day," he says.

When I come back from the latrine, he doesn't even slow down. He's up there in the bunk above me pounding away. "Mind if I turn off the light?" I ask. No answer.

I wake at three, expecting the Hangman, but he doesn't show up. I give him about ten more minutes, then I go back to sleep figuring the mission has been scrubbed for one reason or another. Cavey shakes me awake and I hear the Hangman banging on doors down the hall hollering "breakfast four thirty, briefing five. Come on, move it!" I check my watch. Four thirty-five.

We see Odie loading up on a tall stack of pancakes at breakfast. "This is it, today's the big one," he says. "Magic number is one. I can't hardly believe it. Wish me luck, guys." He stretches and burps a loud one from the deep. "Well, gotta run now. Heavy date. See you guys later, I hope." He trots off to the briefing.

I think back to when I met him on that morning of my first mission. I say to Cavey, "There's a pretty good joe. It'd sure be hell if he doesn't make it on his last one." Cavey says "I bet we have some poor suckers around us having their last breakfast right now who are going to catch it on their very first one. Do you think that's any worse off?"

I know it's stupid, but I can't help it. "Look Caves, not to be morbid or anything, but say they told you for sure you weren't going to make it, and they let you pick the mission. Which would you choose? The first, the last, the tenth, the twentieth — ?"

Cavey says "I'd have to think a while on that one." On the way over to briefing, he says "Not to be morbid, huh. I shouldn't let you suck me into your weird games, but I'd have to take the first. No sense prolonging the agony,"

"No way," I say, "I'd go for the last one. At least you'd have five more months." We argue it back and forth until we settle for the seventeenth, which was our last one.

Cavey laughs and says "How'd you suck me into talking about shit like this. You know you're really some kind of ghoul."

I crouch down and hop around like Frankenstein's dwarf until we come up to the briefing hut. I see Hartak, Cross, and the Hangman wondering what the hell is going on when we clown our way in like a couple of loonies past them. Hartak grips Cross by the arm holding him back, when Cavey says as we go by, "Texans eat shit." I wouldn't swear to it, but I'm pretty sure I saw Hartak grin for a split second before the snarl went back on, but Cross is still fit to be tied.

"We better cut out this stupid shit," Cavey says, "we don't want to get into any trouble. Remember, we're supposed to show fear now." The way he says it makes me laugh more. I slap him on his back and say, "Thanks for reminding me, see you later cowboy." I leave him to join my crew for the day.

The target for today is the Daimler Benz Mercedes aircraft engine plant at Stuttgart. As we bounce along on the truck taking us out to our ship, Bishop asks me questions about Stuttgart. I tell him "Once and for all stop calling me sir, and though it's nothing like Merseberg or Berlin, you'll see some heavy, accurate tracking flak today, and there's always the chance that we'll run into some fighters in that area." It irks me when I see him hanging on to every word I say. He's five months older, but he treats me like I'm some kind of oracle or old veteran.

Maybe it's because we're one of the last groups in the thousand plane bomber stream to go over, but the flak we see today is meager though accurate. It's a mostly clear day, temperature at our altitude minus sixty-four F., only a three tenths undercast over target, almost no wind, and I can see lots of smoke coming straight up. The groups preceding us have given Stuttgart a good going over. We catch a bit of flak at the drop point, and though some of it comes close, there are none of those large black barrages that can paralyze and give me the shakes at the same time. "Looks like they've run short of ammo down there," says Fearless.

We head south out of Stuttgart before turning west back to Bassingbourn. The sun on level with the higher peaks, pops in and out behind the Alps as we cruise by. The deep gorges and valleys in shadow way down below cast off a purple haze. Navigator to crew, I say over the intercom, that's Switzerland off fifteen miles to the left. I don't know who starts it, but soon we have three or four of the guys shouting together, "Switzerland, Switzerland, let's go Switzerland." That goes on until Earl says, "O.K. guys, hold it down. Word just came over that bandits are hitting the groups up ahead." We turn northwest to avoid the flak around Metz. The bandits must have run short of ammo too, because we don't have any trouble all the way home.

NINETEEN

Stuttgart was a good mission. We find out at interrogation that the only one missing from the group today is LL-C from the 322nd. No one saw them get hit, and they didn't radio that they were in trouble. They just slipped out of the formation and haven't been heard from since, although we hear all kinds of probable causes, possible malfunctions, and outlandish theories. There are a hundred and one different ways to lose a ship in this war without any warning. We may never know for sure what went wrong, but we can't help thinking, though nobody says it, that maybe that crew has checked into the Switzerland health spa.

Odie's standing up on top of a table at Interrogation shouting out "Drinks on me tonight. Magic number is now zippo." I find Cavey with a lot of other guys standing around Odie congratulating him. Paul looks happy for Odie. His number is now two. Even Hartak comes over to shake Odie's hand. He sees Cavey and rasps out, "Don't think for a minute that I didn't hear your suggested diet for Texans at briefing this morning, soldier. You're damn lucky I'm from Kansas." He shakes hands with Odie again and takes off in that gimpy walk of his.

When I get back to the room, there's a letter from the Prudential Insurance Company with papers for me to fill out. As my mother's beneficiary and next of kin, I will receive a check for eleven hundred forty six dollars and twenty-three cents as soon as I send in the papers. That's what comes from all those quarters she paid out to that insurance agent who came around twice a month. Next of kin. I'm always spooked when I hear those words. Hell, now I don't even have a next of kin.

Cavey and I are at the bar helping Odie celebrate his graduation. Odie is really tossing them down. He leans on me and says, "You know there's something I've been wanting to ask that son of a bitch for a long time." He points to Hartak at the end of the bar. Hartak sees and responds by throwing him a salute. I try to talk Odie out of it, but it's no use. He shoves me aside and weaves his way down the bar to Hartak. I go with him hoping to keep him out of trouble.

"Hi captain," he says, "how's it goin'? Have a drink on me. My party. I finished up today."

"Yeah, I know. Congratulations." Hartak points to the bottle in front of him. "Thanks, but I'm pretty well fixed here."

Odie stands his ground. "Well, I hope you don't mind if I join you," he says. "You know cap'n, right now I'm the happiest guy on this god forsaken planet, yessiree. Going home. Boy, have I been praying for this day." Odie tosses down a drink then steadies himself by gripping the edge of the bar with both hands. He tries to focus on Hartak and says "But before I go, I gotta ask you something, no matter what."

Hartak's scowl deepens. He looks at me to take this pain in the ass away from him. I tug Odie's arm but he shakes me off. "It's O.K., it's O.K.," he says "everything's under control." He holds on to the bar and holds his glass up to Hartak. "Look cap'n, maybe nobody else around here has the guts, but tonight I figure what the hell, it's now or never. So come on, do me a favor Cap'n, tell me, why do you fly these fuckin' missions when you don't have to, long after your tour is over. What the hell are you trying to prove, Cap'n?"

It's a good thing that Odie's shipping out in the morning, because I see Hartak's knuckles whiten as he grips the bottle and pours a drink. I'm sure that any other time he would have had Odie's ass on a plate, but this time he nods a few times as if he's figuring what he could do to Odie.

Then just when I'm sure he's letting it all slide by, Hartak puts the bottle down and says "Good question. To tell you the truth, and I don't want to make too big a deal out of this, there have been a few times up there when I kind of wondered about it myself." He chuckles and pours himself another drink.

I'm glad it's over with no bloodshed. Hartak looks at me as if he's trying to figure who the hell I am. He turns to Odie again and says "How the hell should I know? That's like asking the dumbshit question about why does a dog lick his balls. That ol' dog does it because he can, and that about sums it up for this ol' dog. I do it because I can. Hell, if it was in the cards for me to go down, they'd have blasted me out long ago. Now I hope that satisfies you." He waves the bottle in the air and his eyes fall on the Hangman. "Hey Ugly," he says "c'mere, have a drink with your old man."

The Hangman comes up and hugs him. Hartak throws his arm around the Hangman's shoulder. "Yes sir," Hartak says, "you can bet the family jewels that wicked, mean bastards like me and the Hangman here, we're going to live out this fuckin' war, ain't we Hangman?"

Those two freaks are made for each other. Back at the other end of the bar Ted Williams and Paul are arm wrestling. "Magic number for us buddies is goddam two," Ted says and stamps his foot on the floor twice. They're both potted.

Paul wants Cavey and I to referee because he says Ted is using an illegal grip. We leave them be, when it looks like they're getting into a real fight over the rules.

We say good night and good bye to Odie. "Have to make this an early night, Odie old pal," Cavey says "unlike some people we know, we have to go to work in the morning."

Odie slides unsteadily off his stool and circles us in his arms. "I guess I finally nailed ol' Hartak," he says and then he whispers as if we're in a conspiracy, "What's your number, guys."

Cavey always looks to me to keep track. "Fifteen," I say.

Odie's face breaks into a wide smile. "Ah, great, duck soup. You guys have it made, made in the shade." He pounds on the bar. "Give my good pals here a drink." He looks sad when we leave.

"Good bye, you lucky bastard," I say. "Drop us a card when you get back to the states." Hansel and Gretel pop out to celebrate ten o'clock. Odie's glass falls way short when he throws it at the clock. "I'm sure going to miss those two little fuckers," he says.

On our way back to the room, Cavey makes three out of five when we stop for him to toss stones at his tree. "Nice shooting, cowboy," I say. He tosses another one, and I hear it hit.

"Confidence, partner," he says, "you have to have the ol' confeedyence. It just shows to go that it can be done. I'm getting the ol' confeedyence that like ol' Odie, we're goin' to make it after all. Just take 'em one at a time. Give me the magic number again, partner."

"Fifteen, cowboy, still fifteen."

There's a knock at the door. "It's open," I say. Before they come in, I know it's Swan and the Hangman. I lean up on one elbow in my sack and say "Get that son of a bitch out of here before I rip his heart out. Get him out of my sight!"

Swan hustles the Hangman out of the room before he can say anything.

Swan comes back and stands in the middle of the room under the light bulb, not saying anything for a while. He watches me staring at Barney Cotton's bombs on the wall. He adjusts his glasses so he can look at them too. He sighs "Ah, that Barney was a good kid," then he leans on top of our bureau and asks, "Which are Cavey's?"

I point to the top and bottom drawers. "The middle two are mine."

Swan lights a cigarette and offers me one. I take it. He pushes with his shoe at the pile of maybe thirty of my burnt out butts on the cement floor. He says, "Maybe you'd like to take a walk, get some air while I take care of this."

I puff a smoke ring at the bombs on the wall. I say, "Nah, it's O.K. I like it here."

"I just thought it would be better for you, being his buddy and all," Swan's voice trails off.

I try to make sense of what he says. I remember the time in Kearney with Minnie and Vinnie and how Caves got pissed off at all that buddy, buddy shit. "So you think it would be better for me," I say. "What makes you think we were buddies? We were room-mates and on the same crew, that's all. Never buddies."

Swan shrugs. He dumps the top drawer on to Cavey's unmade sack, then kneels down to poke around in Cavey's footlocker. "This won't take much longer," he says.

"Hell, don't worry about that, take your time. I have loads of that. Time, I mean."

Swan digs deeper into the foot locker. "What the hell are you snooping for," I ask. "Plans to overthrow the government?"

Swan stands up and goes back to the bureau drawer. He says "Look, I don't like doing this either. I just have to go through his stuff to be sure there are no papers or letters that would embarrass his family. We throw out most of the stuff, but we do send his personal effects to the next of kin."

"That's a great way of putting it, next of kin. Don't you usually call them NOK?"

Swan nods. I sit up in the sack and say, "What the hell would you do with my stuff? I don't have a NOK."

Swan nods again and flips me another cigarette. "Yes, I know," he says. He dumps the other drawer on Cavey's sack.

"You guys have initials for everything, haven't you," I say. "Like I saw him chalked on the board as KIA."

Swan looks at me as if he's checking me out. "Yes, that's the way we're carrying him on the roster for now. Killed in action, though not as a result of enemy action."

"That's a big fuckin' relief."

Swan puts the empty drawers back in the dresser. He sits down straddling the chair, studying me again. "Hartak told me to tell you that you're inactive, off duty for three days."

"Swell. When you see the son of a bitch, thank him for me. You can tell him I'm thinking beautiful, pure thoughts of him."

Swan finds one of Cavey's Milky Ways on the dresser. He offers it to me. I ignore him. He munches on it as he strips the mattress cover from Cavey's sack. I grit my teeth and close my eyes when he bends the bare mattress over in half.

"We're moving Bishop in here tomorrow," he says. "He's been bunking down with the casuals in B block up to now." He removes Cavey's uniform, shirts, and pants from their wire hangers on the pipe and dumps them into the foot locker. I watch him closely now. He didn't get all of Cavey's stuff. Three shirts and his spare coveralls still hang there.

Swan shoves the foot locker out into the hall. "Do you want the light on?" he asks.

"Shit, I don't care. Leave it on."

Swan tries once more. "If there's anything I can do —"

"Yeah, there is. Tell that degenerate lump of shit you came in with, not to come anywhere near me — ever."

Swan leaves the Milky Ways on the dresser when he goes. I spend the day in the sack staring at the folded mattress above me, then switch over to Cotton's bombs, then to Cavey's empty shirts up there, flat sleeved in their wire hangers, then back to the mattress again.

I didn't know about Cavey until we landed. It hadn't been too tough a mission considering it was Hamburg. We had lost one ship during assembly when one of our newer pilots screwed up trying to find our squadron. He fell behind, then cut a corner trying to make up for lost time, and crashed into a ship from the 398th circling under him. They probably never saw each other. We were close enough to shake from the blast of that fireball.

We flew on to target, the oil refinery and shipyards at Hamburg, always heavily defended by cannon from hundreds of ships of the German naval forces. Just about every one of our 17's were hit, some severely, but somehow our squadron came through without losing a ship other than the one at assembly, although I knew one had been hit bad enough to have to force land at Manston on one engine. What I didn't know was that Cavey was on the one that blew up at assembly.

It was Earl who told me soon as we landed. He looked older and more worn out than ever, and I couldn't make too much sense of what he was saying. It was something about Cavey going down. "Cut it out. Only perverts make up shit like that. It's not funny. Cavey was up in the deputy lead ship, and that wasn't the ship that blew."

"Yeah, I know," said Earl and he gripped my arm hard, "but after briefing I was hanging around with Cavey, and Cross told him he was shifting him on to one of the green crews, that he was too wiseass for deputy lead, maybe that would help improve his attitude."

It wasn't until Earl said wiseass that I grasped what he was trying to tell me. I remembered the look on Cross' face at briefing when Cavey laughed and said eat shit, Texans. My heart pounded so hard in my chest that I thought it would blast through, and then a brackish taste came up in my throat. I fought the nausea. Oh God, no! The bastard had to put him on the one that went down! My knees turned weak, and Earl got his arm around me in time to keep me from caving in.

I leaned on the wheel of the ship as I went through a few dry heaves. Then Fearless hooked my arm around his shoulder and half carried me to the truck. I remember how quiet everybody was on the ride going in. By the time we arrived at interrogation I had pulled myself halfway together.

Swan put a drink in front of me before he poured for the other guys. "Take it easy," he said "I can get what I need from the rest of the crew and the other navigators."

I tossed down the drink. "No, it's O.K. Let's get on with it. I'm fine." Earl and the rest of the crew made a fuss over me, saying they would take care of everything. Paul and guys from other crews came around to tell me how sorry they were. The kid Bishop was turning his hat in his hand when he asked "Is there anything I can do for you, sir?"

"No, thanks, it's all right, I'm O.K," and then I said again, "Come on, let's get on with it."

What they didn't know was that I actually was feeling O.K. by then. A weird sense of self-satisfaction built up inside me while I was still back on the truck. I know I should be ashamed of it, and pangs of guilt hit me every now and then when I think of it, but I can't deny it. It's awful I know, but it's as if it turned out that I'm better than Cavey, that I've beaten him in some kind of crazy game, outscored him somehow. It comes over me in waves, and I despise myself for it.

It's growing toward evening. I'm surprised at how hungry I am. I wander down to the mess hall and eat two of everything. Paul and Ted Williams come over to sympathize, but don't hang around long when I don't have anything to say. I know they have only one to go now, and I find myself feeling hostile toward them. I pull myself up short, ashamed of myself, when it occurs to me that they might not make it either.

I can't face hanging around with the guys at the bar, any more than I can deal with the idea of the empty room tonight. I bike around in the darkness until it becomes too cold, and head for the pub in the village. Hardly anyone here tonight from the 91st, which is O.K. with me.

I drift into a dart game with a guy who turns out to be the local dentist. He invites me to have a drink with him and his wife. They wish that this bloody war would end soon, so that we could all go back to leading proper lives. I lift my glass and say, "Amen to that and all that."

"Are you perhaps a churchgoing man?" his wife asks. I think of the flak coming up from the cathedral at Cologne. "Yes," I say "yes, I guess you could say that I am."

I bike back to the base in the cold, drizzly night thinking of times when Cavey biked along with me. I want to feel sad, much sadder than I am. Instead what comes up is that it could just as easily be Cavey biking along here right now, trying to feel sad about me.

I don't have to dig too deep for sadness though, when I come back to our empty room and lie in my sack staring up at the sagging springs and bent over bare mattress above me. I look at Cavey's pin-ups on the wall before I fall into a restless sleep, only to sit up and freeze when I hear the Hangman waking some of the guys down the hall. I wait for him to call my name, then I remember that this is the first of my three off duty days. I tunnel deeper into my sack, and try to keep my mind away from a vision of the Hangman folding up the mattress I now lie on.

TWENTY

I'm still in my sack staring up at Cavey's folded over mattress. Bishop comes in quietly and says "Oh pardon me, I didn't mean to disturb you, sir." He is almost on tiptoe when he brings in his bags. He hangs his clothes up on the pipe, puts the rest of his stuff in the chest of drawers, and drags in his foot locker. I watch him settle in, occupying the room, filling in the cracks and spaces. I turn to the wall when he unfolds the mattress, when he climbs into the bunk above me.

He doesn't shift around up there as Cavey did, and the mattress doesn't sag as much. Bishop is around five eleven and a hundred sixty pounds, nowhere near as heavy as the Caveman. What remains of that strapping, husky body now? He would call it morbid, but I wonder if he blew to bits when his ship exploded, or did he slam into the ground from three miles up? Was he conscious all the way down? I want to scream. I want to throw things. I pull the blanket over my head and snap my fingers until I bring myself back under control. Snap, snap, snap! I fall asleep.

Earl drops in. Hartak has given him three days off too. He starts to talk about old days back in Alex and Kearney.

Bishop jumps off his bunk and says he's sure Earl and I would like our privacy. I tell him it's O.K., stick around.

He's all ears as Earl dredges up old stuff like when we pissed into the radiator on the way back from Jasper, and how Skiles showed up at Kearney with a fat dose of the clap, and the time he marched around with that phony Iron Cross, and old Omar in Labrador. Earl is in his morale building process again. "And how about the time in Iceland," he says, "when the Mouse set fire to that skin he bought—". Earl's voice tails off. He looks at Bishop and says, "That Mouse was one hell of a guy. Couldn't fly a 17 for shit, but he sure was a lot of fun to be around." He turns to me and says, "That Mouse was a card, wasn't he?"

I don't want to be his stooge in this morale building project of his. I know he has the sense not to, but if he says a word about Cavey, I'll throw him out of the room. And then to keep from talking about Cavey, or maybe just trying to be mean to Earl, I say "Yeah and how about JoJo. How come you never talk about him? He went down on the same mission as the Mouse, didn't he?"

Earl puts his hand on my shoulder, then turns to Bishop and says, "JoJo was one sweet guy, never complained, so quiet you hardly knew he was around." Earl seems so, I don't know, earnest in his attempt to buck me up. He slides his hand down from my shoulder, grips my hand in a firm handshake and says, "Don't you worry, old buddy, we're going to make it, you and I. Bet your ass we will, goddam it. I feel it right here." He places his hand flat against his heart and says "You've got to believe." The guy scares me.

The mess hall horn blows for lunch. I don't move. Bishop stops on his way out and asks "Would you like for me to bring you back something sir?"

I pull myself out of the sack. "No, thanks, but I'm warning you, the next time you call me sir, you'll be looking for a new room."

Earl comes over again later and says, "As long as we still have two days off, why don't we go into London. I'll call Annabelle and get us fixed up with her and Dorene."

I've been toying with the idea of using the time to bike up to Caxton's Gibbet, though I don't know how I'm going to handle telling Vivian about Cavey, and I'm still all screwed up about seeing Martha again. I take the easy way out, and right after lunch Earl and I are on our way to London. I'll visit Martha and Vivian next time.

Earl pulled a raid on the PX before we left, and his musette bag is loaded with cigarettes, candy bars, oranges, soap, and from I dont know where, a bottle of Haig & Haig. I ask "Do you think we're going out west to trade with the Indians? Hell, we bought Alaska for less than you have in that bag."

He looks at me as if I were a foolish child. He chuckles and says "Ah, my young friend, you have much to learn. This is a treasure worth its weight in rubies. We must be prepared, no telling what we're likely to run into."

What we're not very likely to run into is Annabelle. There was no answer when Earl called her from Bassingbourn, no answer when we arrive at King's Cross station, and nothing much more when we ring her from our hotel near Marble Arch.

We take a cab down to Piccadilly and amble around in the cold, gray late afternoon. Hundreds of pigeons soar over us as we walk through Trafalgar Square. "What a piss poor formation," I say. Earl cups his hands over his mouth, tilts back his head and yells "Tighten 'er up goddam it, tighten 'er up, where the hell did you guys learn to fly?" Another squadron of birds takes off as we come near them. We watch them assemble as they circle overhead. A white stain with a small yellowish green center lands splat on Earl's sleeve. He shakes his fist and swears at the pigeons, then turns to me. "See, I told you we had it made. We're in the clear." He points to the stain and says "This always means good luck back home."

I don't tell him that back where I come from, this always means you've been shit on. "Better wipe off all this good luck of yours before it eats a hole in your sleeve," I say.

Earl wants to have dinner in a good London restaurant. That seems to be a good idea, although neither of us have ever been close to being inside a good restaurant anywhere. We wander for an hour or so through the now darkened blacked-out streets completely lost until we ask a cabdriver to take us to a good London restaurant. He drops us off at the Cafe Zoltan, Cuisine Hungarica, A Bit of Budapest in Old Soho.

The restaurant, lit by a few candles, is almost as dark inside as the blackout outside. A bald guy with a wide brown mustache and a greasy looking tuxedo emerges from the shadows. He bows. "Welcome m'sieurs, I am Zoltan, at your service."

He leads us to our table. We pass two middle aged women, British colonels' wife types, in strange gypsy costumes. One is cradling a saxophone, the other is seated, wrestling with the straps of an accordion. Zoltan snaps his fingers and they begin a polka that sounds very much like Danny Boy.

Zoltan hovers over our table, ready to take our drink order. When we hesitate, he says "Permit me to suggest a very special '38 Tokay." We nod as if we know what the hell he's talking about.

"That's a strange looking pair of gypsies up there," I say. Earl hands me one of his cigars. "Yeah," he says, "I don't think you ordinarily see too many with red hair." Zoltan comes back with a bottle of wine wrapped in a napkin. He pours a little bit in Earl's glass, then stands there twirling the wine bottle and looks at Earl as if he's waiting for him to say something. Earl tosses the wine down and holds out his glass for another shot. Zoltan sighs for some reason as he gives Earl a refill and I order a couple of beers.

I ask for the bill of fare. Zoltan hesitates, then says, "Ah yes, the menu, messieurs." He hands us a grimy handwritten folded page which we try to decode around all the food and wine stains. Earl says, "What little I can make out on this looks like it's in French." Zoltan rolls his eyes. He pours more wine and says "May I suggest for messieurs the braised squab, a specialty of the house." Earl leans back in his chair, wave his cigar at him and says "That sounds good, we can handle it."

The two gypsy musicians launch into their interpretation of The Blue Danube. It doesn't sound too much different than their Danny Boy. The red headed accordion player reaches behind her chair, pulls out a bottle of wine from under her long skirt, clamps the bottle between her legs, uncorks it, and takes a swig without missing a note.

I hear a clatter and squeak as a waiter in a scruffy tuxedo and smudged white gloves rolls a traystand on wheels to our table. He lifts the cover off a tray, closes his eyes and bows as if he was displaying the crown jewels. All I see is a couple of small roast birds about one fourth the size of chickens. He tongs them on to our plates as if they were vials of nitroglycerin.

The damn birds are 99 and 44/100% skin and bone. We tussle with them trying to find some meat on their pitiful carcasses, and finally give it up as a bad job. We ask for the bill and are a little staggered by the amount written in very clear English. We pay the waiter and as we make our way to the exit I see Zoltan scurry over and whisper to the two gypsies. They break into a rather strange rendition of The Battle Hymn of the Republic. Zoltan is at the door when we get there, rubbing his palms together, bowing and scraping like Uriah Heep in the movie, David Copperfield. "Ah, messieurs," he says, "I trust eveything was to your liking." Earl drops a few pounds in his hand. "Best goddam Hungarian dinner I ever had," he says.

As we walk through Trafalgar Square again, Earl says "I'll bet if they do a count, for sure they'll come up with a pair of missing pigeons. Man, I'm hungrier now than before we ran into Zoltan's." We load up at the first fish and chip stand we come to. Earl calls Annabelle from one of those big red phone booths, but still no dice. "The hell with her," he says "as far as I can see there's no shortage of these here Piccadilly commandos. They come at you in waves, like fighter planes. Keep your eyes peeled."

He's right. You can't walk a block without being propositioned. Most of them are real horrors, but every once in a while you come across one halfway decent looking. "Do me a favor, Earl," I say "don't be too eager. Let's not grab the first one who hits us."

Earl pulls a couple of cigars from his bag of goodies. "What do you take me for, some kind of animal? Tell you what, you do the choosing, you cut one from the herd. O.K.?"

We stroll on, puffing cigars, like a couple of prosperous businessmen. After I decline four propositions in the next couple of blocks, Earl asks "What was wrong with that last one? She was kind of cute I thought."

"Cute? Are you kidding? She was something left over from Hallowe'en. Look, I thought you were leaving this up to me."

He sounds kind of sore after I balk at the next couple of offers. "Who the hell are you looking for, Miss America? Stop being so goddam picky." He blows his top when I ignore a tall peroxide blond in a mannish tailored suit and fox fur collar.

"For crying out loud," I say "she looked like the bride of Frankenstein." He plants himself in front of me and says, "C'mon tell the truth. Do you want to get layed tonight or what? If you're looking for Ginger Rogers, forget it. You're not about to run across her around here. She's out dancing with Fred tonight."

He starts dickering with the next one who asks us for a light. She's dressed like she wants to be taken for Greta Garbo, and talks like her in a deep, husky voice. She wants to know the hotel we're staying at. Earl tells her, and she says the price is ten pounds each. I tell Earl "I dont want her even if it's free." That does it. "See you around," he says and marches off with her. He returns excited a few seconds later. "She says she'll do us both for fifteen, including 'round the world."

"Skip it, she's yours. You're made for each other."

"Fuckin' weirdo," says Earl and disappears into the black-out with her. I drop into a pub, have a few drinks by myself and scoot out when a tall red faced Australian R.A.F. observer throws his arm around my shoulder and wants me to sing *Waltzing Matilda* along with him. I figure it's time to call it a night. The cab driver has to wake me when we get to the hotel.

Once in bed however, sleep comes slowly in bits and pieces broken by wild dreams. I'm between sleeps when I hear Earl stumbling around in our hotel room. I sit up in a cold sweat not knowing where I am, and it takes some time before it sinks in that my dreams were not real.

Earl turns on the lamp. It's half past two, and I can see he hasn't had too good a night. There's dried blood on his collar, and his hand is covering what looks like a head wound.

"Holy shit, what the hell happened to you?" I take him into the bathroom where I try to wipe off the blood from his head with a warm washcloth. He winces when I touch the wounded area. I figure we better have this looked at. I ask the clerk downstairs to call a cab to take us to the hospital.

Earl gives me the details as we ride in the cab. "That floozie I picked up told me that she had a place nearby, a few minutes away. I remember walking down a blacked out side street, stopping in a couple of doorways with her for some smooching around. She had me pretty hot in no time flat, so

I didn't mind a bit when she pulled me into an alleyway and really went to work on me. She had my pants down in no time, and I thought we were about to do it right then and there. That was just about the time I felt something hit the back of my head. It felt like a rock, but it must have been a blackjack because when I fell to my knees, almost unconscious, I was able to make out a guy standing over me who began kicking me until I completely blacked out. I don't know how long I was out, but when I came to, I managed to drag myself to my feet. I'm such a fuckin' dumbass stupid slob. That bitch and her boy friend had me set up from the start. They took me for all I had. I wandered around, beat up, lost in the dark, no money, until I somehow found myself near Marble Arch and made my way to the hotel."

We go to Emergency Services at the hospital and he winds up with eight stitches in that boneheaded scalp of his. He's had enough of London and I never was too crazy about the place myself, so we take an early train back in the morning. Earl says, "The worst of it is, the lousy bastards not only stole my cash, but they made off with all the loot and goodies in my musette bag." He starts laughing, and I wonder if that crack in the head might be more serious than it seems. I ask him "Now what the hell do you think is so funny."

"Oh, I just remembered me telling you back at the base that the reason I carried my bag of goodies was that you never know what you might run into."

We're back at Bassingbourn just when the group returns from a long one to Nuremburg. Everyone's feeling pretty good because although the other groups were hit hard, we didn't lose a ship and had only one abort, a crew from our squadron that dumped their bombs in the sea when it developed engine trouble over Belgium.

Earl goes to his room to clean up, and I go to Interrogation to shoot the shit with the guys after their mission. I run into Paul. This was to be his 35th, and just his luck he had to be on the one that aborted, so now he still has one more to go, and man is he ever pissed. Ted Williams graduated today and he's walking around in a daze smiling, but not saying a word to anyone. I do what I can to help Paul cheer up, but he doesn't buy any of it, not that I blame him.

My three days off duty are over, and I have a strong hunch that I'll be up tomorrow. After dinner, I check the alert list and get further confirmation that I should pay attention to my hunches. Earl and I are listed to fly with another green crew in the morning. For a brief moment there I forget and try to check out who Caves is flying with. Snap, snap, snap!

TWENTY-ONE

I ask Earl if he needs a hand. I have to shout to make myself heard over all the others talking at once before the briefing starts. He is experimenting with his headset, trying to adjust it so it won't pinch the patch bandage covering his stitches. A dozen guys have stopped to make cracks about obvious brain damage, and ask what the hell happened to his head. I tell them all that he's being wired for a secret radar project.

I see Paul up front, at the end of the lead crew bench, making a point of sitting apart from Hartak and his crew, not joining in their pre-briefing capers. The horsing around and chatter cuts off abruptly when Holy Cross jumps up on the platform and says, "Target today, genmun, is the Kugel Fischer Ball Bearing Works at Schweinfurt."

That's the same place where we lost sixty crews on one mission last year. The Germans have completely rebuilt the plant, and now we have to go back to that hellhole again. Paul looks like someone has just given him a swift kick in the balls. Yesterday's abort shafted him into preparing to fly his 35th all over again, but Schweinfurt is really sticking it up with a twist. He deserves a nice easy milk run after all he's gone through, but now he's facing Schweinfurt plus flying with Hartak, a man he doesn't trust and thoroughly despises.

The last one is always the toughest. Every squadron has stories about guys who didn't make it on their last one. I give Paul thumbs up, but he doesn't reply. He stares rigidly at the map and the red twine dodging and twisting across Germany before leading into Schweinfurt. I look up at the map too, but I get a flash that he's going to be a letter home from the chaplain, another folded over mattress. I snap my fingers.

Earl and I bump into him after briefing. "Cheer up," Earl says, "after this one, it's all over but the shouting for you." Paul gives us a weak smile. The way he looks at us, I can't help asking, "Are you O.K. — sick or something?"

"Sick," he says, "why should I be sick? My last one and it's Schweinfurt with that fuckin' madman Hartak and to top it off, it's my dad's birthday. Oh shit, do I want to get this one over with." Earl gives him a pair of cigars. "Save 'em," he says, "one for you and one for your old man when you go home. I'll light yours later when we come back." Paul puts the cigars in his shirt pocket and says, "I hope these smokes don't go to waste." Earl and I do our level best to let him know that's the craziest thing we ever heard.

For once the weather forecast has some connection to reality. We lose no ships on takeoff or assembly, and the only fighters we see are our own, but the flak over Schweinfurt is heavy and accurate as predicted. We lose one ship two minutes short of target, and I see Hartak in the lead ship take a solid hit in the #3 engine two seconds after bombs away. I think of Paul in there when their engine catches fire and they drop from the formation in a steep nose down dive. I can't tell if they're out of control, or it's a desperate attempt by Hartak to snuff out the flames. I watch their ship disappear, while the box barrages of flak explode around and ahead of us. I'm certain once more that we'll be next.

I've no idea what Hartak did, but whatever it was, it worked because four minutes after we drop our bombs, he's jockeyed their ship back into the tail end of our group formation, though flying on only three engines. We have a decent tail wind as we go back, giving us a ground speed of 186. Hartak radioes in that flying on three engines has put too much a load on his #1 engine. He feathers it and they're flying on only two engines now. They won't be able to keep up with the group for long. I feel for Paul back there with Hartak. He must be really sweating this one out.

As far as I can tell, our ship is in good shape on our descent over the North Sea. Schweinfurt has turned out to be not as bad as we feared or as good as we hoped. We go off oxygen and the plane is soon full of chatter and cigarette smoke. Earl calls down over the intercom, ""Pilot to navigator, what's our magic number now?" He knows damn well what it is. I'm about to play along with his game but then I hold back. I wonder if I'd be jinxing us. Thirteen is such a hoodoo. While I hesitate, our tail gunner cuts in with "Hartak's going down!"

Earl says, "Position, navigator." I don't have our exact coordinates. All I know is we're somewhere over the North Sea, maybe twenty minutes from the English coast. I was planning on a fix when we make landfall. I hurry into working out our position forward from where we left the Belgian coast above Ostend. Earl calls back, "It's O.K. Air-Sea rescue has been contacted." I say "Good, anyway we were at 52'24, 02'30 six minutes ago."

I'm pulling for Paul in that ship, but without too much hope. Crash landing a 17 on a wintery rough uneven sea goes against all odds. No runway, only a curling, waving surface that can break a plane to pieces as though it had run into cement.

I see ice floes in a turbulent sea down there with the

wind out of 190 at 32 knots. Even if Hartak can pull a miracle and put that 17 down in one piece, they won't last long in that freezing water, two or three minutes at most unless Air-Sea Rescue manages to find and pick them up right away,

Two ships from our squadron drop out of formation to circle around the spot where Hartak is going down. They won't be able to continue that for too long. We're all low on fuel by now. The rest of us fly back to Bassingbourn.

It's so good to see Great Yarmouth up ahead. Chalk up another win for the good guys. One less to go now. Thirteen may not be my favorite number, but it beats fourteen. For a brief moment, I glide into thinking that maybe I have a shot at making it after all, but I don't dare linger on that for very long. That's a sure jinx. I go back to work, fixing our position, and entering it in the log. I push out of my mind thoughts of Paul somewhere back there below, alive or dead in that frigid grey green whitecapped sea.

An hour later, after we land, I rush into Interrogation and find Swan having tea with a British Red Cross girl. "What's the word on Hartak's crew?" Swan asks the girl to excuse us, as if I was being rude. He pours another cup for her before turning to me. "Unofficial," he says "Hartak and five of the crew were rescued from their dinghy by Air Sea Rescue at 1503 hours. Three crew members M.I.A."

I grab his arm and ask, "Who's missing?"

He loosens my grip. "Take it easy," he says, "I just gave you what came in on telex twenty minutes ago. Nothing since. Try the squadron."

I run out and hitch a ride to the squadron office. About ten guys cluster around a rough handwritten notice tacked outside on the bulletin board. I push my way through and read:

Rescued:		MIA:
Hartak	Michaels	Shmand
Hanlon	Scudellari	Gillespie
Christman	Emmons	Culp

I fall into a chair, relieved that my hunch about Paul not making it was wrong. He's made it the hard way, but he's made it, and I'll bet he's happy right now wherever he is. Tough on Gillespie, a guy who once flew a couple of missions with our crew. I don't know the other two missing guys.

I walk back slowly to the room and pass the spot where Cavey used to throw stones at the tree. Cavey is dead and no rescue for him — ever. A pressure builds and spreads inside me. Something like what I feel in heavy flak, but I recognize the difference. I try to catch my breath and end up sobbing. I pick up a stone and let it fly. I miss. I miss with the next one, and the one after that. I heave a handfull of stones at the lousy tree.

Goddam fuckin' Cavey sonofabitch!

No mission today. We're weathered in with fog, snow turning to sleet, and a slashing icy wind. Earl drops by my room. "Come on with me down to the squadron office," I say "let's check if they have any further word on Paul." We're about to leave when I change my mind. "You check it out, Earl," I say. "We may run into that bastard Cross down there and that could set me off."

Earl puts his hand on my shoulder and says, "You still have it in for him? Like it's his fault we lost ol' Cavey? Time to drop it, bud."

I push Earl's hand off me and say "Why the hell should I? Caves would still be around if that degenerate sonofabitch hadn't pulled him off the ship he was supposed to be on."

Earl says "Maybe, maybe not. Come on, you can't possibly believe that Cross knew Cavey's ship was going down. And suppose we'd lost the ship Cavey was switched from, instead of the one he was on. Damn it, you and he would have probably kissed Cross's ass twenty times and bought him drinks for life. So now you hate Cross, and the guy who switched with Cavey believes Cross is Jesus come to life for saving his ass. Hell, if you want to, you can figure every time he assigns any of us to a ship, he can be killing us or saving us one way or the other, but you know fuckin' well it hasn't anything to do with him. In case you've forgotten, buddy boy, let me remind you when all's said and done, it just boils down to the old fuckin' fickle fingers."

I let Earl drop that on me as if I haven't thought about that, one way or another a hundred times over. Talk about stuff like that always reminds me of how sure I am that I'm not going to make it either. I'm not about to let Earl know that, but I will politely ask him to shut the fuck up next time he delivers one of those preachy lectures of his. Meanwhile I ask him to bring back the news on Paul from the squadron office. I'll wait here. Let him deal with Cross.

Ten minutes later Earl comes back carrying a stuffed briefcase and says, "According to Cross, Hartak and Paul are at the field hospital in Lavenham with the other guys rescued." He waves the briefcase at me and says "Cross asked me to turn this over to Hartak. I've got his jeep. Want to come?"

It's a chance to visit Paul, so I go along on a frigid two hour drive in the jeep over to Lavenham. At the hospital Earl goes to deliver the briefcase to Hartak. I find Paul in a ward with his head and both arms heavily bandaged like the Invisible Man. I ask him if he's in pain.

"Not too bad," he says, "nothing broken, bruises all over and a concussion from where I banged against a bulkhead when we hit the water." He holds up his bandaged arms to show where they sliced off some frostbitten fingertips this morning. He moves his legs under the sheets and gives me a weird grin. "They tell me they took a few toes too." He grins at me again and says "Hey, quit looking so damn glum. I feel great. It could have been all over for me, and now halleleuia. I'm going home. Light me."

I put a cigarette between his lips. He inhales deeply each time as I hold it for him. We don't talk until it's halfway gone when I say "Tell me how it went."

He doesn't answer right off. He looks up at the ceiling for a while before he says, "You know it's kind of weird, I thought I've been trying to shut it out, but now that you ask, I feel like telling everything. Everything I can remember, that is."

His eyes are closed when I hold another cigarette to his lips. His lips pull on the butt as if he's starving. He lets the smoke out long and slow and says, "I guess it's a fuckin' miracle I'm here at all. My thirty-fifth mission and we have that engine fire over the target. I gave up. I was sure we'd never pull out of that dive. Then there was the ditching —" He draws a deep breath and I adjust his pillow.

"The thing is," he says "I was sure we weren't going to make it even after Hartak managed to put out the fire. Hell, we were limping along with two engines out. Then little by little I let myself hope a bit, and when we finally could see the coastline I thought maybe we had some chance to cross the sea and crash land on one of those emergency long runway R.A.F. bases. That little bit of hope didn't last too long. I knew for damn sure it was the end when we lost another engine and started losing altitude fast on the one remaining engine. I could only stare at that icy water when I heard Hartak call out for us to prepare for ditching, but I finally snapped out of it and squirmed my way back to the radio compartment in time to join the rest of the guys who'd made it back there. We were all crouched down and braced against the nearest bulkhead for less than a minute when I felt the plane hit the water, then bounce, and hit again. Then I heard the loudest crashing noise I've ever heard and one side of the plane just broke away and a ton of water came rushing in. Hartak was back there with us by then yelling at us to release the dinghy. I was scared shitless and couldn't make myself move. By the time I tried to stand up, I couldn't make it because the plane was tipped over on its side. I saw and felt the water rising to my chest, so I pulled myself up by grabbing anything I could, like climbing a rope. I saw guys going out through the torn open fuselage, and I wormed my way hand by hand toward the opening."

Paul stops for another long drag on the cigarette I hold to his lips. "Take it easy," I say "it'll keep. Save it for next time."

"No, no, I'm O.K." he says "I want you to hear this. I haven't got to the worst part. It's important. I finally made it to the opening where the guys had jumped out, and looked down at the yellow dinghy with maybe four or five of the guys in it bobbing down below in the waves. I remembered to inflate my Mae West, jumped toward the dinghy, hit the side of it and fell off into the sea. Funny I don't remember it being cold though I know I kept bumping against chunks of ice in the water. Mostly I recall just how dark it was. Then I felt arms pulling at me. I helped by kicking and wiggling myself up, and I saw Hartak was the one pulling the hardest, and he was the one who dragged me up into the dinghy. Once I was in, he handed me a paddle and told me to row. My fingers were so frozen, I dropped the paddle into the water. He cursed and held me as I reached out as far as I could to pull it back in. That's when I saw Gillespie in that damn icy water trying to swim toward us in the dinghy. I reached out to him at the same time I heard Hartak yelling row, dammit, row! I shouted back hold it! Gillespie's out there! Hartak had one of the paddles and he was rowing hard with it. He never stopped.

He kept yelling at Christman who held another paddle to put the fuckin' thing in the water and row, goddammit, row."

Paul holds his bandaged arms in the air. "See, about six inches, six lousy fuckin' inches, that's how close Gillespie came to my stretched out hand. Hartak kept yelling row, row, goddammit, row! That's when the plane slid below the water. I didn't see any more of Gillespie. A 17 was circling over us low, no more than 50 feet above us, and oh man how I wished I could be up there with them. So near, yet so fuckin' far. The waves were bouncing us every which way in that yellow rubber dinghy, and I don't know how the hell we kept from flipping over. Through it all, Hartak kept yelling his row, dammit, row. I don't know how much longer it took before the Air Sea Rescue launch picked us up. Also nobody knows what happened to Shmand or Culp. The poor bastards probably never made it out of the plane."

Earl comes in with a couple of cartons of Parliaments. "Gift from Holy Cross," he says to Paul.

"Tell him to shove it," says Paul. Earl shrugs and drops the cartons on the bed. I brief Earl on most of what Paul told me. He says "I heard all about it from Hartak, although the way Hartak told it, the story came out kind of different even though it had nearly all the same details and Hartak didn't mention a word about Gillespie."

Earl folds his arms across his chest and says "Maybe we should keep in mind that if they hadn't kept on rowing away from the '17 when it made its final slip into the sea, their dinghy with everyone in it would probably have been sucked down or capsized."

"What can I say?" says Paul. "We have no way of knowing, but what I know damn well is though I owe my life to Hartak, he's a fuckin' maniac and his crazy actions have cost us a lot of good guys. I don't know, maybe that's what it takes. Sure as shit if it weren't for him, I'd never have made it into the dinghy, but I'll never forget Gillespie. He didn't call out or anything, just held his arm up toward me. Six lousy fuckin' inches, one more second." Paul leans back in his pillow and blinks. I ask him where to put the Parliaments.

"Oh, you guys can have them. They throw them at us around here three times a day." Earl drops them into his bag and lights a cigar. Paul sniffs it and says "Looks like those two you gave me at briefing went to waste after taking on some salt water." Earl pulls a fistfull of cigars out of his bag and puts them on the night table. "Hell," he says, "we can always come up with replacements." I laugh and say that's what that fucker Cross always says. It turns quiet like we've run out of things to say.

After a while I ask Paul, "What about Lucky Pierre? You said you were going to liberate him when you finished up." Paul snaps out of it and says "Wow! I almost forgot. Thanks for reminding me. Get the bottle out of my jacket in the locker."

I hold the bottle up for Paul and from what I can see, other than missing a few meals Pierre appears to be none the worse for his experience. Paul gazes fondly at the little beast. "Look, he's glad to see me. Damn, I'm going to miss this little fella." He looks up at me and nods. "I guess now is as good a time as any."

I say, "You mean now? Right here in the hospital?"

"Yeah, now. He's sure to find lots of friends around here. Now do it quick, before I weaken and change my mind."

I uncap the bottle, place it on the floor and say "Farewell dear friend." Pierre won't come out. I have to shake the bottle a few times before he tumbles out, walks around in a small circle, then scoots for the corner behind the locker.

Paul says "Did you see him turn that 360? Better than Hartak."

"Lieutenant Scudellari," I say "you have liberated a fellow creature. I'm proud of you."

Earl wonders what the hell this is all about. We try to explain but give up when we see he's not keeping up with us. He plants his feet up on the bed, puffs on his cigar and says, "Aside from resting up and dipping into as much pussy as you can find when you go home, Scud, what are your long range plans, like after the war's over?"

"Long range plans? Hell, I don't know that I have any short range plans other than going home. First, we'll have to see how these turn out." He holds up his bandaged arms. "Then probably the furniture store with Dad until I know what's what. Maybe art school some day, but right now all I can think of is that I'm actually going home. It hasn't completely sunk in yet."

Earl blows a smoke ring toward the ceiling and says, "I always knew you'd make it, buddy boy. Art school, that's swell. I'm hoping to get into college, try for engineering, maybe."

Paul and Earl turn to me like it's a game and it's my turn. I feel stupid that I can't offer them anything. I come up with "Well, if I do make it, which doesn't seem very likely, I'm going to get me a room in a good hotel, hang out the do not disturb sign and sack out for a month." They look at me as if I'm not playing fair. I don't know what more to say, so I give them, "Then I'd like to save up and buy a car when they start making them again, maybe get a nice girl and settle down some day."

I feel better when the guys start talking about cars. Paul favors Oldsmobile who have come out with Hydramatic which let's you drive without shifting gears, and Earl tells him that they're full of problems, he'll take a Mercury any day. Paul says they're nothing but overgrown Fords. They go on like that for a while until it's time for us to go.

"So long guys," Paul says "Good luck. See you around, like they say don't know where, don't know when."

We nod at each other serious faced, like diplomats after

a meeting, as if we've just settled something. I'm sure I'll never see him again.

When we walk down the long hallway on our way out, I notice that Earl has lost some of his zip. He doesn't walk in those quick, short, dancer-like steps anymore. His no neck head is sunk even further into his shoulders as if he's peeking over the top of a fence. Those crinkled up eyes have that weary after-mission look, like he's been ducking flak for a few hours.

He asks me to sit down with him on a bench in the hallway outside Paul's ward. He grips my arm and says "Seriously now as friend to friend tell me what are you thinking about right now?"

I don't know what he's driving at, but I try to come up with something. "Not much," I say "about all that comes to mind is what Cavey used to say, you just can't beat a real good war." Earl seems disappointed, like he expected more from me.

Driving in the jeep back to Bassingbourn, he says "Hartak talked like he was expecting to return to the squadron any day now, even though he's still suffering some from exposure, and his left arm is in a cast for a fracture he tried to hide before it showed up in an X-ray. That guy's some kind of miracle man. He keeps coming back, and when you think of those lives he saved — I tell you boy, we should thank our lucky stars we're in his squadron."

I look at Earl, checking him out. He can't be serious. He is. I say "Yeah, tell that to Gillespie."

He wrinkles his forehead into a deeper frown, but doesn't answer. We drive another mile or so while he chews on that. He pulls off the road, turns to me looking dead earnest and says "Now don't get me wrong. I like you and all that. You're an O.K. guy, and we've been through a hell of a lot together, but I have to tell you for your own good that you can be such an awful jerk when you want to. Sometimes I just can't figure you out."

He looks to me for a reply. I know he thinks he's helping me out again, that this is what true pals do for each other. When I don't answer, he works up a smile to show there's no hard feelings. This is all supposed to be good for my morale. He switches on the motor again and says, "You know what I mean?"

I dig in. I wonder who this stupid bastard is, and how I ever figured him to be a friend of mine. We pass through the little English villages in silence. After a while Earl starts singing Off We Go Into The Wild Blue Yonder but he doesn't know half the words and even less of the tune. He looks at me to join in. I feel like smashing him one in the teeth. He pats my back like we're two good buddies, like that should make me feel better, like everything is under control, like we didn't have thirteen more fuckin' missions to fly.

Oh, Cavey, Cavey, you goddam son of a bitch.

TWENTY-TWO

Miserable flying conditions, but we managed to chalk up a pile of missions early in December. Cologne, Merseberg, Hamburg, Munich, Frankfurt, goddam Merseberg again, plus a couple of other towns in between that I can't recall offhand. Call them Flakenburg. I may have forgotten their names, but I damn well remember those never ending bomb runs where we flew exposed and helpless as geese over a blind. No evasive action during a bomb run. No turning away from those boxes of greasy black flak where we knew going in that we'd have less crews coming out. Just how many less, we'd find out later.

My number is down to seven now. Long overdue for the old fickle finger, and whoever or whatever is tailing me out there. You'd think I'd be able to handle this by now, but it's rougher these days than when I started. I was scared then, not knowing what I was up against. Now I know and I'm beyond scared. Somewhere between numb and dumb. Probably not even a word for it.

The weird part is carrying on as if everything is perfectly normal. I don't know how the other guys manage. I've gone through this whole deal gritting my teeth, closing my eyes, and shaking in my pants, but Cavey was around sweating it out with me. Now I'm supposed to scrub him. That's what everybody else has done, but it's not that simple for me. Nobody talks about him. No mention of his name since they rubbed it off the squadron roster blackboard, but I can still make it out through the chalky gray eraser smear. I catch myself half expecting to see him sacked out up there in his bunk. Those shirts of his that Swan missed when he cleared out his stuff still dangle from the pipe, flat sleeved in their wire hangers just as he last left them. Don't look up there now. Snap, snap. Change subject. Seven to go, and you still have Hartak to deal with, and the Hangman and Holy Cross too. Nice boys. My fellow Americans. Not back on the runway yet, buddy boy, not by a long shot.

Nothing but freezing rain, fog, sleet, and snow one dark gray day after another for the past two weeks. The damp chill gets under your skin, right down to bone. Everyone going around crabby and depressed, and it's not all due to the weather. Just when the infantry boys had fought their way to the border and were ready to advance into Germany, the krauts pulled a surprise counter attack that broke through and made a huge bulge in their line. There's even been talk that they may push them back to the Channel. If we could have got our planes up, we'd have stopped those damn Germans dead in their tracks, but they counted on us not being able to fly in all this gook, and they were right on target there. We haven't had a plane off the ground in thirteen days now.

I log as many hours as I can flat on my back, mostly staring at the walls, sweating out my chances of making it after all. Sometimes I dick around with Bishop assuring him everything is under control, and contrary to evidence and experience, Hartak is basically rational and knows what he's doing, and it's all going to work out fine, just wait and see.

I tell him, "They're replacing our ships with the latest new bullet-proof model B-17", or "they're working night and day on a master plan that will improve the chow and also change the movies a little more often around here." He listens and smiles politely even through crap like that, then he goes back to re-reading his letters from home or curls up there in his bunk with his little Bible. Not what you'd call very stimulating, but it's O.K. with me. I'm not looking for excitement. I try to pick up Radio Bremen through the static on our radio set while flipping through Cavey's old pile of girley books.

I drag myself out of the sack only to trudge over to the mess hall, and once in a while take my bike for a spin around the countryside. The proper thing would be to go up to visit Vivian Lea. She was so decent and kind to me, but I can't bear telling her about Cavey. She's bound to ask about him, and then what can I say to the poor woman when she starts in on her son in the Jap labor camp who I'm sure is done for by now. Mostly though, I suppose what really keeps me away is facing Martha. I'm really all screwed up about that, but the way it stands, in a couple of weeks I'll either be on my way back to the States, drunk, dumb and happy, or else all that's left of me will be little pieces scattered over some German city. Flakenburg? Drop it. Let it slide.

Today, on my way back from biking around, a small patch of blue in the late afternoon sky broke through the cloud cover. The wizards at Operations expect a strong high pressure system to move in, which should finally clear things up a bit before morning. Of course you can't rely too much on weather guys, but let's hope for once they could be right. I want to get this over with.

The alert list tonight shows me flying with Earl and what's left of our crew. Parsons, a new co-pilot, replaces Ted Williams who replaced the Mouse. I don't know the new guy from Adam. Someone I've seen around here without ever speaking to. He has flown nine missions, but was bounced off his old crew because he couldn't get along with his pilot. I've heard some other stuff about him, but all I want to know is whether he's good at his job. It won't take us long to find out if he can cut the mustard. Bishop is in Cavey's old spot. I have to say that the kid has handled himself fairly well up there.

Funny how I think of him as a kid, when as a matter of fact he was twenty-one last month, two months older than me. I suppose after a while you come to look on anybody with fewer missions as some kind of kid around here, and he has 25 or so still to go. Makes me like old grandpappy. I look at each load of replacements coming in and get the willies just thinking about all that's happened since I was in their shoes. No way they could make me go through those missions again. Not for five thousand dollars, not even ten thousand.

I turn in early, but I keep waking to look at my watch every hour or so. When it shows ten after four, I figure the mission has been scrubbed. Maybe the weather has turned bad again, or maybe they're giving us a break because it's the day before Christmas, ha ha. Fat chance. I wake again when I hear the Hangman curse as he bumps into our chair in the dark.

He flashes his light at Bishop in the upper bunk and hollers, "O.K., Brighteyes. Rise and shine, alley oop. Uncle Sam wants you. Briefing at seven. Let's go. Move it, move it, move it!"

Bishop sits up slowly, and just as slowly says, "Yes sir, thank you. I'm up now." The Hangman then prods my shoulder with his flashlight. "You too, lucky boy. Everybody flies, nobody dies. C'mon, ups-a-daisy." He yanks the mound of G.I. blankets off me. I don't even bother to swear at him anymore. I shiver when my feet hit the concrete. I peek through the blackout curtain and see lighter shades of blue low in the dark starlit sky. It's six thirty five, three hours past our usual wake up call. Wherever we're going, it's bound to be a short one. We're starting late and that doesn't give them much time or distance to get us out and back before dark.

The walk paths are jammed full of guys rushing through the wintry early morning to breakfast. The K.P.'s dishing out the powdered eggs and greasy sausages are full of chatter about how this has to be a big one. No stand-downs today. All four squadrons are up.

There are not enough benches to hold all the crews at briefing this morning. We're all squeezed in with guys standing in the aisles and perched in windows. The K.P's as usual were right. Something big is definitely in the works. All four squadrons of the group are here raring to go, boisterous and unruly, like at a pep rally before the big game. I find myself caught up in it too. Two weeks of inaction and we're all a pack of eager beavers. Let's get this fuckin' war over with.

The noise builds with the guys getting restless. I take another swig of black coffee from the thermos Odie left for me when he finished up. Our new co-pilot, a tall blond good looking guy almost like Randolph Scott the actor, twitches and seems more nervous and edgy than I care to see. He sits and fidgets next to Earl who has tried talking to him, but he's too wound up to reply. I figure it might help if I introduce him around. He's Lloyd Parsons from Corona, California and it turns out that Lopez has had some dealings with him back there.

Lopez doesn't seem to be any too fond of him when he asks Parsons "Do you guys still have Pinkertons patrolling around the Parsons orange groves?"

Parsons ignores him and tells us "It's a dirty shame how they let all kinds in the Air Force these days."

I wonder about this guy and tell him that's way out of line. He comes back with "Oh blow it out your ass, this is the last time they catch me flying with such a bunch of sad sacks."

Lopez says "I fuckin' hope so. Maybe you'd rather fly with your Nazi pals in the Luftwaffe." Fearless lights a cigarette for Lopez and tells him to button it up. It's just as well they don't hear Parsons mutter, "Fuckin' little greaseball."

Earl figures it's time to smooth things over. He cups his hands over his mouth like a cheerleader so he can be heard above all the noise as he mimics Arnhem Annie on her broadcast this morning. "Velcome und varm greedings to the men of the 91st Bomb group. Our gallant Luftwaffe and flak battalions have the complete plan of today's operation and vill be vaiting for you. Vunce more so many of your lives are to be vasted. If you ever vish to zee your loved ones again, you must turn back from zis useless effort. Your surrounded infantry forces are trapped. You are doomed. Remember, the Luftwaffe is vaiting."

Earl stops long enough to enjoy the crew's hooting and a few sieg heils. He's really into it as he goes on. "Ve haff no qvarrel mit you. Ve vant peace. You throw avay your life for the greedy profiteers and black marketers on the home front who fill their pockets and go to bed mit your vifes und sveethearts." Skiles throws his arm up in a Nazi salute, then lifts his leg and blows out a long fart loud enough to hear over the noise in the hut.

The crowd parts as the colonel makes his way through. He jumps up on the platform. I've never seen him smile before. He's almost beaming when he raises his arms and announces, "The order of the day — no man, no ship, no bomb is to be spared. Maximum effort. No passes, no leaves. If a ship can leave the ground, it flies. Today, we are delivering a Christmas present to the German that he will long remember. I am proud to tell you that the 91st is putting up 63 aircraft today."

Whistles and cheers as most of the boys stand and applaud. I don't know where or how they dug up all those 17's.

That's almost twice the number we usually put up. I hope our crew doesn't get one of the war wearies, or worse, something put together cannibalized from the crash heap.

The colonel slaps his glove in his palm and says "Remember, maximum effort. No stand downs. The 8th Air Force is sending up two thousand bombers today to thirty German targets. Target assigned to the 91st is the Luftwaffe base at Merzhausen. Those Nazi barbarians have massacred our infantry boys the past two weeks while we've been grounded. Now our group is going to give it back to them in spades. Let's see how those German bastards like it."

Maybe it's all that coffee I'm drinking, but I find myself charged up, hooting and stamping my feet, full of piss and vinegar like the rest of the boys. This isn't one of our grim Merseberg or Berlin briefings. I've never heard of Merzhausen. It sounds like another one of those towns I can't remember. I track the red ribbon on the large map up front when they pull the curtain back. Merzhausen is on this side of the Rhine, hardly any distance at all into Germany. Looks like we have ourselves a bluebird. A milk run for Christmas.

We take it as a good sign that our ship today is DF-G, Paper Doll, one of the newer ships in the squadron. A weak gray yellow wintery early morning light faces us when we exit from the briefing hut, but it sure beats emerging into the usual pre-dawn murk. Eriksen exclaims like its some sort of miracle, "Hot diggety dog. Daylight! Takeoff and assembly in daylight."

Fearless asks me for our ETA for return to base. When I tell him it looks like it will be around two forty, smiles break out among the whole crew. "Short and sweet," says Skiles "a cakewalk."

It takes us much longer than usual to walk the propellers through on a bitter cold morning like this. The oil collected in the lower cylinders has frozen thick, and we have to push hard to turn those props through and loosen up the sludge before starting up the engines.

We take off right on schedule, but despite the daylight, we're having our troubles assembling into squadron and group position. With so many ships up today, we've had to set up all kinds of modifications to our standard formation in order to accommodate them all. An hour and a half after takeoff and we still don't have every ship in its assigned slot. Each group is flying four squadrons instead of the usual three, plus a dozen or so spare ships trying to latch on somewhere. Most of them flying with squadrons other than their own.

I look out at a dazzling blue sky loaded with hundreds of planes clear across the horizon. An impressive sight, but I'm not too keen on what I see out there. Too many ships weaving in and out, climbing on their own, with others cutting across erratically trying to catch up. I've seen one fireball and we've heard reports of two other mid-air collisions so far this morning, and if this keeps up there's going to be a lot more.

We keep circling. From here some of the squadrons look to be in pretty good shape, but all too many look like parts of a disorganized mob. I hear Hartak call in as usual that this is one piss poor assembly. This time he's not just beating his gums, but it's time to shove off. All ships not in formation will either catch up with us over water, or hook on to some other group as best they can. We must move on or risk missing rendezvous with our fighter escort.

We're still pretty much a rag-tag collection of aircraft as we depart the British coast at Harwich, but by the time we cross the beaches above Dunkerque most of our planes look like they're in their slots. It's hard to tell for sure, as we're flying nineteen ships in the squadron today instead of our usual twelve. It's one freaky looking formation.

I feel better when we pick up the fighter escort for our group right on the button three minutes after crossing the French coast. They're a flight of about forty Mustangs scooting around through the thin cirrus above our group. We pass a little south of Brussels and directly over Liege where we correct 15 degrees right to head for our I.P. west of Rudesheim. If the Luftwaffe is waiting for us, they're going to be stood up. Nothing but Mustangs with us at 25800 feet, cruising over a base of 4/10ths low stratus with streaks of cirrus above, a hell of a strong cross wind out of 046 degrees at 57 knots, and it's cold as a a witch's tit up here — minus 62 degrees Fahrenheit. I call for an oxygen check. When Earl checks in he adds, "Hey, this Parsons is a hell of a good co-pilot." Earl, as usual, trying for one nice big happy family. "Peachy," I say, "we're over Germany now."

Hundreds of our bombers and fighters all around as far as the eye can see. An army of about twenty thousand men up here flying unopposed. No flak, no Luftwaffe. We're more than halfway through our bomb run before we see our first flak about nine miles ahead. The black explosions are not too heavily concentrated, and though it may be a bit too soon to tell, I begin to believe that this may turn out to be one of our few milk runs. Bishop, bundled in his flak vest and helmet, twists around toward me and lifts his arms as if asking me to account for the absence of heavy flak.

The few bursts we see are at our altitude, but they're nothing like the usual heavy box barrages we see over major targets. They're far apart, popping up at odd intervals. I point forward and down to remind the kid we're close to target. One of the small black bursts catches LL-Peter, and I stare at her dropping from formation with her No. 3 engine smoking. Not a single trace of flak in the sky when I enter time and position in the log to mark where and when LL-P went down.

Bishop is busy hitting his switches and levers preparing to release our load the instant after we see the bombs tumble out of Hartak's ship. At bombs away I mark the log: Flak - sparse to meager, though I know it was heavy and accurate enough for the poor guys in LL-P. They're the only ship lost out of our group as far as I can tell, but it's hard to know for sure in this botched up formation with all the extra ships we have flying around today. A gaggle of mixed 17's, too many for a squadron and less than a group, bundle together in a halfass formation less than a mile ahead and a thousand feet above us.

Earl calls in that bandits are reported in the area - jet jobs. I see thin contrails up ahead zigging and zagging, twisting and turning back across the straight broader contrails of our bomber stream. Signs of bandits. A 17 spins out of control from that loose formation above us followed by another falling with its wings on fire. Seven or eight chutes open up. I move stiffly to my gun position. My nose is pressed up to the glass as I scan for enemy German fighters that I pray won't show up near us.

Bishop swings his turret back and forth scanning the sky above and below. He points downward in jerky movements to where a chute is wrapped around the tail stabilizer of one of our ships in the low squadron. I see the figure of a guy tangled in the shroud lines and dragged behind like a tow sleeve for five or six seconds before he is torn loose and falls down and away. Large white chunks of his chute remain behind, draped on the tail of the 17. I hope the poor bastard was nobody I know.

Bishop fires his guns at the same time as Skiles calls from his turret, "Bandits! Two o'clock level, closing fast!" Our ship shakes and vibrates as every gun fires at the German fighters streaking by. About a dozen black Focke-Wulfs and five or six brown Me-262 jets. One of the F-W's rams into a 17 in our low squadron. We bounce from the explosion of the fireball.

Skiles cries out again. "More coming! One o'clock!" I see twenty of them with their guns blazing bullets with orange tracers straight at us. Our ship jumps as if it has run into a wall. Blasts of frigid air tear through a jagged gash where the bullets have ripped through the ship's aluminum skin. Earl yells, "Fuck! I'm hit!"

We drop away from the formation. I feel immersed in the paralysis of fear, but I plug in an oxygen bottle and drag myself up to the passage where I can see Earl. Skiles and I reach him at the same time. Earl is holding the wheel in his left hand. His right arm droops loose from his shoulder where blood is spreading down a torn leather sleeve. Parsons is slumped over, bent and twisted in a pool of blood coursing from an open gap of organs and shattered bone where his chest used to be. I go blank, lose complete track of what's going on, until I see Earl struggling to keep the ship level, flying with one arm. I snatch at the medical kit while the plane bobs and weaves all over the sky.

We're still being hit by fighters as I hear our gunners firing away. My trembling hands can hardly tear open the envelopes of sulfa powder and bandages in the medical kit. I manage to scatter the sulfa around and into the hole below Earl's collar bone, and press the patch bandages over it while Earl screams with pain under his oxygen mask. Skiles and I struggle to heave and tug Parsons' body out of his seat. I'm soaked in his blood and he keeps slipping from our grasp until we drop him in the passageway behind his seat. I can't catch my breath and feel like I'm blacking out until I remember to replace my empty oxygen bottle. I call Fearless to come up from the waist quick to take over Skiles' position in the top turret, and to also bring up some blankets. Skiles climbs into the co-pilot seat and tries to wipe away Parsons' blood spread on the spattered windshield. He stops when it becomes mostly frozen smears.

Fear and panic spread through me as real as pain. Nowhere to run, nowhere to hide. I must get away from here. I clip on my chest pack to bail out. I'm about to kick the door open to jump when I look up at Earl. The patch bandages have fallen off, but the freezing air has helped staunch the flow of blood from his wound. His teeth chatter out of control, his body quivers and his right arm still hangs useless, but he's conscious enough to coach Skiles who is gripping the wheel for all he's worth. I jam more patch bandages with sulfa to Earl's wound. I unclip my chute. We're alone over Germany, down to 16,000 feet. Our gunners have stopped firing for now. It's a break, but it won't last long. We haven't seen the last of those German bastards. We're alone up here and they'll be picking us up as a straggler as soon as they've finished with their attack on the group. I drape one blanket over Earl's shoulders, and cover Parsons with the other.

"Can you make it, Earl?" I ask. He nods slowly. I turn to Skiles in the co-pilot seat. "You O.K., ?" He nods slowly. I won't bail out.

I ease my way past Parsons' body when I crawl back to my position. The freezing wind whizzes and whistles through the bullet torn gash in the ship's skin. My chart and maps have been blown around and stomped on. I go through the motions of scanning dials but it's all a blur. I look again for my chute but can't find it. I tell Earl to maintain our present heading until I can figure just where the hell we are. I look out the window for possible landmarks and all I see through holes in the heavy undercast are snow covered empty fields and trees. My watch shows only six minutes since Earl called out that he was hit. I've no idea how the guys in back made out. I force myself to call for a long overdue oxygen check. There's a long pause when it is Parsons' turn to answer until Skiles calls in "Co-pilot, O.K. check."

I go numb again when Bishop points at a pair of fighters closing in on us fast. I hold up my hands to shield the sun from my eyes and a red smear of Parsons' blood spreads across my goggles. The bitter acrid taste of bile rises in back of my throat. I stumble over my chute which has slid from where I stowed it behind the cartridge links. The two fighters are almost in range now. My stomach knots and retches as I drag myself over to my gun position. I pull my oxygen mask aside to shake out the puke. Lopez hollers, "Little friends! Two Mustangs coming our way." They pull up beside us and wag their wings. I crumple to my knees with relief. My hand quivers on the call button. I speak in a voice I don't recognize, "Hey Earl, follow them babies home."

Bishop holds and steadies me when I start to shake.

TWENTY-THREE

I know I must get a grip on myself. I look out at those two 51's covering us, scouting up ahead for enemy fighters then flying lazy S turns to let us catch up. No more signs of the Luftwaffe. That helps me settle down some, though I am still not completely free of the shakes when I go back to work. The crumpled log looks like its been pulled out of a trash can. All O.K. with the crew when I remember to run the oxygen check. When Earl checks in he says "Tell 'em about Parsons." Before I can think of the proper words to say, Zibby back in the tail cuts in with "It's O.K., we got the word back here."

One of the Mustangs radios in that his fuel is running low and he'll have to skip off soon. Those two little friends have done a beautiful job covering us until we're now back over Allied territory. Fifteen minutes later we're down to 11000 feet, cruising at 158 indicated, compass at 282 with Antwerp off our right wing and Brussels a little further to our left. I smell the cigarettes before I'm halfway through telling the crew they can remove their oxygen masks. My face feels as if it had been sandpapered when I slowly peel off my mask glued with frozen puke to my raw cheeks. I wave at the other Mustang as he wags his wings in farewell, before he dives down into the cloud deck and scoots for home too.

When I go up to check on Earl, I divert my eyes from Parsons' body lumped in the soggy blood soaked blanket in the hatchway. I step over him and catch myself almost saying excuse me. Earl is hunched over like an old man in a wheelchair, his face a greenish shade of pale, squinting through eyes almost shut and fixed in a straight ahead stare. He must have instructed Skiles to put the ship on auto-pilot because their hands are off the wheel now.

Our engines and all systems seem to be holding up so far. I ask Earl if he thinks he can possibly land the ship with one arm. He clenches his jaw, biting down on the pain with his lips drawn back baring his teeth like a skeleton. He nods. Skiles sits erect in Parsons' bloodspattered seat. For once he isn't talking. I pat him on the back. He nods.

We see a few groups far off to the north when we cross the English coast at Margate. Eriksen passes on a radio message that Bassingbourn is closed, completely socked in by heavy ground fog moving rapidly eastward. We are to proceed to Bury St. Edmunds before it too is shut down. I peer through the grass dancing across the scope of the G-box and manage to work out our present coordinates. I give Earl the heading to Bury.

We're at 4000 feet descending through heavy strato-cumulus. I'm stuck to the scope taking G fixes every two minutes. We're on course homing in on Bury, but we can't even see our wing tips in this thick sodden mush, nor can we see any of the hundred other ships on the same track in this area. If we do see one, it will be in the last second before we crash into each other. We're down to 1800 feet and thirty miles from Bury before we break into the clear where over a hundred 17's and Liberators are whizzing by in halfassed patterns at low level, all heading for the same runway. Skiles breaks out of his silence to say "I swear we have the whole fuckin' 8th Air Force trying to land here."

I don't see how Earl expects to land our ship with only one arm and Skiles for co-pilot. He says, "Flares, going straight in." We fly a half mile left of the base on a northeast heading and Fearless pumps red flares out the waist window to alert the tower and all ships around that we have an on board emergency. Earl is too weak to maneuver us through a full landing pattern. He creates his own. He makes an abrupt right turn and our ship bounces from the wake of one 17, and we cut across the path of another only fifty yards away. I can't guess how many others we've cut off. We break off on a second turn, and Earl has us lined up with the runway. A flock of ambulances stand side by side waiting on the tarmac. We're descending quickly, now down to 600 feet and only two hundred yards or so behind a Liberator slowly lumbering in. I hope they've warned the pilot of that Lib to get the hell off the runway fast before we plow into him. I call to the crew "Brace yourselves, this is going to be a hard one."

I'm propped against a bulkhead, clutching on to the back of Earl's seat. He grips the wheel with his left hand and his eyes are wide open now fixed straight ahead. The freezing air blitzes through the bullet torn gap in the side of the ship as I holler out the air speed readings to him. I can tell we're coming in way too steep. The runway rushes up to meet us. Earl jockeys the wheel with his left hand, staring straight ahead as he coaches Skiles who clutches the handle over the four throttles in a white knuckled grip. Earl yells out above the roar of the engines, "O.K. Skiles move 'er back easy now - easy - easy - easy now - not so fast dammit - easy - easy - I said easy easy - now cut 'er - goddamit cut 'er - cut 'er hard!"

We hit the ground heavy, tilted over sideways, touching down on the right wheel only. The ship bounces then comes down again on an angle with sparks shooting from the wing tip and the outside propeller as they hit and scrape the concrete before we spin off the runway. We slide and loop out of control. Earl reaches over and cuts all the switches. The noise is deafening until we come to a screeching halt pitched over when the right landing strut caves in. I pick myself up from where I've been slammed down hard against the top turret. Earl sags in his seat with his eyes closed now. I hear him sobbing. I turn away and take deep gulps of air.

A pair of medics from the ambulance climb aboard. They bend down to examine Parsons, but I tell them Earl is an emergency. Our crew huddles together outside the wrecked plane without saying a word when they unload Parsons' body off the ship on a stretcher. Earl is on the next stretcher. The medics carry them off to the meat wagon, then come back for me and Skiles until I convince them that we're okay. The blood matted all over our face and clothes is from Parsons.

We pile up our gear and silently walk around examining the damage to the ship. Paper Doll is tipped over, her landing strut, outside propeller and wing tip crunched and bent under on one side. We reach up and poke our fingers in bullet holes and run our hands over the jagged torn areas in her skin. Eriksen is the first to speak. "They say it's a good landing if you can walk away from it," he says. Fearless pats him on the head. Lopez crosses himself and rattles off some prayers in Spanish with the words Lloyd Parsons coming up every now and then.

The sky is still loaded with bombers above us landing in half minute intervals. "I told you," Skiles says "the whole goddam Eighth is coming in here." Bishop is counting them out loud, seventy-eight, seventy-nine, eighty, like a kid watching freight cars at a crossing. He stops when a cone of pitch black smoke with a fiery orange flash erupts in the sky two miles north. The black cloud rising looks like a large barrage of flak except for the bits and streaks of falling flaming wreckage. We watch the smoke coiling and expanding, becoming ever blacker at its core. I feel the shakes coming on again, so I force my eyes away from the greasy black tower, and scan the outlines of the unfamiliar hangars of Bury St. Edmunds. We've been out here nearly an hour with no truck in sight to take us in. We stamp our feet and swing our arms to ward off the late afternoon chill. Fearless says "I'm about to shoot off another one of those flares. Maybe that'll bring 'em out."

A truck with another crew loaded in back finally pulls up. The driver tells us that we'd better double up. They're short on trucks on account of all the ships landing at Bury today. We throw our gear aboard and crowd in with the other crew, a real happy bunch from the group at Kimbolton. They stare at our wrecked plane, but it doesn't hinder their clowning around. They've had a milk run to Aachen. Didn't see any flak at all, and not a single fighter other than our own. A piece of cake.

Their pilot looks us over and says, "Appears like you're short a couple of guys. I'm Dubois."

A red headed gunner with the most freckles I've ever seen hollers "Yay, that's us. Dubois' Doughboys. Old dubious Dubois. Dooby dooby doo." Dubois shoves him and says, "Come on Reds, knock it off." He turns to me and asks "Which one of you tramps is the pilot?"

I don't answer. He shrugs and says "O.K. never mind, have it your way." Bishop says, "Our pilot was shot. Around the shoulder somewhere. They took him off in the ambulance."

Dubois yells out to his crew, "Hold it down to a medium roar, will you, guys." He then turns back to us and says, "That's tough, so who's co-pilot?" None of the boys on our crew look at Dubois. The question just hangs there until Bishop speaks again. "They took him in the ambulance too, sir. He's dead."

Reds and three or four of their guys in the back are still

horsing around, but most of the ruckus has tapered off. It's not too bad considering there's sixteen guys and their equipment piled in here bouncing around in back of a truck. Dubois tosses his head like a dog shaking off water. He says "Hell, just where the fuck did you guys go today?"

It may be because the truck is so filled with cigarette smoke and we're so jammed together that Fearless' voice is hoarse when he rasps out, "A town called Merzhausen, I think."

Dubois passes around some Phillies and says "Never heard of the place."

The truck stinks from our B.O. and the cigars. We hit a few bumps in the road, topple over into each other, hit a few more and get all tangled up. Some of the guys think it's funny and pretty soon they're clowning around and joking like kids on a bus. Bishop is pushed up against me, and I shove him back. "Move it," I say "give a guy a little room over here, godammit." Then feeling I've been a little rough on him, I say "One helluva day, this has been one sweet helluva day."

"Yes sir," he says, "it sure has been." He wipes a sleeve across his eyes. "Merry Christmas," he says. I can't believe I'd clean forgotten it's Christmas Eve. I shake hands with him. "Yeah, thanks," I say "same to you old buddy and many more." The kid is about to reply but changes his mind. Then he says "Only twenty-four more for me."

"You'll make it easy," I say "Nothing to it. Cheer up kiddo, it's the season to be merry."

The driver drops us off at a large hangar swarming with crews from a half dozen groups. We lug our gear over to where we see a bed sheet stretched between two poles with the words 91st Bomb Gp in large blue pencilled letters. A couple of hundred guys sprawl around lying on the hangar floor propped against their parachute bags. We find the guys from our squadron with Hartak standing over them. He's carrying on a loud argument with a couple of officers from the base here at Bury

St. Edmunds. He spots our crew and stops to say, "Good to see you guys. We thought we'd lost you. Scronch down. Make yourselves comfortable." He turns back to his argument.

We drop our bags and stretch out right on the spot. I'm out cold in a minute with my chute as a pillow until Bishop jostles me awake. Many of the guys in the squadron sleep through when Hartak announces, "I've been fighting these goddam groundpounders for a half hour now and getting nowhere. No food, no quarters. They just aren't prepared to handle us and there's no way we can get you back to Bassingbourn until morning, so we have to make do with what we have here. We'll get you some K-rations, and you flop anywhere you can. If you find a place to hole up in, you're welcome to it, but don't wander too far from here because we're trucking out at 0700 tomorrow, and remember, no stragglers."

I stretch out again lying between Lopez and Bishop, but I can't sleep. I'm starving. When they toss packs of K-rations at us I take doubles. We're all busy scarfing it down when Eriksen says, "That was pretty rough out there today, wasn't it?" He turns to me for confirmation. I don't know what else to say but "Yeah, you could say that."

Lopez says, "Well, one thing you can depend on around here is just when you think it can't get any worse, it sure as hell does get worse." He too looks at me as if he wants my opinion. "Yeah, Conrad" I nod. Fearless and Zibby argue over whether we lose more men by enemy action or by accidents. They try to suck me in but I want no part of it. I tell them "What's the difference. Dead is dead."

I like these guys, but I don't feel much like talking right now. My mind has turned to mush as I try to wipe out what happened today. I doze off again for an hour or so, and know I'm going real dopey when I wake to see Skiles standing over us with a bottle of Dewars White Label in each fist. "A little Christmas cheer, come on with me guys," he says. They get up and I follow them mindlessly like a robot, out the back of the hangar past some warehouses until we come to a small Nissen hut where Skiles kicks the door open.

Zibby and Fearless are shooting pool on a table at the far end of the hut and Eriksen is trying to get a fire going in the coal stove. "Ante up a pound apiece," says Skiles, waving the whiskey bottles above us. "This stuff doesn't come cheap you know."

We're in a hut that looks like it may be the day room for one of the small outfits on the base. The boys found it when they were walking around exploring Bury, and Skiles had the idea of liberating it for the night. We lie down huddled around the stove passing the bottles around.

I wake some time during the night with Fearless snoring in my face. The fire has burnt down in the stove. I get up, stir the ashes, add more coal in the grate. It becomes too hot near the stove so I go to lie down on the pool table. Bishop is lying there awake, gazing out the window. He sits up propped on one elbow when he sees me. He has that look on his face again as if he's waiting for me to say something important. "Move it," I say "give a guy a little room over here, for crying out loud - here comes Santa Claus."

Earl comes into our room on New Years Day to say good-bye. He's heading for London on a three day pass before he goes in for thirty days R & R at the Flak House in Torquay. "Holy moly, Earl, I say, you're looking sharp. You're going to knock 'em dead." He's dressed up in his Class A's, an R.A.F. trench coat folded over one arm, the other wounded arm in a sling. There's the beginning of a Clark Gable mustache, and he's all spiffed up and looking proud like a recruiting poster, a goddam war hero. I'm not being smartass, I'm real happy for the guy when I say "Damn it Earl, I almost feel I should be saluting you."

He pulls out a shiny chromium combination lighter and cigarette case. He flips the case open, offers a Pall Mall to me and Bishop, bends to take one out for himself with his lips, then lights us up, all with one hand. I whistle in admiration.

"Practice," Earl says, "that's all it is, practice. You'd be surprised at what you can do with one hand if you keep at it." He puffs a smoke ring toward the ceiling. Bishop points to Earl's arm in the sling. "I've written home," he says, "telling everyone how you saved us all with that one arm landing." Earl perches himself on our table. He's in no hurry to leave. "Hell, I knew all along we'd make it," he says "until that meatball Skiles leaned against the wheel tipping us over just as we were touching down."

"But," I say, "you have to admit the old bastard came through for us when we needed him. You know damn well we'd never have made it without him. You two were great together. We made it. We're here."

Bishop says, "By grace of the Lord."

Earl says to me, "Why don't you take a break? Hartak said he'd put you in for a week at the Flak House with me."

"That sounds good, but my number is down to six and if I stop now, I doubt I'd ever be able to drag my ass near a briefing hut again. It takes all I've got as it is right now."

Bishop asks "What would really happen if supposing a guy flat out refused to go?"

I signal to Earl to flip me another cigarette. "Hell, that would take more guts than I have," I say. "Nobody knows for sure or if they do, they're not telling. It's something you don't want to talk about around here. I know of a couple of guys on the same crew who did talk seriously about it often, and while I couldn't swear if they actually refused to fly a mission, I can tell you that they disappeared pretty damn quick. I came back from breakfast one morning and they were gone. Swan came around, cleaned out their stuff and folded their mattresses over as if they had gone down. Nobody ever knew where they went or what happened to them. You hear all kinds of stuff like they were hanged, or faced a firing squad, or they're in solitary in Leavenworth. I don't know what the hell the punishment is supposed to be, but I bet it isn't much fun. That's why we have all those crews sitting out the war in Sweden and Switzerland."

Earl says, "I don't know how those guys can live with themselves. What if we all took it in our heads to pull shit like that, chicken out and refuse to fly any missions."

I want to tell Earl that sounds like the best idea he's ever had, but I know I better keep my trap shut. Earl goes on, "Hell, we'd never get this war settled. I know that I can't wait for this arm to recover enough for me to come back. Yeah, I know these missions are rough, but we're making sure no madman will ever start any more wars in the future."

He carries on like that for a while explaining what we're fighting for, almost like he's preaching on the radio. Sometimes I forget how Earl can be. Anyway I feel better when Bishop catches my eye and winks while Earl runs on. That kid is going to be O.K.

Earl finally winds down. On his way out he tells me that I can still change my mind and go with him. "Don't tempt me," I say "and for Pete's sake remember to steer clear of whores in dark alleys." I shake his left hand, the good one. I hope that's not bad luck.

I watch him from the door as he marches off. He turns after a few steps. "Be seeing you," he says. I give him the thumbs up sign, putting a lot into it. I'm not likely to ever see Earl again. Thirty days from now when he comes back, I shall be gone. One way or another.

TWENTY-FOUR

January. The weather, our other enemy, has turned fierce on us. "Weather like this," Zibby says, "and even the birds are walking." Weighty ridges of ice, more threatening than flak, build up on our wings. We climb through thick, foggy mist often unable to see much beyond the wing tips, while hundreds of other bombers assemble with us, shrouded in the same murk. We sweat it out. All eyes straining to warn of the approach of another ship before it's too late. The leaden gray cloud turns milky then hazy yellow before we abruptly break out into the blue. The sun bursts against our eyes like a bulb switched on in a darkened room.

We rarely see the target these days as we cruise isolated from the invisible world five miles below covered under a solid layer of undercast. We drop our bombs by radar. The lead ship in each squadron carries the Magic Eye black box we call Mickey that can penetrate the cloud layer and outline land shapes on its scope. All eyes are on the Mickey ship when we're over the target. When Mickey drops his bombs, we drop ours.

I've gone on a few real beauties lately. One, a long drag to Neubrandenberg where only one ship from the group went down, but we lost two others to icing and dense ground fog when we returned drained and fatigued eleven hours after take off. A miracle we didn't lose more. The group ahead of us didn't drop because they couldn't get their Mickey operational over the target. They left the bomber stream on our way back to unload on a target of opportunity, wherever, whatever, whoever that was.

The mission to Dusseldorf, a real fucked up mess from the start, had to be aborted just before reaching Holland where at 26000 feet we were adrift in cloud-cuckooland, buried deep in stratocumulus the wizards had predicted would top at 9000 and be light and intermittent. One ship from our squadron, DF-R, disappeared on us after the abort without a sign that they were in trouble. It was last seen going into a thick cloud formation, but no observation of it coming out. DF-G ground looped off the runway and tipped over when it hit an icy patch on landing. Four of the guys didn't get out in time. We all watched as it caught fire and blew up. That didn't do much for the old morale, and of course no mission credit for us due to the abort.

My name hasn't shown up on the last three alert lists. A month ago that wouldn't have bothered me one single bit, but I'm down to my last mission now and I'm getting antsy. When I run into Cross, I ask him what gives. "Stay loose," he says, "we're saving you for something big, a blue plate special, a graduation present." I remember how he made Paul sweat out his last one. Pricks like him are the real enemy. I'd like to drop a bomb on him, but for now he's got me by the short hairs, and not much I can do but hunker down and wait.

We don't see much of the Luftwaffe lately. No doubt the weather is as rough on them as on us, but we hear the main reason for their absence is they're hoarding fuel and saving their speedy jet jobs for a mass attack against us one of these days. For now they just send up flights of fifteen or twenty Focke-Wulfs who float around out of range hoping to catch one of our straggler groups. We seldom catch a glimpse of them, but you've had a bad day when it's your group they gang up on. It's only a minute or two, but they'll knock off half the straggling group before our escort can come to the rescue.

Weather hasn't cut back on the flak they throw at us. They've brought back all their guns from France and Russia, so they now have doubled their number of 88's and 105's pointing up, and for sure they're not hoarding any ammunition. Over Hamburg last week the flak was thicker than the undercast. Fearless said, "We could have let our wheels down and taxied on the damned stuff."

There it is - my name on the 1 Feb 45 alert list. Flying with Hartak in the squadron lead for my last one. Lopez is with us as waist gunner instead of his usual spot in the ball turret. No ball turret on the lead ship, where it's replaced by the radar dome for Mickey. It's No. 35 for Lopez too. He's eager to finish up, but none too happy about flying with Hartak. "Mixed feelings," he says "like seeing your mother-in-law driving close to the edge of a cliff in your new Cadillac."

Another one of our breakfast at three, briefing at four mornings. Hartak is late for briefing, his eyes red rimmed as usual, but I'm glad I don't smell any booze on him. He tells us "I've just come from looking over the Telexes down at group and we have a big one coming up this morning. One I've been waiting for a long time. A real hot puppy."

Lopez and I exchange glances. Hartak has his priorities and we have ours, and they're not too often on the same wave length. I look down the bench at the rest of the crew and they're all trying to act like having a big one coming up this morning, a real hot puppy, is O.K., all in a day's work. Hartak narrows his eyes giving us the once over. I fold my arms and try to act as if I don't give a damn. Hartak catches my eye and signals me thumbs up. He's running the mission for the group today from the co-pilot seat of our plane and he can't hardly wait to get this show on the road.

Holy Cross is today's briefing officer and the silly bastard is telling his dumb jokes and laughing it up before the briefing begins like he's having the time of his life. I just know this is going to be a rough one. He hops up on the platform and pulls the sheet aside slowly. The red twine zigzags and stretches out clear across the map. "Target today boys," he says "is numero uno, Big B, the capital. Berlin, Germany." That's what he's been saving me for. A big one, a real hot puppy.

I try to control my jitters by fixing my mind on thinking you'll make it - you'll make it - it's only another mission. Lopez pokes me and says, "Take it easy, you're talking to yourself." Cross stands up there holding that phony smile on his puss while the noise level in the hut fades down to an unusual stillness broken by muttered cursing and a few groans.

Hartak looks like they've called his number at the sweepstakes. "Big B! Attababy, hot dog," he says. "Way to go guys. Hit ol' Hitler where he lives." He walks up and down the bench pounding on us and clapping his hands. My last mission and it has to be with this damned maniac. There has to be a way out. What if I told him I just can't go anymore. He says to me, "Better get this all down. You'll want answers when I call you later." I say, "Yes sir." I pull out my clipboard and copy the notes flashed on the screen from the slide projector:

Stations 0620, Engines 0650, Taxi 0655, Takeoff 0715, Leave Base 0824. Assembly Splasher 7. Leave Harwich 0852. Forecast wind over target 260/48.
4-6/10 cloud cover over target. Base reference altitude - 24000 Interval between groups - 1 minute.

```
1st Division - 12 groups (432 A/C)
3rd Division - 14 groups (504 A/C)
2nd Division - 11 groups 2 Squadrons (420 A/C) Diversion - Magdeburg
Total - 936 A/C (B-17) Berlin          420 A/C (B-24) Magdeberg
```

Swan steps up on the platform and says, "In an attempt to divide the enemy defenses, 420 Liberators from the 2nd Division will precede us by a half hour on the same route, but will break off for a diversionary attack on the synthetic oil refineries at Magdeberg while we continue on to Berlin." The slide projector shows times, latitude and longitude of each turning point of the mission. I map the dog legs on my chart.

Cross gives us our fighter support information. The communications officer and the group bombardier come on after him.

```
Fighter Support
1st and 3rd Divisions - 10 groups P-51's- 66th & 67th Fighter Wings
(664 A/C)
2nd Division - 4 groups P-51's 1 group P-47's - 65th Fighter Wing (294
A/C)
Fighter-Bomber VHF Channels - 701 and 741
Ground Sector Call Sign - Mohair (Channel 741)
VHF Call Signs - 91st Bomb group - Vinegrove 1-7
                        Fighters - Balance 1
VHF Authentification Code Word - Pretty Good
Weather Scouts (en route) 2 P-51's  Call Sign - Buckeye Red
                (over Target) 8 P-51's  C/S - Buckeye Blue
Division Air Commander Call Sign - Cowboy Able Leader
Bomb load  6 - 500 lb. GP's, 4 M17 incendiaries
            1 A/C per group load 1,2, and 6 hour long delay fuses
            Interval setting 150 ft.
Altitude  Odd number groups 25000 ft.  Even number groups 26500 ft.
```

Swan advises us that the Russian lines are only 50 miles east of Berlin as of this morning. It's something to keep in mind if we receive sufficient damage to prevent return to home base. I write in my clipboard

Russian Recognition Signal - Dip right wing 2 or 3 times
If this doesn't work try - Rock both wings 3 to 5 times
If this doesn't work - kiss your ass goodbye

Cross breaks in to say, "We can't vouch for that information, but I hear them Reds are a trigger happy bunch. They haven't seen many B-17's, and you're taking your chances approaching them, but I suppose it's better than falling into the hands of the Nazeyes."

The aiming point assigned to our group is the Tempelhof railroad yards near the center of Berlin. "Fuck that shit," Hartak growls hoarsely to our crew "we're going for pay dirt. The big kahuna." He beckons our crew to crowd around him as he pulls out a folded aerial photograph labelled FRIEDRICHSTRASSE/ BERLIN. The low altitude photo clearly shows streets and buildings. Hartak grins and says this cost me three bottles of good booze and a couple of big favors, but it's worth it. I've been saving this for months. He points to a small red circle on the photo. "Guess what building that is." He nods slowly waiting for an answer as he eyes each of us expectantly. We all stare blankly at him.

He's about fed up with this pack of fools, and pounds his fist into his palm. "The goddam fucken Reich Chancellery, that's what it is! That's what we're going after. Where ol' Hitler is hiding out in his bunker. Get rid of that fuckin' paperhanger once and for all. Who gives a shit about train yards?"

He looks us over as he rubs his hands together and says "I can just about come when I think of dropping our load on ol' Adolph. Knock that sunvabitch off and goddamit the war's over. We win. I've been a long time waiting for this."

He's bouncing now as if he's about to go into a jig. The crew latches on to his energy and we shove and pound on each other. I hope I haven't gone totally flak happy when I find myself caught up in it too. What a great way to finish up — No. 35 — blasting fuckin' Hitler to hell.

We're just about finished drawing up the predicted routes on our charts when they scrub the mission. A solid cold front is forecast to pass through our area this afternoon at the time we're scheduled to return to base. I stomp out of the hut. They had me all pumped up ready to go for No. 35, and now I'll have to go through this shit all over again. Lopez comes out of the hut steaming too. We have a couple of smokes and bitch our way through the situation until he says "Look at the bright side. Hell, they were sending us to fuckin' Berlin. Maybe our next blue plate special will be a piece of cake."

"What the hell are you smoking?"

Hartak is still in the briefing hut when I return to pick up my bag. He has simmered down a bit since the briefing. "Seventy-three under my belt," he says "but this is one I really want. Save those notes. They've been planning on this too long to give up on it now. That damn cold front is moving fast and nothing but clear behind it. Bet your ass they run this same mission tomorrow."

I'd bet the crazy son of a bitch is probably right. It's windy but perfectly clear tonight and the alert list is a duplicate of yesterday's. After dinner I take the bike out for a spin under a lopsided white moon popping in and out behind the sparse clouds racing by. I don't ride very far because it's close to freezing, but I do stop for a while to look up at the steely blue stars pinpointed overhead. I think of the times I used to identify them for Cavey. Snap, snap.

I turn in early but wake often to look at the luminous dial on my watch. Ten after one. I reach over from my sack and draw back the blackout curtain. The moon divides as a few clouds pass by, then comes together bright and clear. Looks like we're going to be off to Berlin in a few more hours. I hope Hartak's luck holds up.

I'm fully awake and switch the light on about five minutes before the Hangman comes around. Bishop is flying today too and he's fully clothed when the Hangman comes through the door. The kid has been sleeping with his clothes on lately. The Hangman faces me, shades his flashlight with his palm and says "Graduation day." He stands awkwardly under the light bulb then shuffles off when I don't answer. He stops at the door, blinks the light, and says "Don't worry, you'll make it." I don't know how to handle this. He goes down the hall pushing in doors and growling his damn breakfast at three. I finish puttting on my layers of clothes slowly, wondering if I heard him right, if his words are good or bad luck for me.

The noise in the briefing hut is pitched higher than ever. The sheet still covers the map up front, but we know the target this time, and we know damn well this one is a green light. No scrub today. Hartak and the Hangman shout at each other in order to be heard. I hear the Hangman roar, "Give 'em hell coach" as he pumps Hartak's hand and hugs him with his free arm. Hartak returns the hug and says "We'll pulverize them bums." He's on fire.

Colonel Close bounds up on the platform and the commotion stops abruptly as a hang-up on the phone. He nods for the sheet over the map to be removed. No surprise there. The red cord zigs and zags at different points than yesterday, but it winds up at the same red blotch near the upper right corner of the map — Berlin. Big B.

The droning undertone of moans and muttered curses dies down when Close raises his arms and says, "You men know your assignments from yesterday, and I'm certain your performance today will reflect further glory on the 91st and those who have gone before. I wish I could be going with you. Good luck, men." He salutes us and marches out. Lopez rolls his eyes and says, "Whoopee for him."

The actual briefing doesn't take much longer as a good part of the information is carried over from yesterday with only a few variations. The radio call signs and frequencies are changed, and we have a completely new weather system and forecast winds, but otherwise we're all set. Nothing can stop the Army Air Corps.

It is twelve minutes to engine time and most of the crew have completed their pre-flight duties. Hartak hasn't shown up yet. Lopez and I walk around the ship looking her over. It's Hartak's ship all right, shiny and squeaky clean as a new refrigerator, not some schoolboy's jaloppy. No scanty clad girl or raunchy name covers her gleaming spick-and-span surface. Only essential markings are visible: the serial number on the tail, the squadron's large black letters DF-D at the waist on both sides, and the group's triangle A centered on the bright red painted rudder. The red paint is to make the ship more visible for spotting during assembly. This ship looks like it's been Simonized says Lopez.

We hear the screech of brakes when the Hangman drives up with Hartak in his jeep. Hartak hops out and the ground crew quickly get busy again scurrying about the plane checking, wiping, polishing, adjusting, pulling here, pushing there. Hartak and the Hangman are in deep conversation when I walk past them to climb into my position. The Hangman seems all worked up because his dog has turned sick. I hear Hartak say "Don't worry, I'm going to take that pup in to the best vet in Cambridge soon as we get back." We're all in position ready to go and they're still out there talking, probably about the goddam dog. At engine time 0650, Sheridan, our pilot starts cranking up No. 1 engine. That gets Hartak's attention. He gives the Hangman a last minute hug and climbs aboard.

He squeezes into the nose with us to make sure the bombardier and I are on track with the Mickey operator, just in case the target is obscured and we have to use Mickey to see through the clouds. We tell him it's O.K. we're on track, then he crawls back to the Mickey to check if he's on track with us.

We take off and head straight for the buncher beacon where we circle with our wheels down to make it easier for the other ships of the group to locate us. The narrow crimson streak along the eastern horizon widens as the sun slowly emerges from below, setting the lower sky aglow. Hartak barks out a continuous series of instructions to the ships in our group as he scans the brightening sky around us hawkeyed, stalking strays, hunting for loose elements in our formation, repeatedly ordering the ships to pull in tighter and tighter.

We circle until Hartak is satisfied each one of the thirty-six ships making up the 91st today are properly situated in their assigned slots. We retract our wheels and are on our way to join the three other groups in our Wing right on schedule, clear all around, visibility unlimited. "Looks like we bomb visual today," Hartak says "No fuck ups on this one. Remember, today's the day we stick it right up Adolph's wazoo."

We assemble with Wing at 9000 feet and head eastward toward the coastal town of Harwich where we start our climb over the North Sea. We cross the Dutch coast two minutes ahead of our briefed time and a few minutes later reach our bombing altitude of 25000 feet. I look out toward the curved horizon fifty miles off. The crystal blue sky is filled with hundreds of bombers around us clear to the horizon in all directions.

Our fighter escort, three squadrons of P-51's join us right on schedule. So far this mission is proceeding exactly as briefed except that the predicted spotty low cumulus has turned out to be a layer of 4/10ths undercast. No problems reported during our oxygen check. Hartak checks in, swearing at the undercast. He calls Tom Whalen, our mickey operator, three times in the next ten minutes to check the equipment. I hear Whalen tell him on the last call that he's having some trouble with the alignment. "Shit, Tommy, get that squared away pronto," says Hartak "we're going to need that baby today."

A strong tail wind is moving us along at a fast clip. Ground speed on our basically eastern heading is 178 miles per hour. If this wind holds up we'll be racing across the target, doing 184 on the bomb run from the I.P. to Berlin. The wind has brought in more clouds below making it now about 5/10ths undercast. Through a hole in the cloud layer I catch a glimpse of Hannover off our right wing about ten miles to the south. I'll bet they're not too unhappy we're passing them by. I mark my log.

Time	Location	Alt	Temp	True Alt	Indicated AirSpeed	True AirSpeed	Ground Speed
1022	52°34′N 09°16′E	25800	-63	26700	148	163	178

Compass	Variation	Deviation	True Heading	WIND Dir Velocity Drift	True Course	Remarks
104	+2	-2	104	210 38 -11	093	Hannover 10-mi S.

My heat suit for a change is still working O.K. and the cabin heat is turned up all the way, still it's freezing in here with the outside temperature down to minus 66 Fahrenheit. Forty minutes to target and no flak or fighters yet. That won't last too much longer. I've been so busy that I haven't given much thought to what we're bound to face over Berlin. Whalen calls in to say "Mickey is working O.K. now."

Five minutes to the I.P. and the bombardier and I help each other put on our flak jackets. I tell him "This wind is going to give us a hell of a fast ground speed over target. Less time in flak." I look down below. All I see is fields of snow where the ground is visible through holes in the undercast which has now increased to 7/10ths coverage, maybe 8/10ths. The ships change formation, narrowing down for the turn at the I.P. My last bomb run. I keep repeating, only one more, let me get through this one, just this one. We make our turn at the I.P. Ten minutes to Berlin.

Whalen calls Hartak, "I can't get a fuckin' thing on this heading!" Two seconds later Hartak is squeezing his way to the Mickey with a portable oxygen bottle clipped to his pants. The first patches of flak up ahead increase in frequency and size as we fly closer to target. Six minutes to Berlin. The oxygen regulator blinks faster as I draw quick breaths with my heart pounding. Fuckin' Hartak is taking us into the thick of it — right into the goddam Reich Chancellery.

We're over Berlin now. A minute and a half to target and the sky is dark with boxes of barrage flak. I cringe as I stare at the bursts, numb and dumb again. Hartak stops at our nose compartment on his way back to his seat. He pulls his oxygen mask aside to speak to me and the bombardier. He gives us the thumbs up sign and says, "Mickey fixed. All O.K. up here?" We nod.

He's smiling as he waits for me to return his thumbs up gesture. I don't know when I've seen anyone look so happy. He reaches out to pat my shoulder with one hand and pulls the mask back on his face with the other. The flak is all around us now. I see the orange core inside one blast, and another a few yards ahead rocking the ship. I force myself to slowly raise my hand for the thumbs up Hartak is expecting. He turns toward me as he starts to climb back to his seat. His head jerks back as if it has been yanked. He sinks to the floor. I bend down to help him. His eyeballs are rolled back and a line of blood leaks out of his helmet. The regulator on his oxygen bottle isn't blinking. I lurch to my position to call for help, but Whalen is on the intercom with the bombardier. He's saying "There she is. On scope. Hitler's hide away." Soon as he stops I call in, "Hartak's hit, looks bad."

Sheridan, our pilot, says, "Christ we're at target now. Do what you can, call back." I crouch down to Hartak just as the bombs are dropped. He hasn't moved. I try to check his mask and oxygen bottle, but we go into a sharp diving turn to the right and I fall away from him. When we level out, the top turret gunner comes down with the first aid kit. He unzips Hartak's jacket to feel his heart. He shakes his head and says no use, he's had it. He points to a gash in Hartak's forehead just above his eyebrow. "Fuckin' flak," he says and closes

Hartak's eyes. We straighten Hartak out and cover him with a blanket. Hartak looks as if he's asleep and I feel dead, as if they've thrown a blanket over me.

My left hand clamps my wrist trying to steady it enough to make an entry in the log.

We're out of the flak now and I'm still numb when a speck of feeling breaks through enough for me to sense that I've actually made it. No. 35! I'm lightheaded and lean against a bulkhead for support. I wish I could feel good about it, but I know I don't. I look at Hartak lying there. A heavy sense of failure, of fault, drags on me like a weight, and my eyes are locked on the blanketed heap that used to be Hartak.

The numb feeling returns. This mission isn't over. We're still in Germany, not on the runway yet. Anything can happen. I'll never make it. I tell the crew over the intercom that Hartak is gone. It's a long ride back with the same strong wind, only now it's facing us as a headwind bringing our ground-speed down to 128 miles per hour. I avert my eyes each time they slide over to fix on Hartak lying there as if asleep.

We plow on westward following the long white contrails streaming from a thousand bombers in a line extending more than a hundred miles over Germany. We see no more flak, and no opposing fighters come up to challenge our fighter escort flying above the contrails. We slog along bucking the strong headwind for two and a half hours before we're finally out of Germany, then start our descent over the North Sea ten miles south of Helgoland. They send up their usual flak, but we're safely out of range. It's a routine tactic of ours to get them worked up and waste their effort and ammunition. One of these days some damn fool will fly too close. I want to shout down to those gunners at Helgoland and maybe to the whole fuckin world — that's my last look at flak.

We're off oxygen and Whalen comes forward to have a smoke with me. He looks at Hartak's body and says, "I can't believe it, ol' Hartak felt so good, on top of the world when he got the Mickey going again. I was thinking how lucky we are to have a guy like him when I saw Adolph's bunker come up on the scope."

I ask, "How do you think we made out?" He shrugs and says, "Let's hope our cameras were working. We dropped O.K. but in all the commotion I never saw where they fell, but I know we had that damn building square in the scope, right in the cross-hairs. I don't know how Hartak did it, but he got that Mickey working just in time. Then this has to happen. Son of a bitch."

He kneels on one knee and prays in Latin over Hartak's body. I turn away. The odd sense of fault returns. My eyes burn. I squint against the sun straight ahead and try to hold on. Whalen finishes his prayers and says "Last one for you and him, except you made it." My voice cracks when I say "Oh yeah, I made it all right." I turn away from him quickly.

TWENTY-FIVE

We cross over Great Yarmouth at 6000 feet and soon see the villages, towns, and countryside sliding by beneath us. That has always been a welcome sight, but never more so than today. Nine hours four minutes after takeoff our wheels touch down on the runway back in Bassingbourn. The tower directs us to a hard stand where an ambulance pulls up beside the ship before the propellers stop spinning. Cross and the Hangman dressed in their Class A's step out of a staff car with the group's chaplain. This has been a long, bad day and it looks as if it's not over yet.

I drag my ass over to where the crew stands bunched together in a small shaft of sunlight on this cold, dreary February afternoon while waiting for a truck to take us in. We watch the medics climb aboard and take Hartak off in a stretcher. Cross holds up his hands and halts them a few feet before they reach the ambulance. He calls out to our crew, "All right men, shape up, let's get over here."

We're slow to stir. Cross comes over to us and says "O.K., you heard me. Don't make me order you. Now move it." He glares at us as we mutter and take our time grouping around him near the ambulance. The medics grow uneasy standing there holding Hartak's body on the stretcher. There's no telling what the hell this character is going to think of next. One of the medics asks Cross "Is it O.K. to place the body inside the ambulance?"

Cross says, "Now hold it right there, you move it when I tell you to, soldier." The medics stare back at Cross, shift their weight, and for a short moment it looks as if they're about to dump Hartak's body on to the tarmac. Cross is fuming when they lower the stretcher to the ground. He then gives a signal to the Hangman who stumbles his way over to the stretcher while carrying a new folded blanket. I can smell the booze on him as he has trouble placing the blanket over Hartak's body. He almost knocks off his hat when he raises his hand to touch his visor in salute, and we snicker as he trips up trying to do a smart about face. Cross who has been standing stiffly at attention through it all, scowls daggers at him, then at our crew slouching against the ambulance. A couple of the guys stamp out their cigarettes and stand a little straighter, but the rest of us just look past him.

The chaplain hands Cross an American flag tightly gathered into a triangle. Cross marches up to the stretcher, unfolds the flag and drapes it over the blanket covering Hartak's body, then holds his salute as the chaplain recites a psalm. While a bugler steps up from behind the ambulance and blows Taps, a gust of wind whisks the flag off the blanket. It lands in an oily puddle near Lopez. He gathers it up and hands the flag back to Cross. My eyes are fixed on the grease stains running across four of the red and white stripes on the flag. Cross tries to tuck the flag under Hartak's body so the stains won't show, but many of the streaks are still visible. Cross signals the bugler to play Taps again. More saluting, more glowering at us tramps. We're all relieved when Cross nods to the medics.

They lift Hartak's body into the ambulance and drive off. Cross' little ceremony is over.

He grabs my arm and says, "I'd like a word with you if you don't mind." He's red assed furious and I'm none too happy that he's singling me out from the crew for a chewing out. I pull my arm away and follow him back toward the tail of the plane. This has been a bad day, and I've had about all I'm going to take from this shithead. He surprises me by offering a cigarette, then he says, "They tell me you were the one with him when it happened, right?"

I nod. Cross gnaws on his lip and asks, "Didn't he say anything?"

"No."

"Nothing, nothing at all?"

"Nope, as far as I know he never knew what hit him."

Cross' eyes are moist. He jams his fists deep into his overcoat and says, "Tell me everything and don't spare the details." I tell him. Nearly everything and some of the details. When I finish, he punches the side of the ship hard enough to put a dent in the aluminum and barks out, "Why did that bastard leave his seat? Couldn't anybody else fix the goddamn Mickey? Christ, seventy-four missions and he ends up wrapped in a fuckin' army blanket." Cross stiffens up again. His mouth twitches and his eyes narrow to slits as he squints through the cigarette smoke at me. Those questions were not for me to answer and I know that black look. I know damn well what it means. It's what I felt about him when I was told that Cavey went down. He'd damn well give anything to have me in that blanket instead of Hartak.

I fold my arms across my chest but don't say a word. We lock stares at each other until he says "Dammit I want a full written report on my desk in twenty-four hours." I give him yes sir but we both know the war will long be over before he gets that report from me.

Sheridan, our pilot, pulls the crew aside before we go into interrogation and says, "Look, we don't know diddley about going for Hitler's bunker. We went for the rail yards as briefed, right? We don't want any inquiries or shit about Hartak deliberately disobeying briefing orders. Let's keep it clean." None of us have any problem with that. I doctor my log, and that's the story we give Swan. Other than questions about Hartak, it's a routine interrogation. Swan tells us, "It appears to be one of our more successful missions. Strike photos from the groups who went over before us show excellent bombing results, complete destruction of Tempelhof terminal and marshalling yards, although quite a few crews from our squadron have reported that our group dropped at least a minute past the briefed target."

Swan refers to his clipboard and says "These early scouting reports confirm a complete wipeout of the rail yards, and according to this supplementary report, the government buildings along Wilhelmstrasse appear to be also heavily hit with large fires and heavy smoke around the Air Ministry, Reich Chancellery, Foreign Office, Gestapo Headquarters, and Goering's Office in the Haus den Fliegen. This particular damage could be attributed to our group dropping late. Any comments?"

None of us have any information to add. He nods slowly, looking us over. giving me a long look, letting me know he's not fooled, not for a minute, but the interrogation is over.

Lopez hugs me and says "Damn, I can't believe we made it. You and me pal, we're actually going home."

That grabs me. I too can hardly believe we made it, but when it comes to going home, I'm at zero. No home, no family. Not even a next of kin. Swan cuts in on my mooning by tapping me on the shoulder. He wants me to stick around for a few more questions after the others leave.

"Dropping on the government buildings was Hartak's

idea, wasn't it," he says. "You're doing the talking," I say. He pours me a drink, then shoves the bottle over to me and says "Congratulations, keep it as a graduation present." I drop the bottle in my bag. "Thanks," I say "that's for later. I don't feel much like celebrating right now."

"Hartak?"

"Yeah, I still can't believe it, but it's more than that."

"Anything you can tell me?"

"No, not that I know of. C'mon, let's get this over with. Shoot."

He too wants everything I can remember about what happened to Hartak. "Why don't you ask his asshole buddy, Cross?" I fill him in on the show Cross put on for us. "He even had the chaplain out there," I say "and the Hangman was so piss-eyed drunk he couldn't stand up straight."

"Yes, he's taking it hard," Swan says. "That mutt of his died on him today. Look, I know you're worn out, but you're the witness and I need your statement for my report."

I talk slowly as he writes down every word. When I finish, he gives me the carbon copy of what he's written. "Take this," he says, "you can use it as your report to Cross."

"Forget it, I wouldn't give that little prick the satisfaction."

"Take it, he won't let you clear the base without it. He'll keep you here for the duration plus six months." Swan folds the copy and puts it in my jacket pocket. I'm so bushed I stagger when I start to leave the hut. Swan slips a chair under me. I close my eyes and see Hartak in the blanket, and again feel that blanket weighing over me dragging me down. I see The Mouse and JoJo, even Parsons, but not Cavey no matter how hard I try. There's something important I want to say, but no one I could say it to even if I could find the words.

Swan sits with me, watching me carefully. "You were mumbling," he says "I couldn't make out what it was."

"Nothing, nothing at all," I say. "Thanks for the bottle. Be seeing you." I pull myself to my feet and give him thumbs up.

Bishop is curled up with his little Bible taking his post-mission nap when I get back to the room. The sun is setting as I flop down just aching for sleep. I wake in the darkness with the sense of having had bad dreams. I pull the string turning on the light. It's ten of eight and Bishop is gone, probably to dinner. I'd have to be a lot hungrier than I am to lift my beat up carcass out of this sack.

I pick up my Lardner book and start reading Haircut again. It's one of my favorites, but I don't get far into it before my eyes focus on my thumbs holding up the book. I see Hartak standing in the hatchway giving me thumbs up and waiting for me to return the gesture, and me so stiff with fear it takes forever to raise my arm, and I see his head yanked back, and I see . . . And I see that if I'd only raised this thumb a fraction of a second sooner, if I hadn't been so yellow, he would have been on his way back to his seat instead of slumped bleeding dead on the floor.

I pull myself out of the sack and go to the latrine. I wash my hands and face and force my mind on to other subjects. I sit down for a crap which won't come, but Hartak shows up clear on the scope of my mind. Maybe I have the whole thing wrong. I remember our first night here when he told us at the meeting that fear was healthy, that it could save our life. Well the son of a bitch was right all along. Maybe he just didn't have enough fear today. I did.

So maybe if I hadn't been so scared and if I was able to stand up and raise my thumb a second sooner, that fuckin piece of flak would have caught me instead. I think up a lot of ifs. It doesn't change the fact that Hartak is dead, and though there are a million little ifs and maybes that he or I or anyone could have or should have done before to change that, noth-ing, not one single goddam thing can change that now. I kick the door of the toilet cell loose from its hinges. I wash my hands and face again. It doesn't help much.

It's too late for dinner, but I scrounge a couple of ham sandwiches from the K.P.'s in back of the mess hall. I skip the bar. It would mean endless bullshit on what happened today, and there's not much more I can take of that. They post the alert list and my stomach goes into knots again until it hits me that my name isn't on it and will never be on one again.

Back in the room I pour myself a stiff drink out of Swan's bottle. I crawl into my sack and try to pick up where I left off in my book. I manage to finish the story this time, and am about to turn off the light when Fearless and Zibby show up carrying a cake. They had the cook bake two, one for me and one for Lopez, and want to present me mine with the compliments of the crew. Lopez would be here, but he's bombed out of his mind right now with Eriksen administering to his needs, Skiles has an emergency in Cambridge who just can't wait, and Earl, of course, is living it up at the flak house.

Fearless and Zibby are on the alert list. I tell them they're sure to make it in a breeze. We talk over old times back in Kearney and Alex, making sure we don't bring up anything about Cavey, the Mouse, and JoJo. The cake isn't half bad, and when Bishop comes back we have no trouble polishing it off along with Swan's bottle and some Johnny Walker that appears when Fearless says abracadabra and waves his hand around his overcoat pocket. Bishop is on the alert list too, and climbs up into his bunk. We carry on bravely without him and think he's conked out, when he sits up suddenly with his eyes closed and rattles off his prayers. I can't tell if he's plastered or not when he falls back on his pillow out stone cold. I guess I didn't last too much longer because the next thing I know the Hangman is in the room flashing his light. "Good," he says, "a triple play. Bishop, Fosdick, Zybisko, hit the deck! You're on today. Move it." Zibby and Fearless are lying on the floor. They both look completely baffled when they pop their heads out like turtles from under their overcoats. They can't figure where the hell they are. Bishop and I give them a hand in getting oriented. It takes a while and I end up going along with the three of them to briefing.

I feel like a stranger in the briefing hut. I should be with these guys sitting on a bench, not standing aside here against the curved wall. Cross pulls the sheet away from the map. The target today is Merseberg. I draw my breath in, my stomach tightens, my nails dig into my palms. I grip the back of one of the benches and regain my breath only when it sinks in that this is not for me. I'm not going. Damn it, I've made it. I don't pay attention to much more after that. It's as if this is all some kind of dumb show written in a language unknown to me. When the guys shuffle out after it's over, I catch Zibby and Fearless. I tell them "It's O.K. You guys are going to make it." They look at me the way I'd look at them if the situation was reversed. They know I'm pissing in their ear. I'm no longer one of them. "Good luck fellas," I say, "happy landings." We shake hands.

"Yeah, see you around," says Fearless.

The hut empties out. I have nowhere to go. I light up a smoke and drop into our crew's old bench. An empty briefing hut is one spooky place. I look around the hut for the last time and it brings back more than I want to remember, I catch hold of myself before I drift too deep.

I bump into the Hangman on my way out. He falls in step with me and offers me a cigarette. "No thanks," I say. I wish the bastard would get lost, but he stays with me walking in silence until he says "I told you that you were going to make it." We pass near Cavey's tree. I make a snowball and throw it at the tree. I miss by a mile. He makes one, gives it to me and says "Here, try another." I take it and miss again.

"Sorry about Hartak," I say.

"Yeah, thanks, he was a great guy, but the way he was going, it was bound to happen sooner or later. Do you know I also lost my dog today?"

I think he means the dog is missing. I've forgotten that Swan had told me the mutt had died. Before I can catch myself I say, "Oh, she's sure to turn up at your door when she's hungry."

He has tears in his eyes when he says, "No, no, Flak has gone to her rest now beyond all suffering. I pray we meet in heaven some day if they'll take in a sinner like me."

"Oh, you'll make it," I say, "absolutely no question about it, a piece of cake." I knew the guy was loony the first time I laid eyes on him. I make a snowball and give it to him. He throws and misses. We stockpile a load of ammunition and keep throwing at the tree. After four or five more misses, I hear the solid thwack of two hitting at the same time. The Hangman gives me thumbs up.

My shipping orders came through today along with a surprise birthday card from Bishop. My birthday is three days off, but I'll be gone by then, so he figured he'd give it to me now. It's a home made thing with a large 21 in red crayon. Under it he wrote it's our magic number, you are 21 and I have 21 missions to go. It's been a long, long time since anybody remembered my birthday. Not since I was a kid. I truly hope he makes it.

I leave in two days via ground transport to Liverpool where I'll be boarding a boat for the Zone of the Interior. Army talk for the U. S. of A. That's going to be one long ride and I'm making it alone. A far different trip than I had flying over with Cavey and Earl and the Mouse and Fearless and Zibby and Lopez and JoJo and Skiles and Eriksen. Ages ago. I didn't know then what I was getting into and I don't know now. I guess I never will.

I'm all packed and ready to go tomorrow. It's quiet on the base with the group out on a mission. The day is slightly overcast but not as cold as it has been. I bike up to Caxton Gibbet. It's been two months since my visit there. I find Vivian Lea in the barn applying liniment to a horse. Her red face beams a welcoming smile as she says "I'm sure you'd be more comfortable waiting in the parlor until I'm finished with Elizabeth. It will be but half a mo'."

I hear her calling for Martha when she comes into the house to change. I don't know how I'll handle this. They come into the parlor together. Martha takes my hand in both of hers and raises it to her cheek. "It's so good to see you again," she says, "I hope you've been well." Vivian leads me to a large upholstered chair near the fireplace and says "Tell me, how is that fine young chap from Wyoming? Carvey, I believe."

"Cavey," I say. "I'm afraid he didn't do too well."

Vivian sucks in her breath, gives a short cry, and her palms cross at her throat. I'm angry at myself for talking like that— afraid he didn't do too well— shit, he died in an exploding, burning B-17, and there wasn't a piece left of him large enough to identify, but I can't tell Vivian that. Hell, I can't tell anybody that.

We're quiet for a moment until Vivian tells Martha to bring in the tea. I can't believe how my hands are trembling. I know I should ask her about her son in the Jap prison camp, but I don't dare, not now. She dabs at her tears and says, "This bloody war." She leans on the corner of the table and says, "I'm sure you must miss him very much."

I nod. "Yes, I miss him." At least I said that one right. I say it again. "Yes I miss him very much." Martha wheels in a tea-cart with cheese and crackers, jam, and some kind of liver spread, and a large blue tea-pot. She is most polite as she pours a cup for me. Vivian asks "Is this is a short visit or can you spend the night."

"I can't stay, I'm leaving for the States in the morning."

They both are genuinely happy to hear this. "Oh, your family must be overjoyed over this happy news," Vivian says. I don't bother to deal with that. I think of the ditty that goes, "We're the Battling Bastards of Bataan, no father, no mother, no Uncle Sam." I don't hang around too much after that. They ask me to write to them. Vivian says, "I fully intends to visit the Grand Tetons as soon as the war is over." I then ask her about her son. Not a word since the card nine months ago, but she prays for him every day. I give her a goodbye hug, but I will not be the one to tell her that it will all turn out all right.

Martha walks with me down the path when I leave. I take her hands in mine and say, "I'm sorry I never had the chance to properly thank you. You were very kind to me." She is blushing. When we're out of sight of the house she puts her arms around me and gives me a hard kiss. "God bless you, find a good woman when you go home and be kind to her." she says and then runs back to the house.

I bike back to the base in time to see the squadron return from the mission. Target was Frankfurt, nine returned safely, one down over target, one crash landed in Belgium, and one unaccounted for. I scan the list of MIA's. I'm glad I don't recognize any of the names.

My last morning in Bassingbourn. I've been up since four when the Hangman came for Bishop. Before that I was up at two and three and a few times in between. That's nothing new for me. I let myself think about Cavey last night instead of my usual tricks to force him out of my mind. I'm in my sack thinking about him now. I can still see his barrel chest and long dangling arms and legs, and how he popped out of his clothes that always looked tight and short on him, and the goofy way he bounced when he walked as if his knees were buckling under him, and the crew cuts we gave each other. I remember how much he wanted to have a car some day. What I can't see is his face, no matter how hard I try.

That's gone. Dead and gone for the real duration with nothing left to remind us, unless somewhere out there, that sweet whore Annabelle is still keeping him safe and warm in her locket. Not very likely, is it Cavey, you goddam son of a bitch.

I hear a jeep pull up outside and then a voice down the hall calling out my name. I open the door for a T/5 who picks up my foot locker and says "I'm here to take you in to Royston for the train to the repple depple" I'm to stay there until they find space for me on a boat back to the States from Liverpool. The T/5 waits patiently at the door while I stand there taking in all the details of the room — the bunk beds, the bureau, the little radio, the pin-ups, the scrawling on the grimy walls, a pair of Cavey's shirts still dangling flat sleeved from the pipe where Swan left them that day.

I know I should be feeling pretty good right now. No more Flakenbergs. I've made it after all. So why do I feel so down and blue, so isolated, like flying off alone without maps or charts to a target unknown. I grab the upper bunk to steady myself, then remember to leave a note for Bishop. *Good bye, good luck old buddy. Keep a tight asshole. You'll make it.* I drop the note on his bunk before managing to drag my ass out of the room.

I toss my bag into the jeep, and I'm back again to that dark cold morning when the Hangman flashed his light in my eyes and bawled out breakfast at three briefing at four, then took me on that mad ride to my first mission. "Just a minute," I say to the driver, "there's something I forgot to take care of."

Back in the room, I reach down and fold over my mattress. That does it. Swan won't have to turn this one over. One last look around. I grab one of Cavey's shirts, roll it up under my arm, then close the door slowly behind me. I climb back in the jeep and give the driver thumbs up. "Yep," I say as if I knew where I was heading, "let's get the hell out of here."